After the End
An Eye for an Eye

R.J. Lynch

Two Hands Media—Mukwonago, WI
ISBN: 978-1-73453230-2
Library of Congress Control Number: 2020901348
Title: *After the End: An Eye for an Eye*
Author: R.J. Lynch
Digital distribution | 2020
Paperback | 2020

Dedication

I would like to dedicate this book to my dear friend Garrett Carlson for being the one man who stuck with me through this process. I dedicate this to those who struggle as Rob does with mental difficulties. Most importantly I dedicate this to my loving parents Cindy and Bob Lynch who have supported me and my craziness no matter what, your boy made it.

Table of Contents

Part 1: Despartian

Chapter 1
A Meeting of Fate

It was a somber early summer night, and the city of Despartian was silent. The trouble which seemed to plague the city had finally taken the night off. Over the past week, the city had been ravaged by storms causing damage to houses that barely stood before their arrival. Now few people were afraid of the storms, but every crack of thunder reminded the people of the bombs that nearly obliterated the city several years ago. The lightning that preceded blinded those whose only memories were that of muzzle fire and grenades. The tragedies of the past were still fresh, so storms like the ones that had just come through always seemed to open fresh wounds.

The tragedy that was imprinted on all of their brains was not unique to Despartian. They were not the unlucky recipients of some singular moment of terror or cataclysmic event. No, they suffered the same fate of the rest of the world. Their city had been engulfed by a war that didn't rewrite history but obliterated all traces of existence prior to it. Given that truth, the people of this city may have actually had it easy compared to other parts of the world. The people of Despartian still had ruins of a city, unlike many people around the world who just had ash. Although for some the city's lifeless existence is more of a burden than a blessing it curses them with the thing mankind always searches for, hope. Every day, every week, people started to search for something better because they thought it was possible.

People don't talk about the War very often. It was ugly as war tends to be, but this one was relentless and unlike anything ever seen before. When they do talk about it, they refer to it by a nickname it earned towards the end of it, Finis Temporis a Latin phrase referring to the end of time. It was an idea that mankind often pondered, what would bring their end. There were predictions from religious fanatics, Mayan Calendars, and scientific probabilities. In the end though they didn't need acts of god or the mythical they just needed one another. They just needed time to grow so far apart that they no longer cared about the survival of one another. They destroyed their own world because of their own pride and refusal to work with each other. The world today is nothing more than the remnants of the past mixed with the survivors attempts to create something new again. Now in an era where the world population is a quarter of what it was just ten years prior all people can do is survive instead of thriving like they did before.

On this somber night, two men sit on a rooftop overlooking the city. These men had seen everything that this world had to offer, but they were still amazed by their city. Its resilience was beyond comprehension. There was no reason that this city should be standing after what it had gone through. Especially given the fact that many prominent societal hubs like New York, Beijing, London, Sydney, and Cairo looked like Chernobyl. Now before the War, these two men were just average people with no connection to one another. They would have likely passed through this life without leaving a mark on the history books. The War changed their fates and intertwined them indefinitely. It made them two of the most influential people in the city and outside of Despartian they were war legends. Becoming these men of influence was not easy and different for each of them. One moved to the city at an early age and it became home long before the War ever started. The other followed the first to the city after it was already in ruin. No one could figure out why he came, but his arrival led to the rebirth of the city. Despite their different origins both men seemed to love the city equally, as each one has continued to fight for the city. Though at times they seemed to be fighting each other with their methods.

"How did we let this happen," queried one of them at last to break the silence? He was wearing a tattered ebony colored cloak to disguise his appearance and was holding a small flask in his left hand. He kept his back turned to the other man and used his cloak to shield him from the other. He refused to look at the other man as he took a quick sip from his flask.

"Tell me, my old friend, how many nights have you wasted drinking and toiling over that same question? More importantly, how many times have you avoided answering it knowing that the truth is frightening," the second figure responded? This second man was the polar opposite of the first. While the first lurked in the shadows the second man bombarded one's senses with his own signature flash. It included a dark sleek suit, with a blood red undershirt that glowed in the blackened night and his hair blended in with the night sky. Maybe his most noticeable feature, despite his expensive clothing choice, was his skin, which seemed to reflect what little light was in the sky. He was paler than the moon above them his complexion resembled that of an albino snake and would make a vampire jealous. His voice was low and hissed. The cloaked figure did not respond. Instead, he chose to look over the city, while he swirled his drink.

"Even now I can sense the fear in you as you continue to run from the truth into an open bottle. However, I just don't understand why you're so scared. I mean you were shot at, nearly blown up, and should have been killed numerous times, none of which ever seemed to faze you, but these insignificant words scare you. The truth terrifies you," the pale man stated as he mocked the other, "There is great irony in that, as it was fear of words and ideas that caused this. It was a fear of differences, which led to a lack of compassion and this."

"Life isn't fair. That is one of the simplest truths we know, but it is people who make it a true nightmare. People were afraid of each other rightfully so, as we see what they were and are capable of. The funny thing is that they should have also feared themselves. So, my old friend you asked how this happened? It happened because instead of love we embraced hate and ignorance. Instead of compassion and understanding we embraced fear. We chose to focus on the negative and that is what did this. You can run through the scenarios over and over again in your head, but you will keep finding the same answer and what is terrifying is that there is nothing we could have done about it. It didn't matter how hard we fought if no one else was willing to look at themselves and change." The cloaked man continued to listen, he did not argue or protest he just accepted what was being said. It was odd, since most of the time when these two were together all they could do was argue, but maybe deep down he knew that the words being said were the truth or it was possible he was just ignoring the pale man completely. Regardless of what was going through his mind, the pale man was infuriated by the complete apathy being demonstrated in front of him.

"Ten years I have known you and still you find new ways to get under my skin," he yelled, it was clear that the newfound frustration entertained the other man! The yelling brought a smirk to his face and he nearly started to chuckle at his old friend's irritation. This in return just enraged the pale man farther. Then finally, after a few moments he decided to answer the pale man:

"It is funny when you sent me the invitation to come meet you, I couldn't help but think back to the last time we were in the same room. If my memory serves me right that last thing, I said to you was very derogatory and to get out of my life forever and yet here you are again." At this statement, the pale man walked over and placed his hand on his friend and tightened his grip.

"Now it has been a couple years since then and my memory is a little foggy from that night. Things that I can recall include something like two, three, maybe eight tequila shots, but who was counting. Due do all that alcohol things are not quite picturesque so, did you say that before or after I put your ass through that poor man's table," the pale man replied in a cold tone with a face filled with detest? This opened up the wounds in the cloaked man's memory, causing his eyes to grow intense and his fist to clench around his flask. In response, the pale man tightened his own grip even further to maintain his dominance. He was well aware of the skills possessed by the man in front of him and a fight on the rooftop would not benefit either of them at the moment, even if the cloaked man was no longer sober at this point.

"Why am I here," the cloaked figure finally asked, "We haven't spoken since that day and I was pretty content never seeing you again since you stabbed me in the back that day and made it clear that our brotherhood was over! Now be honest with me and tell me what you want," the cloaked figure yelled thinking back to that last meeting and the hate he has fostered since that day!

"Quite simply, I'm here to offer you a job," the man uttered with an emotionless face. This phrase though simple in wording carried meaning that drove the cloaked figure to throw off the pale man's hand and grab him by the collar of his nice suit. He held him against the edge as if he was ready to throw him. His eyes, which peered through a ragged unkempt beard that was graying far earlier than it should, were no longer intense or glazed from whatever was in the flask, they were now just filled with blind rage and malicious intent. The two men now connected by the grasp of one stood and stared at each other for what felt like an eternity. Their eyes locked and they peered into one another's soul.

The pale man had lifeless emerald eyes void of any meaning and holding nothing, but anguish from years of pain never discussed. Looking into them was to see the envy for a life taken from him. The cloaked man on the other hand had eyes that glimmered like a clear sunny sky. Their blue was pure like the Mediterranean Sea as his whole life could be seen in them. On the surface there was an innocence on display despite all the tragedy they had seen. Yet when the pale man looked deeper, he saw the truth. He saw the loneliness from years of poor decisions and pushing people away. The pale man may have had eyes of anguish caused by years of life kicking him around, but the cloaked man had the worst look of all, that of self-hate. His pain was self-created and he had lived that way for so long there seemed to be no way back to the man he was years ago.

"I'll take that as a no," grinned the pale man, "but I would feel as if I cheated you if I did not inform you that I am getting the band back together, the whole unit is coming back even Commander Gene. You know Gene personally asked me to extend an olive branch to you despite our recent personal history. You were always the old man's favorite despite your inexperience." When that name Gene hit the cloaked man's ears he hesitated for a moment and he smiled for a moment. Gene was the one person from his old squad that still meant the world to him, but the hesitation only lasted momentarily as he remembered the man in front of him. He could not let the devil gain any advantage now that they were combative.

"You overestimate my desire to see a group of traitors and homicidal maniacs. Three years ago, in that nowhere bar, the men I called brothers and trusted more than anything in this world made their decisions. They chose you as they left me alone drunk and bloody in that village where we couldn't even speak the language. They were the ones who cut ties with me and I have zero interest in repairing them. In all honesty, I think it would be better for me and the whole world if I just killed you now," the cloaked man declared as he held his old friend a little farther off the edge only to bring him back and let him go. The pale man dropped to the ground with his back up against the edge. The next thing did was to start laughing, but he didn't have a normal laugh instead it was a haunting and echoing sound. The laugh was terrifying and made the cloaked man physically upset, he even began to shake as it grew louder.

"I thought…HehHeh…I thought you were going to drop me. I was so excited! I thought that you found your old self! I'm mean you even had the look of a killer again, that was… exhilarating. God, I do miss the old days when we were going shot for shot kill for kill. No hesitation and no remorse as bodies dropped around us. We were the definition of a killing machine. No one could stop us and our legends will never die because of it. On top of that, if I remember right, I won our little contest with 185 kills to 173. What happened to you? I've heard that you barely even fight anymore, even when drinks are spilled on you or your honor disgraced. You've turned into this soft fool who can't kill one man who you think is a danger to the people you care about or do you think I'm not a danger to them because you think there is no one left that cares for you. I mean I understand how you could think that, since you are nothing, but a drunk whore monger. However, trust me there are still people you should be worried about especially that girl you were ready to marry," he explained as the blood-curdling laugh continued. The cloaked man just stood over his former squad mate while the taunting laugh grew louder and louder.

He wanted to strike back and respond to the comments, but there was a part of him that thought he was right. Ever since the War ended the cloaked man had transformed from a war hero to man, he could barely look in the mirror at, he was disgusted by his own reflection. He no longer knew who he was and had lost everyone close to him. He had pushed everyone away, but there were still those he could not lose if he wanted to maintain the little bit of sanity he possessed.

The silence in the air was suddenly broken as a shot rang out piercing the cloaked man's shoulder. He fell to his knees grasping at his left side, the pain was tremendous for a moment. He may have been shot several times before this, but there was something different about this one. It was more excruciating than anything he had felt before, but then without any reason, the pain ended. He looked at his shoulder in amazement. What had just happened he wondered? With the pain gone he prepared to rise again when his body gave out and fell to the ground. He was unable to move or respond in any manner.

"I cannot believe that after all this time you thought I would take no for an answer. You know better than anyone that I always get what I want eventually. Someday soon you will come to me and on that day, you will become part of something bigger than yourself. My plans never fail. Until then I'll wait and let destiny decide our time schedule.

Now I bet, you're wondering why your body is seizing up. How could you be stopped in your tracks like this? You see that bullet expertly placed by our old mate Dave is coated with a paralysis serum that I've developed and wanted to test out before the show begins. You'll notice as it affects your body, your heart rate is slowing to the point that you will not bleed out and your nervous system has been sent haywire unable to connect signals for movement. I'm really proud of this one and hope you enjoy the ingenuity of it. Now it shouldn't kill you, because my math is never wrong, and neither will I as that just wouldn't be fun. And since the drug has left you useless this conversation is over so I'll see you around Rob... HehHeh," laughed the pale man as he started to walk away, specifically making sure that he stepped on Rob's shoulder.

A few hours had passed since the pale man had left Rob on that rooftop and he was slowly regaining his bodily functions. Unfortunately, the pain of being shot also returned with them. He had hoped over the multiple exposures he would grow used to the pain, but despite his hopes, he was in utter agony. As he fought through the pain he gingerly began to crawl to the edge. He wanted to lift himself up again so that the wound would be above his heart lessening the chance he would bleed out, but with every inch he moved, the pain overwhelmed his body. Inch by inch he crawled fighting the urge to scream and give up. That serum had a nasty side effect of returning all the pain the victim should have felt during the initial moments. It felt as if he had been shot multiple times now instead of just the once. After an intense effort, he was able to return to an assisted sitting position. Struggling to re-catch his breath he reached for his pocket and pulled out a bulky phone. During the War cell phones were often destroyed and networks decimated in order to limit communication. However, recent breakthroughs revived the industry as it was making a comeback, but things were still a long way from pre-war conditions. As he fought through the pain, he was finally able to reach the one man he trusted more than anything.

"Philip, I need you. I ran into a bit of an issue, and I may have been shot," Rob grunted into the phone as he gritted his teeth.

"So, no contact from you in over a week outside of a note about a meeting with John and this is what you call me about. I guess I've gotten worse calls before," replied the voice over the phone.

"I love you man, but right now I need help I'll listen to the lecture later. Now if you could come to pick me up, I'll be writhing around on the roof of the old science building," he responded.

"Shall I call for Ms. Anna as well," queried the voice? The question was met by silence at the other end. When two people spend as much time together as Philip and Rob do, they become able to read silence as well as they understand each other's words. It was easy to tell that he was ashamed of the state he was in and wanted to keep things as private as he could.

"I'll bring the medical supplies then; I should be there in no more than fifteen. Try not to die on me," the voice explained. With that, they ended the conversation and all Rob could do was wait. The pain was overwhelming, but he had survived much worse during his war days.

While he sat on the edge of the roof, he gazed at the skyline in front of him. Despite the War and the tragedies that had engulfed the city to him, it was still home. It was the place where he became attached to the world. Regardless of the disarray, to him, it still maintained a certain mysticism. He had seen every corner of the earth, but the way the heavens met the earth in this city was magical. Nature was at its purest and most dominant here he had always believed. The river that flows on its easternmost edges remained fierce and unyielding to the world. It had never faltered or slowed despite any attempts to change it. Enclosing them to their west were the bluffs covered with the new growth that had arisen from the ashes of the old city. Both forces of nature each had their own form of stability. Years ago, men had thought they were the river's master, but the dams and bridges were washed away, while the river continued to flow. Men thought they conquered the rolling hills, but the houses and roads have turned to rubble, yet the bluffs still stand tall. Despite all of man's glory, it was nature that survived not them.

Between the two mighty giants of nature stood the city. While the natural monuments preached unwavering determination, the city was an agent of chaos. The War had dismantled the city that once stood, but like the phoenix, it was rising again. Despartian remained though only barely. The people were now attempting to rebuild with nothing more than rubble and dreams. The sad truth that brought a tear to Rob's eye was that despite the destruction the people had yet to learn how to give without taking. All the lessons that should have been learned from a history-altering war had been ignored. While many people worked hard building everything up from scrap, others still chose to take. Making the problem worse was the fact that one repercussion of the War was the total distrust of any form of governing body, so what was once crime now could not be labeled in such a fashion. There was no organized force to stop or regulate the people, despite the best efforts of many to contain without the trust of the citizens' nothing real could be done.

Lost in a trance he became startled when a loud gong echoed through the city. One of the few monuments that remained was an old clock tower. It was finally midnight and Rob closed his eyes listening to each strike. There was familiarity in it and with each strike, the clock grew louder and prouder until it reached what would normally be the seventh ring. Instead of the usual gong, there was silence, the only damage the tower seemed to take during the War. No one could understand it every other hour rang true, but the seventh remains quiet. Maybe the answer to the tower's flaw is simple, but in these times the simple often becomes overlooked.

Rob was still listening to the echoes fill the streets of the city when the door to the roof flew open. He smiled as he saw a monster of a man step out to greet him. Philip was both long and large filling up every door he stepped through. At first glance, he looked sturdy and strong, but upon a deeper look, it was clear that years of hardship had worn his body down. He was ten years or so Rob's senior and the War made the distinction even greater. His once jet-black locks and beard had faded and were now sprinkled with grays and silvers. His face was warm yet his eyes showed nothing, but exhaustion from working harder than his body should attempt at his age.

"You look horrible," he smirked as he surveyed Rob's body, "how did you manage to get yourself shot again? Your note said this was going to be a nice civil conversation between old war buddies. Although given your history I guess this could be considered civil. I guess the more important question should be why I let you go alone. I knew about your history and that you were in the middle of one of your bad weeks, yet I didn't come to stop you."

"Yeah you really dropped the ball on this one Philip," responded Rob as he smirked with a slight grimace.

"Last question, why did I come to get you? I could have had that nice house all to myself never needing to worry about a thing again," he said looking off into the distance both of them aware that it was a joke to lighten the mood. They were too loyal to one another for Philip to leave Rob behind. Coming back to reality he pulled out an old tackle box with several crude medical devices within it.

"So, do you need me to help remove the bullet or have you mastered your technique after the thousandth attempt," asked Philip as he pulled the tools out, handing them to Rob.

"With the placement of the shot I can handle the stitches, but with all the cutting involved I better let you take care of the removal. I really don't feel like taking my arm off tonight," admitted Rob with much distaste knowing he was unable to do what was necessary. The pair combined to removes his cloak and undershirt revealing the mess that was hidden underneath. No doubt that he was a physical specimen that could intimidate many weaker men, but he was severely damaged. Every inch of his torso had been torn up by years of brutalization. He was covered with scars from stabbings and shootings he survived. On top of this, he had several areas of burnt flesh that had barely healed correctly. The scar tissue consumed his body giving him the appearance of something that wasn't human.

"I'm surprised that the bullet didn't just bounce off of you. Whoever shot you was a great marksman to penetrate this crocodile hide of yours," Philip commented as he tried to keep things light at the start of the procedure. All Rob could do was sit there gritting his teeth while the bullet was being extracted. Thankfully, there was still something left in his flask to disinfect the area and numb his pain.

"You'd think that after so many injuries that this wouldn't bother me anymore, but nothing has changed, I guess. Maybe I should try and just get shot at less," chuckled Rob as he writhed in pain.

"I've been telling you that for a while now. I'm sorry to inform you, but you are still mortal, pain does affect you and you are still going to bleed like the rest of us," lectured Philip.

"Hey, I can pretend to be superman can't I," Rob responded with a slight chuckle given his current condition.

"You can try, but remember just because you are emotionally hollow doesn't mean your heart is useless," he replied with a stern voice causing Rob to fall silent for a few minutes.

"Well, Mr. Big Mouth are you done removing it yet I need to get myself stitched up before work in the morning," Rob said with all the enthusiasm sucked from his voice.

"Really? You have a battlefield medic as a friend who you refuse to call when you need help and then you criticize an old man for not removing a bullet fast enough. This wasn't exactly in my job description you know," mouthed off Philip shaking his head, "give me just a minute." The bullet hit the ground soaked with blood. Rob slowly rose to his feet still grasping his wound as he limped toward the tackle box. Philip watched as the stubborn fool pulled a needle and some thread from the box. Slowly he started to stitch himself up, he was too prideful to ask for help despite how difficult it was to move.

"You really do make a mess, don't you? Now, how the hell did one little bullet take you out, I thought you were some kind of tough guy," Philip finally asked looking at the beaten body of his friend?

"Laugh it up big guy that bullet was laced with some kind of serum. If it hadn't been you would have had about four more to remove or you would have just had a corpse," Rob said with hesitation in his voice.

"You're afraid I can hear it in your tone. What did he say to Rob," probed Philip as he looked at the terror in his friend's eyes?

"He offered me a job and when I declined this was his response. This whatever this is, is far from over. John talked as if he had some sort of plan and knowing him there is no good that could come from any plan of his. I've been a part of many of them and every single one of them ends with a trail of bodies. This means my only job now has to be getting ahead of whatever he is planning I don't care about what he has done for this city. He has always been a loose cannon who enjoys chaos more than anything," he responded gazing at his city.

"Maybe you're right, but right now you need sleep, sir. You still have a day job and there are a lot of people counting on you. Come now," Philip was able to draw a smile from Rob's normally stern appearance with that reminder. Philip helped Rob down the steps to the car he had waiting out front. It had been a long night with an early morning still to come.

Chapter 2
The Medics Plea

After a pain-ridden sleep, the 5 a.m. alarm came like nails on a chalkboard. Rob slowly made his way out of bed holding his shoulder and fighting off the pain that tried to overtake him. After, dressing himself gingerly he made his way to the kitchen where Philip awaited him as he did every time Rob found himself back at his home.

The house wouldn't have been anything special fifteen years ago, but in the new world they lived in it was virtually a mansion. Three-person houses like Rob's were rare even in Despartian which is one of the supply richest cities left. However, they were still dealing with constant supply shortages forcing people to live in group homes and deal with tight spaces. Rob did not come from or hold any kind of great wealth, but he was a hero to many people in the city thus they felt it appropriate to give him the best they had.

During the War, the city had been ransacked and nearly burned beyond repair. In response to the enemy's attack, Rob came in with his own army to drive the enemy out. His efforts in both fighting and the recovery were crucial in the city's ability to stay afloat. He was the homeboy who saved and helped rebuild the city, on top of many other feats. Now Philp and he shared a working companionship where each one felt indebted to the other. Rob saw Philip as a mentor from before the War and as someone who has saved him many times such as the previous night since the end of it. Philip, on the other hand, remembers the boy he helped grow and simultaneously the man who saved his life when the city was under siege.

Philip had been trapped in the destruction and when he thought all hope was lost Rob was the one that ended up saving him. The two men are now completely loyal to one another and nothing could come between them despite the jabs that the two often throw at one another.

"So, what's for breakfast? Lobster maybe," joked Rob knowing that after last night's adventures things would be slightly tenser than normal.

"No, lobster is only for those who don't look like homeless bums fresh off the street. However, I decided to still spoil you with some flocons d'avoine otherwise known as oatmeal, eat up," he answered plopping down a spoonful of brown goo, "If you're good I might be able to find some peanut butter hidden around here somewhere."

"Aye, so what are you up to today Philip? If you don't have anything else, I heard that the northern fields need an ox for plowing," smirked Rob as he began to munch on the goo.

"It is good to see that the bullet didn't affect your humor at all. Now if you actually want to know I'll be in the kitchen today...," Philip began before getting interrupted.

"God help those poor souls you feed," Rob mouthed off again. Making himself laugh and stopping Philip in his tracks

"Well sounds like I don't need to find that peanut butter," Philip responded causing Rob to sulk down in his chair, "Now where are you off to today, you pretentious prick?"

"I'll give you prick I have my days, but I'm not pretentious," scoffed Rob as he shuffled in a spoonful of his breakfast, "There is a four-family home on State Street that has been under construction for the last few days if you really want to know."

"Well, hopefully, that keeps you out of trouble for the day. Now can you try not to tear out your stitches while you work? All of your shirts are covered in blood and I'm tired of washing them."

"No, I still have the yellow one... oh no I remember now. I was wearing it that night I found out that chick was a guy and that didn't really end well. I should probably just buy red shirts from now on," Rob responded as he started to reflect on his mistakes.

"It would help if you left Mrs. Pennel's house before Mr. Pennel returned home. Trust me from experience it is easier to make your exit when you aren't worried about getting caught. You also tend to lose fewer shirts, pants, and socks that way," Philip responded as he stirred his own breakfast.

"It was a mistake Philip, can you get over it," Rob muttered knowing what was likely coming next.

"Once is a mistake, but after the fourth time you are just an idiot," Philip responded as he sat down with his own bowl.

"Maybe you're right Philip maybe I am an idiot, but that woman knew things that made me go wild. When she used to put her hand..." Rob paused for a moment to see Philip's expression had gone blank, "I forget sometimes. I'm sorry Philip I wish we could have saved her. I'm going to head out then have a good day." Philip stayed silent as Rob walked out. Once his friend had left, he pulled out a locket with a picture of him and a beautiful woman. He could not help himself as he began to cry for the woman he lost.

It was a beautiful late June morning. The sun was glistening brightly in the sky and the weather was perfect as it had neither become too hot nor stayed too cold. As people walked through the streets you could hear the birds singing in the air above and he was just close enough to hear the soothing rush of the Mississippi. Days like this often-brought tears to the people of Despartian. It reminded them of the days long ago past when the children would spend all day outside. It reminded them of the days when they were younger and carefree. They would spend the whole day down by the riverside causing problems. Those carefree days were nonexistent now.

Things were different, with hundreds of repairs required to rebuild the city from the rubble, everyone was forced to work. If they were able-bodied, and even in some cases when they were not, that was the expectation and that's what they did often driving themselves to near death from exhaustion. They wanted their lives back to normal and did everything to make it happen. It was not easy, but people learned and did whatever came naturally. For others, they did what at first was not so natural. The War had taught its survivors that they were capable of more than they had ever imagined. When the city needed them to adapt, they adapted and thrived.

Some of these people found their calling teaching either they had worked the field before or they had a deep love for the children. The basic requirements to be a teacher had changed as the whole system of education had changed. No longer was the system based on ideas of standardized testing and stress. Now they focused on problem-solving and embracing mistakes. The War was due to people avoiding failures in life so in this new world they wanted the children to see that mistakes were not worthy of punishment, but instead were moments of growth. They wanted the kids to learn that you do not avoid failure you embrace it and use it. More importantly than that, they focused on the idea of human decency and what it meant to exist in a world with others.

The biggest employment field was day laborers. They were the strongest people who could rebuild the city with pure brute strength and resourcefulness. The new laborers didn't have set plans or fancy models they arrived on site found whatever resources were available and made the best house they could as they knew someday it might be theirs. As age or injury caught up with them, they turned to the fields and kitchens to nourish those who were rebuilding the city. This was the role that Philip and many from his generation now occupied.

The last group is referred to as the 'stars'. This isn't a name given out of affection, but instead one of hatred and sarcasm from the rest of the workers. The name is derived from their work with Ascension Corporation. The 'stars that help us ascend again' are the men and women who were hand-selected to return technological loses to the world. Up until two years ago the company was sputtering and stuck in a rut that it could not overcome. Then John arrived and brought life to the company. His biggest and most heralded accomplishment was resetting the electrical grid and returning light to the world after it had been dark for so many years. With that accomplishment, Ascension has risen to be a global sensation making John one of the most influential men in the world despite his unwillingness to show his face to the world.

Rob made his way to today's workplace passing many people moving like lemmings without question. When Rob looks in the eyes of the people, he sees the love in the day workers who are just trying to survive and pave the way for the future. They are the group that learned from the mistakes made prior to the War, but to every yin, there must always be yang. That distinction belongs to the 'night crews' who take advantage of the lawless lands and take whatever they desire. All too often the day workers would work long and hard just to have their work destroyed at night. The night crews had learned nothing from the War and continued to make the same choices that led to the destruction. The balance between the two sides was in constant flux with both of them terrified of what loomed on the horizon. The day laborers thought that if they didn't continue to fight their futures would be doomed, while the night crews saw demise as inevitable at this point, so they chose to live for the current moment. The truth was that neither side knew what would come and this created constant tension in the city.

About two hours into the newest construction project Rob's shirt had a bloodstain growing on it. He had been sweating hard enough that he never noticed the feeling of blood dripping. Unfortunately for him, it got bad enough that someone eventually yelled at him;

"Hey Bub you're bleeding pretty badly there you'd better get that looked at. We don't need you falling apart on us and getting more of us hurt here."

"Damn, Philip is going to kill me," Rob whispered to himself. He hated it when he was interrupted at work, but the laborers would not continue if one of their own was injured. With the dangers of this reborn world, they had to look after one another. They lacked many safety features once used in construction and in order to ensure that everyone left the projects alive, they all needed to be at 100%. They all knew that even a small injury could eventually lead to a catastrophe for all at the site. He had tried arguing with them in the past, but learned quickly how stubborn they could be, so knowing there would be no sense in arguing Rob meandered down to the medical tent. As he walked down to the tent he started to work through the doctor and nurse rotation. One of the few blessings from the War was that it spared most of the medical field, and to a point created a surplus. Thousands of medical professionals were trained during the War in an attempt to save as many lives as possible and those who were already trained tended to be the last ones into battle with a decreased chance of death. Now that the War is over those trained rotated through different work camps in order to stay as fresh as possible. Today he was really hoping for one of the cute blondes that recently moved to the city.

"That's right you're on today, well at least I got the cute part right," Rob mumbled as he pulled the tent's curtain back to reveal a young woman patching up another worker's leg.

"How lovely what brings you down here Rob? Did you get caught with another man's wife again," the woman's voice replied as she finished taping up the worker?

"I was only caught once and with the way that man moved I honestly didn't think he could catch me," defended Rob as he started to flash a boyish grin, "How are you doing today Anna?"

"I don't want to know what you're thinking about Rob, but whatever it is get it out of your head because it isn't going to happen," she responded. Anna was an awe-inspiring enigma, she was built like an Amazon, carried herself with the majesty of a queen, had the intelligence of a chess grandmaster, and was as friendly as a puppy. Anna was an enigma to most as she was not what anyone would expect. Her strength made her a force during the War. Her beauty attracted to the eyes of everyone who saw her, with her blonde hair that glowed, even under the cheap light of the tent. The most striking feature was her intelligence that rivaled everyone in the city and unlike John or Rob, she used hers only in an attempt to help others. She began to remove his shirt to take a look at his injury. Her hands moved gently across his back as if a feather was moving across it. She may have been strong, but she knew how to restrain it. She looked at the busted stitching and all she could do was shake her head.

"Why is it that every time I see you, you manage to look like you're in worse shape? I mean the shaggy beard that makes you look homeless, and of course more bullet holes with drunk stitching. Do you just let people use you as target practice or is this what you need to help yourself relax nowadays cause if that is the case I know a pretty good psychologist that might be able to help," she stated as Rob's face turned to disdain at the last few comments? Anna looked over the wound again and finally began to work.

"A little bit of both I guess. I did actually sleep in my own bed last night because of this," Rob responded trying not to be a smartass while she had a needle at his back. He had learned over numerous occasions that he is best served keeping his mouth shut.

"You are a piece of work Rob and you should really shave that mess," she ordered.

"Yeah, it has been getting a little scratchy. I just haven't had the time," he told her as he winced at the occasional stitch.

Anna never thought she'd be a doctor; it was never even a thought in her head despite her genius-level intellect. She was going to help people, but her concerns were more about the youth. She loved those who often had no one else to love them. The War threw a monkey wrench in her plans and she quickly learned that she had a knack for keeping people alive, along with comforting those who were at their lowest. Since that change in profession she has saved hundreds of lives, but she still remembers the first which just so happened to be Rob.

The pair have shared many experiences both before and during the War. She was there for some of his most atrocious injuries. Of those, the ones that broke her heart were the ones he sustained the night he fought with John. It wasn't the injury that she remembered it was the look in his eyes. Near the end of the War, Rob's gaze continued to grow farther and farther away. He continued to lose those that mattered to him and when his team betrayed him, he was gone. His will had been broken and the pursuit of the bottle followed quickly. After that night he started to push people away, but she was one of the few that he couldn't shake. This friendship saved his life more times than he could count and he would do anything to pay her back for all she has done, yet she often refused his help citing hers as a mere duty. Although there was truth in that it was also a lie. She saved hundreds, but it was obvious that she paid special attention to him.

There had been rumors throughout the War and after that, there was something between the two of them, but those were only spread by those who didn't know them. They cared for one another and Rob often flirted with her, but it was more of a playful flirt. The two of them were more like siblings than anything and cared for one another as such. That relationship started when they were in college together. The War intensified that relationship.

Arguably the defining moment of their relationship was the first time she operated on him. The media at the time referred to that battle as the 'Memphis Throwdown'. Media outlets always loved giving catchy names to battles, so they would be remembered even though no one fighting them wanted to remember.

The War as a whole had two specific phases in it. It started as the second American Civil War. After years of tense racial and class relations, a pivotal election was held to determine the newest president of the United States. Neither option was considered the best and it likely didn't matter who won as the end result would have still been the same. The election divided a fragile country and two opposing sides began to rise. Theses sides grew more violent eventually leading to one orchestrating a naval bombardment of Los Angeles. The city was nearly burned to the ground and the country drew its battle lines.

The second part was an all-out world war that broke the planet. Seeing the weakness that had befallen one of the strongest countries in the world enemy nations began to take advantage. This led to allies intervening, however, due to the chaotic nature of the Civil War, there were allies and enemies that had different investments in who would win. This eventually led to the War disintegrating borders and relationships leading to what exists in the present.

Now the Battle of Memphis occurred early during the Civil War portion. Memphis being in the heart of the country was an area where the social and racial tensions were more intense compared to many cities. The battle would go on to become one of the bloodiest and most drawn-out battles. Anna had only been in the field for two weeks and she was still green in every sense never tasting a true battle.

***

It was the morning of October 7th and it had been a quiet morning early on. The sun was bright and there was a crispness in the air for that time of year. Rob was fighting for the side known as Unity and was a member of the 12th division at that time. Sometime late in that beautiful morning the base Rob was stationed in fell under attack. The position he had been assigned to was a critical location for Unity's ability to take Memphis, and it was just as critical for the opposition to drive them out of it. Within the first few minutes of the siege, twenty were already dead and another forty were severely injured across the facility. The battle for the base turned into a ten-day blood fest that would birth not one, but two legendary figures upon the third night of the siege.

During that day's conflict Unity's forces were spread thin. They not only had to guard the base, bit protect the nearby areas and the truth that they did not want to face was that they just didn't have the manpower. This, in turn, left Rob and solely one other soldier to guard the west entrance of the fort. Now to the higher-ups, this wasn't a mistake at first because it had been one of the entrances untouched by the enemy until a blast finally destroyed the door they were guarding. This killed the other guard instantly leaving Rob to fend for himself/. The rest of the story has gone down as legend and told by both sides.

Rob was deeply injured from the blast with his leg was torn up by the shrapnel from the door. He could nearly immobile, but still able to find cover. Legend says that for 10-20 minutes he would battle twenty some soldiers. They tried everything to get past him and take a foothold within the base. He never wavered and there was no chance that he would let them kill him, he had too many people relying on him. During that battle he had one mentality: he was going to fight to his last bullet and use his bare hands if he had to. The odds never mattered to him while he stared death in the eyes. He just kept going knowing that if he didn't, none of his fighting would matter. That was the day that a boy from Despartian became a hero that was always willing to fight and was always ready to die if the moment called for it.

After twenty minutes of brutal fighting reinforcements finally arrived and drove the invaders out. Once the area was secured, they rushed the young soldier to the medical bay where all the doctors were already swamped from the previous battles. The only one available was Anna, but she had no experience all she had done was the prep work. She had gone through all the practices, simulations, tests, and completed all the studying she needed, but the last test was supposed to be operating with an experienced doctor to help her in case of an emergency.

She had been sent to Memphis as it was suspected that it would soon turn into a war zone and she would have her opportunities. Unfortunately, the battle escalated faster than anticipated and swamped the regular doctors. She had been ordered to delegate herself to an assistant until the battle wound down. She was deemed unfit for any form of intense surgery especially one that involved saving the leg of a man she knew personally. Not knowing what else to do she started going through the basic prep work hoping that someone else would finish and be able to help. She continued preparations even after they were all finished, but there was no one. She was all he had. The gravity of the moment began catching up to her until she suddenly stopped moving completely. Her hands began shaking nearly dropping the tools. She was turning into a wreck, not only could this man die on her table as her first patient, but she would also lose a close friend at the same time. When a life is in a person's hands all the studying and cadaver practice becomes mute.

Even the smartest person in the world can look like a child learning to walk for the first time.

She tried to calm herself and him by making small talk about the old days, but it just wasn't working for her hands only started to shake worse. He understood her hesitation as he laid there, but then the pain meds wore off. Once he could feel his leg again his cries grew louder and he became aware of how close he was to losing his leg. He looked deep into her blue eyes and pleaded;

"Anna, you need to start the procedure. If we wait much longer my leg is gone and possibly more. If this shrapnel is infected than regardless of what you do, I'm done for. It's your move."

"I... I can't Rob I've never done this and I don't want to lose you. If you die by my hands, I'm never going to be able to look Iris in the eyes again. You two mean so much to me and I can't handle that," she stuttered as her hands clenched tight.

"God, why is it that every woman I know wants to argue with me... I'm likely to die either way Anna. If I sit here waiting for another doctor my survival rate plummets if your screw-up, I'm dead. I don't like either of those, but at least the second completely relies on you screwing up, which you won't," he assured her trying to bring her confidence back, "Now listen to me closely. I've watched you for years now, not in a creepy way like that might sound. Over that time, I have come to realize you are one of the most intelligent people around, far greater than myself. I mean just look at the current situation I'm out there getting shot at while you stay in this nice guarded room.

The second thing I learned was that you are not only intelligent, but you also work harder than everyone else. Most of these doctors had this dream since they were young and spent their whole life studying for it, you, on the other hand, were thrown into this out of necessity and have thrived because of that ethic. Most people in that situation would have settled with being just okay, but not you, you became the quickest graduate of the program. That takes something special that no one else here has.

The third thing I noticed was that nothing can get in your way. You have potential and something special deep in you that will make you one of the best ever, I know that and promise it. If there was anyone, I'd want to do this surgery it would be you. Lastly, you have a spectacular ass," they both chuckled at his last observation. With what little energy he had left he put his hand to her face and wiped away a nervous tear that had fallen. He finished with a proud declaration, "Now shut up and get this shit out of my leg you big dummy!"

That day she went on to perform her first surgery. In the process, she saved Rob's leg and life. It was not a perfect, textbook surgery, but they rarely are. What was impressive was her ability to respond to the hiccups and in the end that was what created the sense of faith, she would use for the rest of the war. If it was not for her Rob likely would have been dead that day or a number of other times after that and then all the heroics would have gone undone. Without each other, they would never have heroes. This newfound faith, given to her by Rob, also allowed Anna to become greater than she ever imagined. She eventually went on to become one of the greatest surgeons the war would see just as Rob predicted. She was not only a medical savant, but she also was an expert at maintaining a calm and collected composure despite some of the grotesque injuries she would face. Without her and the special unit, Rob would go on to join the tide of the war would have shifted far differently than it did.

***

As Anna finishes up the newest stitching job concern consumes her face. She begins to run her hand over his many scars, burns, and defects. He has destroyed his body through the years to the point where now he feels like a topographic map of the Himalayas. She has repaired many of these wounds, but for each one, she has helped with at least another two existed. Then she looks at the beard and smells the stench of booze from his past week. She worries about his physical body but knows he has had another one of his bad weeks. They have been coming more frequently and growing far more intense each time. Even to the point where he is showing up with a bullet wound. She knows that no matter what she does for his body there is no cure for his heart.

"Your stitching is done," she starts with a quiver in her voice as he begins to rise, "do me a favor though I really don't want to see you in my tent twice today so go down and see if they need you at the school. I know the kids are always happy to see you. Do it for me, please." They both understood the deeper meaning in her words, but neither wanted to talk about it. She knew that no matter how far gone he got; the kids always sobered him up. He loved them and always tried to be the best role model he could be for them.

"I thought you enjoyed these little moments that we get to share together. I mean who else keeps you on such high alert," he chuckled as he struggled to put his shirt back on, "On the other hand, Philip did say I was running out of clean shirts. Maybe this time I'll actually listen to you and not piss off Philip." He rose to his feet with a smile, as he tried to hide the pain.

"Wow, you're actually agreeing with me. That might be a first. Now promise me that you'll try to stop in and say hi when you're not bleeding, dying, broken, or running from trouble. I do enjoy seeing my friends much more when they don't require stitches. Also shave that bloody beard. It makes you look like a bum," she said, putting her hand on his shoulder.

"Will do, but I'm going to need some shaving cream," he started as she threw some shaving utensils at him. She faked a smile as they nodded goodbye.

"He is going to get himself killed one of these days, but I don't think he cares. I just hope that I'm not there to see it," she whispered, but she could not think about him for long. It was a busy day and he wouldn't be her only patient today. They all needed attention and they all mattered.

Chapter 3
The Future and The Past

Rob made quick work of the beard before he left the worksite. It had grown irritating and scratchy over the past week and he was tired of the comments, plus it wasn't a good look for going to see the kids. He often tried to keep himself clean-shaven and neat a habit taught to him during his military training. However, he has had several weeks as of late that were rough. He has been struggling more than ever with his past which has led him deeper into the bottle. It was very possible that he would not have made it back from this bender had it not been for John's summons. This realization probably made things worse for him because it means the man, he hates more than anyone saved his life, again.

Now that Rob was back to his sober self, he was back to listening to someone with far more sense than him. He had learned over the last fifteen years that she always had his best interest in mind and despite his continuous need to fight he respected her opinion more than anything. She was one of his oldest friends and with how he has acted he still couldn't believe she has stuck around so long. He had thought that it was out of duty considering they were often on the same missions, but she still fights for him after the Wars end. Maybe it was her sister like bond to Rob's fiancée Iris, but since he returned from the War, he grew distant from her. In the end it was likely just loyalty to a friend she felt sorry for, despite his stupidity.

He slowly hobbled closer to the building that housed the school. It was nothing special, but it accomplished what it needed to. It was a small, old brick building not much bigger than an auditorium. Much of the color had faded from the bricks making it look filthy and rotten something some overprotective parents would have sued about back in the pre-war days. The most distinctive element was the brass bell placed on top that many from older generations insisted on out of nostalgia. It was one of two schools in the immediate area, the other resided on the southern side of the city. They were placed in manners that would limit how far the children had to travel, but with a limited number of teachers two buildings were all that could be maintained which still forced many children to cover large distances and often skip classes.

When he arrived, the younger kids were at recess playing in the field next to the school. All of these children were born during the waning years of the War when the area was far more peaceful which made them ignorant of what the world was like prior to it. It was truly beautiful to see how they lived without a care in the world. He stood in amazement watching the joy in their eyes when a sudden yell rang out;

"Rob!!!" He turned quickly to find the source. However, the first thing he saw was a young girl flying through the air toward him. Reacting quickly, he flung his arms out to catch the girl and give her a big hug. He held the girl tight. Her name was Alexandra and she was a young school girl that lived with one of Rob's former friends, among other things. She was born just after the War had started. She had bright blue eyes that shined like diamonds and glowed with an energy Rob could barely comprehend. That dirty blonde hair of hers flowed as she flew in the air towards him and fell gently to her shoulders when she stopped. Topping things off was her infectious personality that brought a smile to even his darkest days.

"I missed you so much. Why don't you come to see Aunt Lisa and me anymore did I do something wrong," the young girl asked with her big blue eyes pouting?

"No sweetie, it isn't you. I've just been really busy lately that's all. Trust me, I was starting to miss you too cutie," he replied setting the girl down and looking her in the eyes, "Now what is behind your ear girl?" Rob reached behind her ear and showed her a piece of chocolate that he had been hiding. The little girl's eyes grew big at the sight and her smile stretched from ear to ear.

"Now I'm not a chocolate expert or anything but I'm pretty sure it's supposed to be in your tummy, dummy," he said as his own smile grew to match the size of hers.

"I didn't put it there," she defended as she reached for the chocolate with her big goofy smile which was missing one of her canines.

"Really, who put it there then, the chocolate fairy," he questioned as he handed her the piece?

"You did silly," she answered as she swayed back and forth as young kids do.

"Ah, you think too much of me," he smiled patting her on the head while she consumed her magic chocolate.

"Alexandra where are you," called a loud voice?

"I think she left Gerald. I tried to stop her I swear, but she's just like her aunt stubborn to the end," he hollered back as he winked at Alex who was now giggling. The man he called Gerald turned a corner to find them. Gerald is a big and tall man with an even bigger heart. He is one of the few people who still seemed to hold a positive attitude despite what had occurred over the last few years. The moment the man with the golden heart and hair to match saw Rob he ran over to him and hoisted him off the ground with a giant bear hug. It was easy to see the discomfort the injured man was feeling as he was suspended in the air.

"God Gerald, between you and the little squirt there I think I would've been safer just going back to work," he gasped as he tried to regain his breath after the hug. Curious at the comment Gerald looked at his friend who was now loosening his bad shoulder. All Gerald could do was shake his head; some things never change, he thought.

"How've you been buddy? I haven't seen you for a couple of weeks now. What's new," Gerald queried ignoring Rob's injury? Gerald had a special knack for people and learned early to treat each one as the unique human beings they were. This included Rob most of all. He has learned that prodding wasn't going to get him anywhere. Rob was always the type to deflect and reply with sarcasm so, instead, he just went into happy go lucky mode. That personality and social awareness of his is why he was put into the schools. With his body build, most people would assume he'd be working with the laborers, but his heart and brain were too valuable to not let him inspire the next generations. Every time Rob snuck by the school and would overhear one of Gerald's lessons, he became filled with hope knowing that at least these kids would turn into better people than most of their parents and grandparents who created the world they lived in.

"You know the same old same old just working to rebuild the city. Then last night I got shot in the shoulder, so nothing too exciting," he shrugged in a nonchalant manner.

"Ms. E was looking for you Alex, hurry back to the classroom so that we can start the lessons," he said shooing the little girl away, "Alright now that the girl is gone what did you do this time?" He knew that he couldn't ignore what Rob had just said and had to prod despite his better intuition.

"If you must know I went to have a meeting with John last night and...." he started knowing that a lecture was soon to come.

"Just making sure we are talking about Ascension John also known as the guy who sent you through a table the last time you saw him after I recall you punched him. Great plan as always Rob I couldn't imagine a scenario where that ends poorly," Gerald interrupted with a sarcastic grin on his face.

"He asked me to meet with him and I was kind of curious. I mean our last meeting wasn't particularly good, but things can change. Instead, I learned that he's still an asshole, just now he has a lot more money and greater influence. I also discovered that he is working on something big, I'm just not sure what yet," Rob responded with a concerned look in his eyes.

"I should be shocked. I mean people don't get shot a whole lot these days, but for you, this is just par for the course isn't it? Now I'd love to know what you said that would cause him to shoot you, but I have a feeling it is best that I don't know," Gerald started as he shook his head looking at his buddy, "Also do me a favor don't say that the man, who has done more for this city than anyone else, is up to trouble too many other people. Especially right now when the smell of alcohol is still on your clothing. Now you are my friend and I know you are telling the truth, but it is a hard truth for most people to swallow. Luckily, even those who are not your friend recognize you as a war hero, but John is much more important to this city right now and if you go telling stories it will blow up in your face. I don't want to see you get run out of the city Rob." Gerald placed his hand on Rob's good shoulder. Rob reached for Gerald's hand and moved it away from his shoulder. He acknowledged and appreciated the concern, but as always had to do things his way.

"You know all about the adventures John and I went on together. We fought to save what was left of this country and planet doing things that were cruel and vicious, but effective. I trusted him deeply and he slowly became a brother to me as we saved each other's lives. We were inseparable at the end. People began to hear legends and ran when they saw us. Back in those days I never could have imagined regretting that decision, but as the missions went on, I began to see the darkness in John. He could be the greatest man you knew and then turn around to become the devil. He took vicious to the next level as villages burned at our feet. Even with as close as we were, it always felt like he was holding something back, something he didn't want me to know. There is something about that man that can't be trusted no matter how sympathetic he makes himself feel. Now he is planning something again and I know it is the devil inside of him running it. He let the darkness consume him entirely that night he put me through the tale and now I have to find a way to stop him because I'm the only one who can," Rob replied looking out in the distance toward the Ascension headquarters where John was operating.

"I understand Rob I just want to make sure that you don't go around getting more holes pumped into you. I really do worry about you. With that said Ms. E has been looking for you too Rob. The sisters have missed you," Gerald said trying to change the subject knowing that nothing he did would change the path Rob was going to follow.

"Well I don't have anything to say to her," he proclaimed. Even though Gerald had not said their names Rob knew the implication of any conversation and had no interest in having one. The happiness Alex had brought him had vanished entirely and distress became visible in his expressions.

"Good, I didn't want to listen to your drunk ass anyways. I just need you to hear me out," called a woman's voice from behind him. Rob dropped his head knowing whatever was about to be said was not good. The conversation he wanted to avoid was inevitable at this point so, he turned to greet the voice trying to fake a smile to lessen the blows he anticipated. The source of the voice was a lean woman with a disgusted look on her face. The woman still had the figure she once had years ago thin, but with a healthy amount of muscle. Other parts of her had changed however, she once had long blonde locks that flowed and always seemed to cover her eyes. Now she kept her hair short and tied tight in a bun on top of her head and though the students would never know she dyed her hair a much darker tone to give her a more mature look.

"You sir are a brute and a royal pain in the ass. I mean you run around this town as a virtual vagrant and think that there is no consequence to it. You think that the world revolves around you and that the rest of us can be damned. Now if you were anyone else, I wouldn't care, I'd let you do your thing as long as you stayed out of my way, but your stupidity affects the person I care about more than anything in the world. My sister loves you and your antics tear her apart daily. Just because you have the luxury of running away and avoiding things doesn't me, we do," the angry woman yelled at Rob as she avoided actually grabbing hold of him.

"I'm not avoiding her because I enjoy it, Ali. I'm doing it because she is better off never seeing me again," he fired back as sadness filled his eyes. He didn't cry, but it was clear he wanted to do nothing else. The angry woman was Iris' sister Ali and had always had her back. She was angry about Rob's actions because technically they were still engaged as there was never an official break-up, he just stopped talking to her.

"You say that, but you are only what you've made yourself through this downward spiral you've been on. You have to understand that what happened to Jenny was not your fault and neither of us blames you for it. You have to forgive yourself for that tragedy and all the others that you carry in your heart. The whole world was plunged into chaos and you can't try to carry the burden of it on your shoulders alone. You have to let others in and if there was anyone that you should talk to it is the woman that loved you more than anything. Move on and go see your fiancé again. It has been far too long," Ali pleaded as her words of anger turned to those of desperation. Rob had no answer so he did the only thing he knew how to anymore he walked away from the problem, "She still has the ring you know. She refuses to give it up despite my best efforts, not without an actual ending from you. She is such a beautiful, kind, and intelligent soul that could do much better than you and at the very least deserves an actual good-bye!" Rob didn't answer he just walked away ignoring Gerald as he tried to wave good-bye. There was truth in what she was saying, but if he acknowledged it, he'd have to face it full force.

"You can't run forever Rob, especially when you're running from your own past," she added, trying to get him to stop.

"Watch me," he responded at last as he continued to walk away. Gerald placed his arm around Ali to comfort her and they both just shook their heads while he disappeared. Gerald looked at the school behind him. The classes would soon be starting again, but he feared that his fellow teacher would not be much help anymore.

"Why are men such idiots," Ali finally said as she recovered from the interaction with Rob?

"It isn't a man thing this time. It may have started that way as an evolutionary stance of him being a man needing to protect his family, but we are far beyond that now. Even before the War he always tried to be the strong friend who could take everyone's troubles on so that they could thrive while he suffered. His heart may have been greater than any of ours, because it had faced so much pain. He refused to let us be alone because he had been solitary forever. He had this desire to make others happy no matter the cost. Then the War made it worse, he had such a strong affinity for life I think the War broke him when he had to take life to protect it," Gerald said as the pair started to head back towards the classrooms.

"But he doesn't have to be that way anymore he can come back to us again and be at peace again," Ali claimed still unsure of what Gerald was saying about Rob.

"The thing is that his mindset is completely different. You have to understand that during that war things happened to him and he did things. Maybe more importantly he saw things that scared him. He saw the darkest side of mankind, stared into the abyss that was death and he is still trying to deal with it. His soul is etched with death and until he finds a way to cleanse it, he will always be running, thinking he isn't good enough despite what we might tell him. Maybe just as important as his desire to protect us from what he saw out there.

Now letting your soon to be wife's sister die along with her best friend's boyfriend on the same day is hard for a man who just wants to protect people. Then after that tragedy having their shared best friend, Danielle go missing during a battle could have only broken him farther. He is shattered and despite what it looks like he is trying to put himself together again. This is something he has to for himself, so for now all we can do now is help him the best we can and hope that he chooses to change before it is too late," Gerald explained as he looked up at the sky to say a prayer for his friend.

"Well enough on him let's go help some kids Ali," Gerald said as his demeanor changed from a stern philosopher to a joyful teacher again.

Chapter 4
Bridge of Passion

Given how his day had gone so far Rob decided that his best option was to wander through the city for the rest of the day. At this point it felt like anywhere he went he'd be yelled at and was growing tired of it. All he wanted to do was escape the criticism, in truth he wanted to wander into the bars again, but after his conversation with John, he knew he had to sober up. He had to be ready whenever John made his move, so instead he wandered and thought. He thought on what Anna had done for him and felt guilty that he continued to put her through unnecessary pains. Then he considered Ali's words and the truth she had shared. It had hurt him to hear her pleas because he did care for her and Iris, but they deserved better than him. He knew all of the lectures were his own fault and that they only said what they said out of love, but he didn't want to hear it anymore.

He didn't understand how he could still be so loved despite his best efforts to push them away. He was trying to protect them from himself, but even at that, he has failed. He has spent the better part of the last three years drinking and sleeping around avoiding his past and any form of commitment. Yet despite all that, there were still people that believed in him and to his own displeasure considered him a hero for the actions he took during the war.

He hated that word, hero. With the things that he had done, there was no reason for him to be classified as a hero. He had killed numerous people, felt the lives of countless people be extinguished, and watched many more die in front of him unable to save them. The acts he committed should never have been considered heroic and if people ever found out the details, they would look at him in disgust. Heroics exist in war, but he did not perform them. In his mind he had been nothing more than a brutal liberator on a good day, on his worst he was a tyrant. He understood why people called him one and why they wanted him to be the hero they told stories about.

They needed him to be the shining light of hope to come from the brutality. They wanted their hometown kid to be their champion. Even though he understood that he still hated it. There were thousands of men and women he fought with that deserved the title much more than him, but they never made it home. They never had their moment of appreciation outside of a few mass funerals.

The people of Despartian told stories of his amazing feats that the children adored, but he could never sit around long enough to hear the finish because they left out the ugly parts. They didn't know about the ugly moments where his moral compass became blurry and those outweighed any accomplishments. His team committed some of the greatest atrocities during that seven-year war. They started out as an elite squad that went on suicide missions, but they just kept succeeding at them. Every mission was expected to be their last, but it never was. They orchestrated the complete destabilization of governments at every level, planned the razing of several cities, and eliminated countless valuable individuals. They were the best at what they did, but none of it was truly sanctioned. Every mission was given to that was covert and had they been caught they would have been disowned. Despite all that it didn't matter to Rob at the time. He was fighting in a war that was unprecedented and it all felt normal at the time.

That last bit was the part that bothered him the most now that the war was over. He had either ruined or killed countless eyes without ever batting an eye. This is the very same man who hated to kill insects prior to it. He had seen the demon inside himself, he had seen it blossom, and he saw himself change beyond recognition. A man with a demon, like his own, didn't deserve the title of hero. Beyond that, he was haunted by the fact that a man with the title of hero should be able to protect those precious to him. He was no hero.

After some time wondering, Rob finally made his way to Federation Bridge. He often came to the bridge to think as it reminded him of what he calls his great failure and for him, nothing motivates him more than the memory of what happened. Prior to leaving for the war, he made a promise to his fiancé that he was doing so to protect her and the ones he cared about. He also told her that if anything would ever happen to the city he would be there, but when it fell under attack he was not there. The city succumbed to the war in the second year after avoiding any form of confrontation for as long as it could. During the battle, the Federation Bridge's sister bridge that sat next to it was destroyed in an attempt to slow the enemy down. The idea was to force them onto the smaller bridge where the local guards could stand a chance versus an unstoppable force. Now it did work for some time, but just like the Alamo numbers win. They had prayed throughout the siege that reinforcements would come, but the nearest was headed by Rob's team and they were on a far more important mission. They were only able to return to the city when it was rubble.

Nowadays he sits on the bridge from time to time wondering what it would be like to fall off. It seemed every day the thought would cross his mind, but he just couldn't do it. There was still something that kept him going. He was not depressed, but the traumas and memories he carried with him made some days unbearable. He wanted to finally escape them, but in the back of his mind he wanted to keep going because he wanted to make it to the day that he would be free of the pain, so instead, he reflected and embraced the pain of his memories for the time being.

"Are you going to jump at last," asked the voice of a woman? The sound of her voice made him smile it was one that was soothing to his ears. It was a comforting one that had been there for him even when he was at his worst. She was a critical part of his life because unlike all his other friends she never critiqued him or told him to change. She was the one that accepted the parts of him that were broken because she was just as damaged.

"Nah, I think I'll stick around another day. Besides the view up here is just getting good," he smirked with a flirtatious smile spreading across his face. She laughed as she approached him to sit down. She was a slender woman that was more legs than anything else and her clothing choice was not particularly conservative either, which always made Rob's day.

"For once I'd have to agree with you. Now how are you doing today," she finally asked?

"Well, I'm here at the bridge so I'm doing as well as you could expect Kendra. And since it appears that you've left Carly and the others behind early tonight you must be doing just as well," he replied softly as he raised his hand to her face to push aside some stray hairs that covered her tantalizing smile.

"No, it's not actually like that. The other girls already have jobs lined up while I struck out. Carly even landed a job with one of those rich brains that work for Ascension," she replied quietly as she looked up at the clouds overhead.

"Hopefully she is safe tonight, those guys that work for Ascension are just trouble. Most of them are cocky, punks who think they deserve something because they work at Ascension," Rob interjected with disdain for the company. Kendra just shook her head knowing that Rob was only lashing out at one of the people at Ascension.

"You are quite the overreactor and deflector. Plus, I'm sure that she is fine, it isn't her first rodeo. Now I actually came here for you Rob. I had heard that you've had quite the last week and I know that tomorrow is the anniversary of that day. I figured that you'd want someone to talk to and even if you refuse, I wanted to talk. It has been a rough week for me too," she explained as she leaned over to rest her head on his shoulder. She had a long distant look in her eyes that looked far beyond the horizon.

Kendra led a difficult life even by modern standards. Her beauty was her only asset and because of it her and her roommates participated in the world's oldest profession which hadn't improved in its long history. She wasn't the most intelligent woman around but had a big heart that just cared about people. Unfortunately, that big heart and job were a horrible combo which is why she often feels alone and like damaged goods. She hadn't been through the horrors that Rob had, but she still carried more problems than she liked to admit.

"I forget sometimes that you are one of the few people outside of my immediate teammates that know the truth about that day eight years ago. I've been running from it for so long," he started as his mind wandered back to the days before Despartian was destroyed and the decisions he made.

"I still couldn't imagine carrying around a burden like that, but as I've told you before they would forgive you. Maybe, more importantly, Iris deserves to hear the truth from you," she explained to him knowing that he would soon brush the advice off.

"You are starting to sound like everyone else Kendra. Don't do that. I need you to be what you usually are. Now please can we just talk about our weeks," he pleaded as he deflected her earlier comments.

"You're right. If I start judging you then you'll do the same and I really don't want to deal with that right now, so can we just start tonight over," she asked? He simply nodded his head and their familiar routine took hold.

The two of them sat on the edge of the bridge and she began to tell him stories about her week. Meanwhile, he just sat and listened to her. He never interrupted or injected his opinions. The floor was all hers and that was all she needed. Her whole life she had people try and tell her what to do and more often than not their advice left her miserable. She wanted to do things on her own, but during these conversations on the bridge, she wanted someone to truly listen to her so that she didn't feel alone. Once she finished, he started to confide in her. He told her the stories that were cluttering his mind and sent him on the benders like the one during the week before.

These talks were exactly what they needed and it was something that they couldn't do with anyone else. They shared a connection; they were two broken souls that felt connected to this world through one another. They talked for hours as they looked out over the river ignoring the people passing them as they headed to work or home. The talking continued all the way until sunset when all of a sudden, they became silent and just absorbed the majesty of nature. Neither ever explained why they would stop talking, but every time the sun set or rose when they were together, all conversation stopped. It may have been because in the insane world they both lived in the sun was the one constant and it would bring them the peace of mind that they treasured so deeply.

The same feelings they held for the sun could describe their relationship. It was a constant existence, when one needed the other, they were there, but they didn't need to be. This was not a romantic love they did not yearn for one another the way lovers do; in truth, they were just in search of the physical release and the consistency. Neither struggled with the physical aspect as both had their share of partners, but no one connected with them in the same manner. Now it was not consistent in the regular sense however, for them it was the knowledge that they were both always broken and would never try and change one another. After the sun fully fell, he reached over and stroked her cheek just before leaning over to kiss her on it.

"It's getting late do you want to head out and see what Philip is cooking up tonight," he asked knowing that the invitation was not just for food, but for the other things besides emotional support that they craved from one another.

"Yeah, but I need to stop by and feed Baxter first," she replied after a brief hesitation knowing that this night would end like so many others that they had shared. She knew that their relationship was flawed and she hated it, but like a drug she wanted it. She needed the connection she felt when the two of them were together even if she wasn't sure how he felt about her.

Kendra's house was a rundown mess of a building like many in the city. It was especially common for the area she lived in, but it still saddened Rob every time he saw the condition of her home. The house had a rustic color to it and the windows in the upper floors were cracked. Weeds crawled up the side of the building filling in all the holes that had worn off the building. It was not much, but it kept five people and a dog semi-comfortable which is really all that people could hope for these days especially if they didn't receive help from Ascension. Though Rob felt sorry for Kendra she was proud of the shack because she and the other five earned the building and the freedom it gave them.

They walked up to the front door and Kendra flung the door open when the pair was rushed by a giant German Shepherd. The creature was massive standing just under three feet when it was on all fours and easily eclipsed the ninety-pound mark. It was a ferocious beast that could intimidate the bravest of men once it flashed its jaws.

The dog rose onto its hind legs and put his front paws on her shoulders. It was at the point where the dog could look her in the eyes and with all its excitement it would have put Kendra on the ground if Rob had not been there to catch her. Despite the appearance, Baxter was the definition of all bark and no bite. Whenever he saw a friendly face, he turned into a puppy again. Even with his massive size Rob still found the dog adorable. Kendra had found Baxter as a puppy all by himself wandering the town alone and starving, so she took him in and put some weight back on the dog even though it took some food out of her mouth. After those first few days the dog grew protective. It knew her sacrifices and thanked her every day for them. This led to an interesting first meeting with Rob when he ended up with the nine-month-old German Shepherd's jaw clenched on his ass. Since then, Baxter has apologized and taken a liking for Rob as he knows he only wants the best for Kendra and would never hurt her intentionally.

"Hey boy! do you want some food," Kendra asked smiling as the pup finally returned back to all four? The dog's ears perked up immediately at the sound of food and he rushed into another room. Almost instantaneously he returned to them with a giant silver dish in his mouth and the poutiest of eyes. Even though he had been spoiled his whole life you'd never be able to tell by the eyes he can give when hungry.

She took the dish from him and they headed to the kitchen to find his food. While Rob waited for her to return his curiosity overwhelmed him and he decided to go snooping around. After some time, he stumbled upon a recently taken picture of Kendra, Carly, and her roommates all gathered with a girl he had never seen before. She was different than what he was used to seeing, especially with the crowd that Kendra usually follows. This girl wore a pristine dress that stole the image and drew your attention from the others. She also had something that was not often seen in the city anymore. She had this youthful glow to her along with a mischievous smile.

"Kendra who's the other girl in this picture," he asked mystified by the picture? He knew it likely wouldn't matter, but it was rare for him to see a woman he had never seen before. As expected, he had slept with many of Despartian's eligible bachelorettes and even the ineligible ones, but outside of his escapades, he had acted as a watchman for the city. He had made it his duty to always know what was going on inside the city so that he could protect it from any more disasters. That means that if someone new had entered the city he needed to know their intentions.

"Girl? If anyone is going to recognize the girls of this town, I thought it'd be you or do you need a picture of her ass to unclog your memory," she answered back confused about what he was talking about, but also in a slight condescending manner knowing she couldn't pass up the opportunity to insult him.

"Ouch, I expect comments like that from Philip, Anna, Ali, Gerald, and just about everyone else in town but you, come on now," he hissed back offended by the accusation, "Honestly I have no clue who this woman is I've never seen her and that is what worries me the most." Now curious about what he was gibbering about Kendra made her way towards Rob and when she arrived, he pointed out the source of his inquiry.

"Now I get it, this one is younger than eighteen so she hasn't hit your radar yet," she joked now that she understood what was going on.

"Ha, thanks for the heads up, but seriously who is she? She doesn't seem like the usual crowd you hang out with; I mean no signs of drug abuse or being 'well-traveled'," he said causing her face to scrunch a little as she absorbed the insult.

"We were working around Ascension looking for new clients and she just ran into us," she answered trying to redirect the conversation in a more serious manner.

"I still hate the fact that you girls work around Ascension I worry about what they may be up to. Especially John, I'm telling you he is planning something," Rob responded with a worried face.

"Yeah, we know, but sweetie Ascension is where the high rollers live and we need the money. Those guys spend a lot of time in those offices and need company when they are done. Plus, the word on the street is they are kind of weird which costs them extra. Now back to the original question, that girl. You see just before we finished fishing around the building we happened to run into this sweet little girl;

"'What are you wastes doing here,' she asked us. Okay, she wasn't that sweet, but we have gotten used to that especially from other women so we rolled with it and Carly calmly answered her.

'We are working doll-face. Trying to make some money something I'm assuming you really don't have to worry about. Now if you'll excuse us, we were just leaving.' That's exactly what we did we just started to walk away when she yelled back to us.

'If you need work, I might have something for you. One of the guys here has been bugging me for things and let's just say he isn't my type. I'd be glad to give you his number if you'll get him out of my hair.' Carly went and got the number from the girl who was too young to be approached by the men here, but they still tried their hardest to get hard.

Now that I think about it that creep, she spoke of should be the last one Carly is visiting tonight, so I guess I'll have the full details tomorrow. After hearing about some of the sleazeballs in the office we all began to feel sort of bad for her so we just started talking and she explained that despite her age her Uncle John had given her a job in the company," this comment by Kendra drew terror and disgust to Rob's face.

"What was her name," he asked still dumbfounded staring at the girl in the picture.

"Trisha Mayland," Kendra said quickly, seeing how Rob no longer cared about the rest of the story. Rob just continued to stare trying to memorize her image. There was no way that this niece's arrival was coincidental. Kendra tried to grab his arm and pull him to the door. She knew this fascination was not going to be a healthy one. At first, he wouldn't break concentration, but eventually, he looked back up seeing this beautiful woman trying to take him home and returned to his senses for the most part. Before he shut the door behind him, however, he took one last look at the photo baffled that this girl was related to his antithesis.

During their walk to his house, they kept their conversation shallow and avoided any sort of depth or gravity. They had their deep talk on the bridge and now they just needed lightness. Plus, Kendra wanted to avoid the chance that Rob would ask about Trisha and any connection to John could send him on a spiral. She knew things about their connection that he would never admit, and she knew it was best to avoid the topic.

"I'm back and brought some company along with me," Rob called out as he finally entered his house. Inside Philip was putting the final touches on tonight's meal.

"You usually do so I'm prepared. So, who is the, I want to say lucky but can't do it, lady tonight? Is it one of my favorites," Philip answered not breaking his concentration as he finished laying out the dinner?

"It's not one of the favorites it is your favorite," Kendra yelled back!

"Oh, my I'd recognize that voice anywhere," he said finally coming out of the kitchen to greet their guest, "if it isn't my sweet Kendra. I love it when you come over, but I must admit that I always hope you find somebody better than that chump over there. Now come give me a hug." The two embraced as Rob stood watching two of his favorite people in the world come together. The three crept to the kitchen as Philip and Kendra talked to see what feast Philip had prepared.

It was a wonderfully prepared meal by Philip. He had put together a feast worthy of royalty and they ate it like they had their crowns. The three laughed and talked for a brief time as they enjoyed his food, but it did not last long. The two of them had a specific thing in mind and that is all they wanted to do. They cleaned up their plates, excused themselves to his room, and once they were finally alone instinct took over.

They removed each other's clothing with tenderness and with each item that was removed another burden fell with it. They would carry nothing when they laid together and everything would be exposed. It was a terrifying thought to be that open as the demons inside were terrifying, but they accepted each other's flaws. Once they were completely naked, they looked into one another's eyes and saw their souls laid out just as bade as their bodies. If they had wanted to hide something from one another it was impossible. The thing that was truly beautiful is that each had flaws across their bodies and souls yet the person looking at them didn't care because they each understood that these flaws made one another truly special. Knowing this they felt entirely free from all the pain and the pressure that surrounded falsehoods.

This was the only time that he didn't need to be strong, he didn't have to protect anyone, nor feel guilty for his failures. He could be in this moment and this moment alone not running from the past that haunts him. Across from him, she did not have to be afraid anymore. In her line of work, she was exposed to the worst people in the city who wanted nothing more than to use her. They didn't see her for the person she was, they did not see the beautiful soul he saw when he looked into her eyes. Her life was based on serving the depravity of man and she did it well, but it broke her a little more every day. Then in this moment and all the ones, she spent with him she forgot all of that. She stood there looked into his soul and felt peaceful for the first time since they last met.

Now with their souls exposed they used them to write living poetry and their bodies moved in perfect unison. They had such familiarity with one another's body that they made sex look beautiful. They had been with each other many times, yet somehow each time still felt like the first. There was extreme familiarity as they knew what each liked, but there was still bewilderment as they continually tried to surprise one another. Sex was the easy part of their time together; it was the soul searching beforehand that was difficult. Despite this ease however, there was still something missing, love. No, there was no love between them. They went to each other not because they see a future together, they do it because of the momentary high. At face value, their relationship could be mistaken for love, but it was an addiction. This was their drug and they hated that they needed it. They had tried to move on. They tried to find other people, but their relationship had the perfect formula for addiction. It was a dangerous game that they played, but it was one they were unwilling to give up on. Nothing else seemed to work the same and no one else brought out the same kind of peaceful euphoria. It was never just the sex for they each had a plethora of partners, but the bareness was irreplaceable. The two of them were completely damaged and in this new world of rebuilding, people always expected them to fix their problems, but with one another they accepted the brokenness. They embraced the jagged edges no matter how much it cut them. It was just a quick fix and, in the end, there was no winning there was just postponing the pain.

Once they had gotten their fix, they laid sprawled across his bed. He rests on his stomach with his arms clasped beneath his head. She is still partly on top of him and as she tries to sleep, she runs her hand across his back. She feels every scar that plasters his body and when she reaches his newest one, she isn't in shock like the others no she just holds her hand over it for a moment. She is becoming acquainted with his new addition and her face holds a somber look. She never asked him about his scars because she feared he would ask about hers. Instead, she would engrain its feeling in her mind so that she knew about it the next time they met.

"I bet everyone freaked out about this, huh," she spoke softly while prodding the area around his new scar.

"Yeah, but what can you expect? People worry a lot these days. I take it that you don't," he replied in his normally reassuring tone.

"Why would I worry about you? Ever since our fourth encounter like this, I stopped worrying about these scars of yours. I realized that the physical scars don't mean anything to you. These aren't the things that will kill you," she started as he rolled to his side to look her in the eyes, "The thing that is going to kill you are those scars you carry on the inside. Your soul is barely limping along. I still don't understand how you are still alive honestly. I figured that you would have died of a broken heart by now. Now that you've been broken so many times, I'm nearly brought to tears whenever we return to this arrangement you deserve much better than this you know. We all want to help you, we all want to love you. Yet you keep shutting us down, you refuse our help because you are afraid that we are going to get hurt. One day you'll have to forgive yourself, everyone else has, but it's like there is something that you're not telling us. Knowing that though we're both damaged so I'll keep this up, I want you to realize if neither of us changes one of us is going to end up in a ditch somewhere. Until that day I'm not going to miss a night's sleep just because you added a new scar."

"Sleep tight," he added kissing her on the forehead as they both closed their eyes.

Chapter 5
Nightmare Past

"Where were you? Why didn't you save us," the screams yelled out as Rob ran lost through an annihilated city? The screams grew louder and more daunting with every step he took. Bodies were scattered on every street corner and the stench of death filled the air. All he could do was run, but he was going nowhere. He was searching for those he loved in the chaos yet every face he saw was blank and empty. His city of Despartian was burning to ash and he was helpless. Every turn he took lead to a dead end or suffering. After what felt like an eternity, he found his friends lying motionless in the streets. Meanwhile others were missing limbs and holding onto the last breaths they would ever take. Familiar faces were burned to a crisp, and there was nothing left for him, his world was falling apart around him.

He had failed all the people that counted on him. His failure and his decisions led to this destruction and every corner he turned he found more pain. He could not run and he could not help, it was the most powerless moment in his life. It was his lowest point and all he could do was run faster.

"Slow down kiddo there isn't much you can do now," a voice called! Rob looked around to find the source it was one familiar to him, but one that was not there when the city had actually fallen. Out in the distance, he noticed John sitting on a box playing some form of board game acting like there wasn't a care in the world. Rob was dumbfounded. John was never in Despartian, he wouldn't join Rob for months. He shook his head as he tried to refocus himself on his burning city, but the city was gone and he was now standing in a rundown old shack in the middle of a rainstorm. The fire was crackling inside the building as rain seeped through the rotting ceiling. It was a sight he was familiar with yet he was still unsure of what was happening. He was cautious of John and approached carefully. As he crept closer, he saw the shogi board that his old

friend was preparing for them. It was one of John's favorites that he taught Rob how to play and often in their slow days they would play game after game with the student often beating the teacher.

"Why don't you sit down it looks like you've overworked yourself again," John suggested as he motioned his hand towards a seat opposite him. Rob was still weary, but took a seat anyways. With few other options he moved his first pawn and the game had officially begun. However, in the back of his mind all he could think about was the burning city he had just seen and his dying friends.

"Why am I here with you? My city was burning and now I'm stuck playing a dumb game with you of all people," Rob was frustrated and it showed in the aggressive style of play. John on the other hand was calm and moved with precision.

"You're here because you need to be here. We are always in the place we need to be, unfortunately it just isn't always where we want to be. I thought you would have figured that out by now, but you are a fool I guess," John replied.

"Yes, I believe you've said that a couple times," Rob answered back as he tried to calm himself back down. It may have just been a game, but he still refused to lose to John.

"Alright, then you should also remember that the first thing I taught you after movement patterns is the idea of strategic sacrifices. In this game we play if we take a piece, we can turn it against our opponent so at times a pawn must be sacrificed to collect a knight or if we are lucky a gold or silver piece. These are essential strategies not just to this game, but war itself. You understood that once. You grasped the concept very well you told me. You knew your enemies wouldn't give-up Minneapolis without a fight. They were bunkered in, but greedy. They wanted a foothold in Wisconsin and you gave it to them. Suggesting that Despartian should be used as bait was genius. It was a cold, calculated decision, but the right one. You sacrificed a few lives in order to undermine the enemy's northern front. It was a tough decision, but it had to be made Rob you have to stop regretting it.

Everything worked exactly as predicted, but then you got soft. You left the forces to go assist the pawns that you had grown attached to. Then you acted surprised when they were all gone just as you knew they would be. That changed you and when I found you, you were weak and broken. Now you play your pawns close to you as if you think you can protect all of them. That is pure arrogance! No one can protect everyone and you cannot hold yourself accountable for a sacrifice that saved more lives than it cost! Yet you still believe that despite all the carnage you can have everything you want. That naïve idealism and arrogance of yours is what will bring about your end. This thought that you are responsible for everyone will cost you Rob, remember that and you can lose more than you can imagine. Remember that we are only as strong as our willingness to sacrifice," John lectured as he grew close to a victory.

"People aren't pawns John! This isn't some sick game where you can just throw out the pieces that don't further your own victory. They each have purposes and lives of their own! They are human and are just as important as you and I," Rob retorted as he grew increasingly frustrated!

"Yes, they each have a purpose and for some it is sacrificing themselves for people like you and I. You know that some people are more important than others, it is just life. You understood it once. You knew what it took to win when things were ugly and no one else wanted to accept the responsibility. Life is just a game; Rob and we have to play by the rules we are presented with. Most people know that they are just going to die a meaningless death after an even more meaningless life. If they are lucky, they get sacrificed for some kind of greater good. Some grand purpose. That is the merciful thing for them, so don't get attached to these pieces, Rob. You are not one of them. You are more like me than you'll ever know so use them," John demanded!

"I can't, I'm not you John," Rob answered again.

"Then you'll end up all alone," John smirked as he looked down at the board. He had taken all of Rob's pieces except for the king and in response those pieces were now being used by John. Meanwhile all Rob had to show for it was a few of John's pawns, "Now I may have lost some insignificant pieces, but unlike you I'm not alone and I'm not going to lose it'll be interesting to see what I take from you next!"

***

Rob jerked awake his body sweating heavily. His breathing grew shallow and quick, with his heart racing. It was all a nightmare, yet it felt all too real. The guilt was eating away at him and it haunted him. Opposite him Kendra still slept peacefully. Thankfully he had not awakened her, as he did not feel like explaining his nightmare to her. He gently put his hand on her naked back and ran it down her smooth body. She was real and that is what he needed right now. He slowly fell back asleep still wary of what might be waiting for him there.

Chapter 6
When the Sun Rises Shadows Grow

The sun rises and the birds are singing their good mornings. With the natural alarms singing constantly a man begins to rise from his slumber. As he shakes off the rust from the night's rest, he removes his silk sheets from across his slender frame. The room he sleeps in is the most glamorous in the city. The sheets are a violent blood red and the bed's frame glimmered a gold tint that contrasted the rustic gray of the rest of the city. Throughout the rest of the room he had old wooden furniture scattered. It was a random assortment, but they were rare, so he had to have them.

"Jefferies," the man yells, "I'm awake, now bring me my breakfast on the double!" The voice was commanding and echoed throughout his chamber. He demanded his assistant's presence regardless of whether he needed it or not.

"Yes, sir," replies a meek voice belonging to a brittle gray-haired old, "What is it that you need this morning Mr. Kore?" The old man was in his late sixties but his fragility made him seem older than that. His movements were slow and rigid as he tried to perform whatever duties John required of him.

"I need you to send my niece in here immediately," John demanded! His eyes were still tired as his gaze swept across the room looking at his possessions. There was no feeling in his gaze for a man that seemed to have everything he rarely seemed genuinely happy. It was always as if there was something missing, something he couldn't have despite his greatest efforts. Mere moments passed before young Trisha walked in. There was an urgency in her steps as she knew when her Uncle called for her, he did not want to be kept waiting. When she arrived, she was wearing a floral sundress complimenting her frizzled platinum blonde hair. The dress was a navy-blue piece that hung down just below her knees and was covered with several roses. Her face was as stern and emotionless as her uncles with just a hint of fear. Her skin was porcelain and perfect, but her dead eyes looked as if they had seen pain beyond her years.

"What do you need this morning Uncle John," she queried? As she spoke to him, she refused to make eye contact. Her gaze traveled across the room even though his darted straight through her.

"You must have gotten up quite early to look so beautiful this early my dear," he replied completely ignoring her question. At his comment, she began to adjust her dress and fix mistakes she was only imagining. He slowly started to remove the sheets from his body rising from his bed at last. Once he was standing tall, he started to creep closer to her, she began to take a step back but was afraid to go any farther than a small movement.

"No Uncle, honestly I never made it to bed last night. A problem arose last night and I was forced to stay out longer than we anticipated," she answered in a robotic tone. Something had occurred of great importance, yet there was no feeling in her voice. Her fear of her Uncle did not even affect her tone, yet she still couldn't look at the man approaching her. Her past with him was a troubled and it was clear in every interaction.

"The plan is still in motion I take it," he stated in a forceful demanding manner as opposed to a question, "You know that if even the slightest detail is off, I may have to kill you! I will not take the fall for your failures!" As he approached her his eyes grew intense and his steps more impactful. He was not as large as he was during the War as he had slimmed significantly when he took over as the owner of Ascension, but the intensity he walked with was the same from those days.

"Despite the mishaps, everything is still going according to plan. I can assure you of that Uncle," she replied, trying to hold her composure as her fear started to take over her. She took another step back trying to avoid whatever might come next, but there was no getting away now. He placed his hand on her shoulder and he slowly started to stroke the hair that rested on it.

"That is exactly what I like to hear. Now we just need to wait for the final pieces of Hope Tower to be placed and I will have everything I've dreamed of," he smiled, somehow, he had shifted all the intensity to gentleness as he played with her hair, but then the smile vanished as he tensed up grabbing her hair viciously. "But Trisha I want you to remember something if you fail me or worse betray me, I will make your life miserable and I can guarantee that you will beg for death. Now remember the fate that your parents faced and understand that would be a merciful end," he exclaimed as he threw her to the ground and started to walk away!

"I understand Uncle. I will not fail you; I will not fail you I promise," she yelped trying to hold back her tears as the terror consumed her. She instantly began to think of the atrocities that had taken her parents and she began to shake at the thought. It had only been a few years since he had taken her away and the memory still burned in her mind despite constant conditioning performed by her Uncle.

"Good now, off to bed. You must be exhausted from your adventures last night," he calmly stated. His voice shifted from the violent terror he had just been to a tender caring uncle in a single moment. He had made several complete personality shifts within seconds not once, but three times over mere minutes. Those close to him knew that his personality was unstable and there were questions on whether or not he was fully in control of his own mind at times.

After she scurried out of his room, he turned his gaze out to look upon the city he had made his home. From his room, he could see the whole city. He stood on the top floor of Ascension's main building which was housed within the old university. Outside his window, the main figure he could see was a vast tower that stood higher than every other building in the city. The great tower stood next to the river, it was his baby, and it was Ascension's Hope Tower. He stared at the majestic beast that he was responsible for building and marveled at his own achievement. Much like his bedroom, it glittered on the skyline compared to the brokenness of Despartian. The steel being used was the first new steel in the city since the start of the War and it was provided by affiliates of Ascension. This new steel gave off an extra glow when the sun rose in the mornings and a majestic silhouette when the sun set behind it. The world said that a building of its size couldn't be built in two years with the current state of technological development, the world called his vision insane. Now they said nothing for it was just days away from being finished.

That day two years ago always remained fresh in his mind for it was one of his greatest accomplishments:

****

John had arrived in the city of Desparitan with intentions to change the world, though many were unsure whether it was for the betterment or worsening of it. John had always been ambitious and outgoing, but he had a way of hiding his motivations. Though he always worried those who knew him. They knew that regardless of what he aimed for he would make major moves and run through any roadblocks that people threw in his way. John knew that despite Ascension's faltering it had the resources required to accomplish his own goals. Once John selected Ascension as his target, he began a methodical takeover using their failures to sway the disgruntled employees to his side. John had always had an incredible memory and used it to inspire more breakthroughs than the company had accomplished in a year over his first month as a supervisor. Impressed by the breakthroughs the board of directors started to promote him and this just moved their downfall farther along. They thought it was a good idea and that it would promote good faith within the company. They thought he was their cash cow, however unbeknownst to them John's allies within the company were consolidating their shares of the company and selling them to John. The company was becoming his without the knowledge of those above him and by the time he entered the conference room of the founders he controlled over half the company and was ready to make his final moves on a rainy afternoon.

"I'm disbanding the board. You will all clear out of here and find new work immediately," the upstart John proclaimed as the rain rolled down the windows of the room! The darkness of the room was only broken up by the occasional flash of light in the sky.

"What makes you think that you have the authority to do something like that," asked a frail old man with terror in his voice? John looked at the man in disgust as he began to answer.

"It is very simple really; I was given the authority by you and the workers! You sniveling imbecile! I arrived here and brought you wealth so quickly that you ignored my other moves! You missed me befriending your employees and buying their shares! You were oblivious to me hiring my allies when you gave me the power to do so and most importantly you lost track of how many shares you had

given me through promotions. I knew the price would be high, but with as many strong contacts as I have, it did not take me long to piece together half of the corporation. The funny thing was, that most of my power came from the people that you trusted because I did a better job than you. They left you and you never knew. You wanted my ideas, but failed to investigate my ambitions. That is just good business on my part and sloppy business by you," John explained to the board. They all seemed confused by what they had just heard. Never in a million years could they have imagined something like this was going on. Things were finally looking up for them and they never wanted to imagine a disaster like this.

"But why would they turn on us like that? Why would men and women we hired give you our corporation," one of the men asked with a quiver in his voice? Though he was the only one to speak it was clear that the entire board had the same thought. They started this company from nothing and gave hundreds of people jobs. They couldn't understand what was happening.

"It is simple really after they saw my accomplishments, they realized that all of you stall prosperity. You had made them a promise that if they worked hard their shares would be worth something, but they were meaningless until I came along. You over-promised and had them working basically for free, that is how you lost them! Now you make this company less than it could be, so for their sake, I am removing you from office. There is always a chance that you could fight this. You could try and turn the employees back to your side. That is very possible, but you see several of the intellectuals I filled this office with have other skills and will make sure that my ambition is accomplished. For any of you that still have any plans to oppose me, despite that bit of information I want to remind you that while you all sat around and hid during that war my friends and I set a standard for killing efficiency," John smirked with great detest in his voice as he scanned the room looking at the sorry excuses for men that sat in front of him. All the men in the room fell silent and all they could do was look at one another hoping that one of them would be brave enough to oppose the hungry tyrant that stood before them. Slowly the despair took each of them over and one by one they accepted their fate hanging their heads.

"Now that we all understand the severity of the current circumstances; I would like to offer an olive branch. I think all of

you are useless worms and parasites whose singular ability is ruining others' lives. I fear that with this sole talent you will cause me more issues than you are currently worth, so in order to avoid anyone from interfering with my goals, I have an opportunity for all of you. Now listen closely because this will be your only shot and I highly recommend that you choose wisely," the men gathered around the table still silent. Their silence was only broken by the occasional crack of thunder. They looked to John hoping that he was offering them mercy, *"I need men to fill advisory roles to help with a smooth transition from all of you to me. The role of an advisor is very simple you do nothing, but act as a figurehead to show the city and the world that I am a good man. The outside world would be very concerned with an unplanned change in leadership during such as time of prosperity, so they have to feel like this was a plan. Lastly, my advisors will use all of their connections to gather support for my greatest undertaking. You will not waver in your support no matter what the public says and if you fail to support me you will be terminated from your position. These are my terms now what do you all have to say."* No sooner had he finished before three of the eleven board members had already risen to support him. The rest remained seated as they pondered the choice set before them. Finally, one grew brave enough to ask what all the others were afraid to;

"What is this project, the way you speak about it is that it will be some great controversy. I refuse to stand behind anything that could harm those that come after me. They are more important than any title you can give." The old man who spoke seemed strong in his convictions, yet there was still a quiver in his voice. He knew the legends about John and his viciousness, if he grew violent none of the men would make it out of that room alive.

"Funny how you care about the world now. You all have been driving one of the last great companies into the ground all but dooming this world, but now you care. Now you want to take a stand against something. Look outside those windows boys the rain is trying to put out the fires you have started. I wonder is my idea of change causing you to fear profit loss? I mean I know this 'righteous stand' isn't about the kids or their future. I read your personnel files, sir! You have been married five times with seven children between them, but every single one of them you call illegitimate.

After learning this I had some of my people uncover your will and found and found that every one of them was left off. If the future was your concern you would take care of the people you are supposed to love so don't you dare bring the children into this you slime," he yelled as he stared at the man with his cold green eyes, "Now despite my hate for all of you, I will still answer his question. You all will convince the city to put over half of its resources into building a tower that will be larger and far grander than anything currently left in this world. We will make it the symbol that draws the world to our city. It will be a monument to my ambition and most importantly it will be finished within two years' time."

"Impossible," called out one of the members! John's heartless gaze fell quickly on the man shutting him up in an instant. The rest of the room knew that resistance was futile. John would put an end to whoever stood in his way.

"It is possible, I assure you. I have calculated my plans out to the day and my plans never fail. This tower which I shall name Hope Tower because people love the sentimental shit like that, will be finished on time. Now you all have a decision to make join me or effective immediately you're terminated." Half of the remaining eight men rose, but the four that remained seated refused. John was puzzled he never expected these men to stand for some moral principle, but nevertheless, he had two large men come in and remove the rebellious few. Those that had decided to stand remained still as they watched their co-workers disappear. All John could do was smile as a new era was starting, his era.

***

Those two years had passed and as he promised the tower was near completion. His plan was slowly unfolding just as he had predicted it would. The tower was the most prominent figure in the skyline, the city was being revived as he allowed it, and the people loved him for the supposed help he gave them. The only person who he still needed to fall in line was Rob and, in his mind, Rob would be compliant by the end of the week. At last a smirk strung across his face as he looked out the window, he felt nothing could stop him anymore. With good reason as everything had fallen into place without trouble up until this point.

55

"Sir, your breakfast is ready," Jefferies announced as he entered John's room disrupting his master's concentration. John turned to him and looked at the man, many years ago this frail old man was a strong soldier who fought in hellish battles across jungles that stretched across the world, but those years had long vanished. He had fought in some of the meaningless battles of the past, winning several awards for his courage, but those medals meant nothing after the War. They were nothing, but rusted dirt in a closest, and now he could barely muster the will to move as he was consumed by intense pain from the years of battle. Until John found him, the old man was barely surviving the harsh realities of the new world, so he had little complaint as he worked just to survive. He vowed to serve John faithfully no matter how cold-hearted John was on any given day.

"Have it or give it to the dogs, I no longer need it. Next, I'll need you to call my advisors and have them meet me in the conference room. We all need to have a discussion with the grand opening only days away," John commanded as he left to go change into something more befitting a man of his stature! Jefferies took a piece of toast that had been prepared and place it on John's dresser. Jefferies had been there for John since he first took over Ascension and regardless of how demanding he was there was still a part of him that wanted to see his master thrive. Most importantly he had learned that despite his master's denial, he would need some form of food to get him through the day.

Sometime after John had made his order, he finally entered the conference room with a piece of toast in his mouth and marched to the head of the table. While the rest of the men were dressed in dull worn out suits, John commanded the room in a pressed black suit top and a scarlet undershirt that accented his frame. He made it clear that he ruled the room and no one in it would question him. The seven men from two years prior still remained in their positions and stood at attention as they waited for John to take his seat. All of the men now looked like lifeless husk as if it had been ten years versus two.

"Gentlemen I had heard rumors swirling that you needed to talk to me about something so now's the time to spit it out," John ordered as he surveyed the room.

"Well you see it isn't anything particularly important, but we thought that we'd clear up some small formalities before your baby is finished," one of the husks stammered as he tried to avoid angering his boss. John remained quiet, but the man knew that he had to be careful as he proceeded.

"You see this has to do with your old friend Rob. There has been a rumor that he has been insulting your greatness and calling for a boycott of the tower. He seems to think that it is some sort of trap sir," the old man insisted.

"Now normally we would ignore little things like this, but that man as you in all your wisdom knows carries weight still in this community," another man began to explain when John refused to reply to the first, "We have spent a lot of money in his discretization, but people still follow his charisma especially the children who in turn convince their parents that he is telling truths. We believe as a board that for your great dream to achieve its potential we need to unify this city so; we believe it would be best if you two make public amends." John leaned back in his chair and put his fingers together to think for a moment. He was silent for an abnormally long time before he finally arose from his seat. The men in the room sat in terror knowing that when he was silent things rarely ended well for someone.

"My mother was a very strong and independent woman," he started saying, "She raised my brother and me all on her own after my father died a soldier's death in war from my childhood. She was also a wise woman. No matter the situation she always had her two cents to give about it and she wanted to ensure that the two of us grew-up understanding this world and its unfairness. Now I have forgotten many things she said and maybe that is my own fault for never listening like she wanted me to. Yet, there was one thing she said that stuck with me. She used to tell me as we would walk down the street.

'Son look around you. 90% of the people alive think they are somebody, they think that their life is groundbreaking and the world should admire them. These are the fools that the world eats up and spits right back out. They all die worthless deaths and within a generation or two are completely forgotten. They are useless for they neither accomplish anything nor do they ever help others become great. Then about 9% of people know that they are dirt. They know that they are simply a cog in history's grand machine. These people help push our world further by accepting their fates, but just like the other 90%, they are never remembered. This is your brother and I;

we are not world changers just pieces to push others forward. On the other hand, you my son, I've seen things and I know that you are the remaining 1%. You will be the subject of whole books; you will revolutionize the world and change it beyond recognition. Without you, the world would not fulfill its potential so do not let fools stand in your way.'

Now my poor mother died when I was only sixteen years old and she died believing that, so I will not disappoint her. I can assure you, gentlemen, I am aware of Rob; he is simply a fool in my way and I have already begun to recruit him in order to smooth this process out. He has been a little resistant at first, but I promise you by the time that tower is finished he will be willing to die for me and everything that tower is meant to stand for. Now all of you can leave and I also wanted to inform you that the board will be dissolved at the finishing of the tower. You have fulfilled your purpose and I no longer need you," he exclaimed pointing towards the exit! The old men shuffled out of the room as quickly as their bodies could move, they didn't want to be in the same room as him any longer than they had to. There were no complaints as the company they built no longer meant anything to them and were prepared to move on for good.

"Making amends will be hard after you had me shoot him," a raspy voice said after the board had left the room.

"Trust me, Dave, it is all part of my plan. I needed him to feel the urgency. You see the only way my plan succeeds is with his help and the only way to get that drunk off his ass is to make him hate me. After that everything is need to know and all you need is your list of targets. Now is everyone here or are we waiting for anyone else after last night's debacle," John asked as he returned to his chair at the head of the table?

"We are all here sir," a stern voice answered back. Four more men and Trisha entered the room. They each moved with precision, with no wasted movement from any of the six. All of them surrounded John and sat in a particular order as often they would pass open seats. Each was silent as they waited for John to speak.

John sat at the head of the table; his pale body popped out of his sleek black suit. Directly to his left sat his niece who still barely looked awake. Like most days she dressed in a beautiful garment that her Uncle had bought her, today it was a yellow strapless dress that made her tanned skin glimmer in the light. She was accessorized completely with aqua bracelets, Pluto suede pumps, and turquoise earrings. Despite still only being seventeen she could command a room as well as her Uncle except she held them with her beauty. The only thing that out did her beauty was her cunning. Directly to her left sat Dave the infamous sniper whose mere name caused platoons to run and hide. He was not nearly as dressed up as the other two, but he made a fair attempt at it. His blue polo barely fit over his shoulders, but it was clear that it was the only eloquent thing he owned as there were a few holes near the bottom of it. It seemed as if he never blinked and his eyes always held steady never shaking. There was a reason he was the expert marksman he was. The last man on the left side was the long lanky Chinese fellow known as Chen. He was known for his ability to navigate any vehicle with the utmost expertise. The legend goes that no man ever escaped his pursuit nor did anyone ever catch him. He wore an old leather jacket and cheap sunglasses that he says his father gave him along with the egotistical grin he always carried. Without him, the squad would have likely died 100 times over.

Directly across from Chen sat the smallest man, Rick. Rick was a working man, the old lab coat that he wore was covered in oil, dirt, and what looked like blood though whose it was no one, not even Rick, could be sure. He had a constant twitch in his left eye from all the chemicals he had inhaled over his years. Rick was known as a scientific genius with a dark side to him. People claimed that he could deceive any opponent with different illusions and tricks. His experiments though were known for being highly illegal and morally questionable. Next to Rick sat a lean and fierce looking black man. He was known as Jackson and his lethal skills were sought after by many. The stories that were told about him drove many mad. They say he once threw a knife at a fly and pinned it to the wall without killing it from 50ft away. Other legends claim that Jackson once cut a man in half in a single strike and then gave the man's pet hamster a haircut with the same blade without nicking it. The last man who sat directly to John's right was Gene. Gene was a grizzled old vet who had seen his share of battles. He was the man who first trained all these men except for John and then he led all of them as their commander during the War. He now had long gray hair which he often kept in a bun and a burn scar that went from his left ear down to his chin. Gene was believed to be an Urban Legend. In truth the whole squad wasn't supposed to exist, their feats were beyond human so, to think that he trained them all was incomprehensible to most. On top of being the one who trained these inhuman beasts, legends say that he once defused a whole minefield himself and reset it around an enemy fortress trapping them inside. His explosive expertise was unmatched in the War.

These men who were all thought of as myths and now worked towards achieving John's ambition. The War had turned them all into brothers and afterward John helped them all find work when no one else would. It was, for this reason, they all swore to fight for him now no matter the cost. This loyalty was important to one another, but even with the title of brother, they knew not to trust one another. They couldn't not after the day they all turned on Rob who was considered the heart of the team. After that betrayal, they could not truly love or care for one another maybe they still wanted to, but they couldn't their hearts had turned cold and emotionless. Their meetings often consisted of them sitting in silence rarely making eye-contact waiting for someone to say something and there was constant tenseness to their meeting as they knew anyone in that room could kill the other without remorse. This was business now and they all knew it. They were here because this was the only work, they could find in the new world.

"Now that I have you all here, I want to assure you all that things are going exactly as I planned. There are a few more dominos that need to fall before all is said and done, but I trust that all of you who still have a role will complete it. Now Rick has something to show all of you and I must say it is quite impressive. Rick take it away," John stated as he motioned his hand to Rick.

"Yes, it took a lot of time and cost a lot, but it is all finished. After this breakthrough the world will never be the same," he stated with a slight snicker in his tone. A door opened and the thing that they all saw shocked them. The coldest men alive were struck with fear and disbelief. Trisha was in complete shock all she could do was shake her head and hold back tears. John put his feet on the table, leaned back in his chair and laughed.

Part 2: A Lost Girl

Chapter 7
A Loved Girl

Over on the poor side of town, Rob and Kendra went their separate ways early, with Rob returning to working on homes the next day despite Anna's disapproval. It was a hot and humid summer day with temperatures in the mid-nineties and heat index much higher than that. The work was moving slow nearly coming to a halt at several points. The men wanted to stop for the day, but those who still needed housing were desperate especially during weeks like this. They knew that with all the suffering they endured others were facing much harsher realities. This helped them push on despite the haze and constant flirtation with dehydration. Even Rob who was known for skipping his breaks once a project had begun opted to rest about midday.

Philip knew of the heat to come that day and packed a rare lunch for Rob that day knowing he would need something. Despite sitting down in the shade, the sun still beat down on him making life unbearable, he was miserable as the sweat dripped down his body. His eyes slowly made their way to the sky and clouds above him. The heat was playing tricks on his mind and eventually, he found himself dozing off, slowly entering his fantasies. Thanks to Ali's scolding the day before he had been thinking about Iris and then she began to flood his dreams again. He saw the two of them together again as he thought about the days that he missed the most. He saw those few fleeting days where he was happy for the first time and deeply in love with Iris.

***

He could still picture those beautiful summer days when he wasn't much older than 22. She loved summer the most out of all the seasons though there were very few things she didn't love. He started to remember the day he knew he was in love. It was one day when they went for one of their famous walks that everyone talked about. They would start on the edge of town and keep walking for what seemed like miles and all they did was talk. Their conversations would revolve around family, school, friends, whatever they felt like or needed to discuss. This was their time to be together and was their way to become intimate. This meant the distance they would walk never mattered to them. With each walk they grew closer and received another chance to enjoy their love for as long as possible. They had a very pure love that made many of their friends jealous and when they looked into each other's eyes there was a connection that few ever have. It was to the point that they could have a conversation without ever speaking a word and knew that they could always trust one another.

Their biggest problem was that the two of them were always busy. They worked hard to achieve the grand dreams they each had and seldom had free time so when the days came where they could just cherish one another they seized the opportunity. They were like most modern people of the time they put too much emphasis on what was ahead. They had vision and ambition, but lived too far in the future and wasted days worrying about what would be insignificant instead of one another.

Iris dreamed about becoming a doctor saving people's life. There are many people that dream of becoming M. Ds, but fall short due to the rigorous nature of the schooling. However, the days of studying barely phased Iris. Now she had bad days, but she also had this superpower that allowed her to smile and stay happy even in the face of the most difficult circumstances. With that said she was like any young person filled with stresses buried deep below, but no matter how hard she tried to hide it from everyone else Rob could hear it and was there for her even when she thought she didn't need him. With that superpower and her support system she was well on her way towards becoming a doctor far greater than Anna. However, unlike Anna the War stopped her from completing her bachelors and halted her ambitions. She instead had to watch one of her best friends live out her dream and become a hero

The War was still months away however on this day and there is little reason to dwell on it. That is why on beautiful summer days, they put their ambitions aside and belonged solely to one another. Rob knew how lucky he was because this was love in its purest form and the woman, he was with was one of the kindest he had ever met. Her soul was pure despite numerous tragedies that had struck it. Now the relationship was never perfect, but real ones never are. They had their moments where their relationship was on the edge, but it was in these darkest days that their relationship grew stronger. The two of them were experts at communication and were able to work through the differences they had. Others around them could never understand, but the two of them knew simple truths about love. They knew that it is easy when somebody seems perfect, but in reality, perfect is often one partner faking who they are and it creates a tension that destroys relationships. That is why love is about finding the quirks that make the other person special that nobody else gets to see. Maybe it is their goofy eyes that she makes every time you want a nice picture, or maybe it is their forgiving you each time you leave a dresser drawer open despite her constant reminders. Love is ignoring the times their brilliant mind turns on the wrong burner on the stove and wonders why the water isn't boiling. Maybe they have this goofy laugh that only comes out when they're embarrassed, but while they turn red at its sound you hug them and remind them you love it. The big things are important, but at the end of the day it is everything else that makes a relationship whole. She didn't remember every date he had ever taken her on, but she loved to tell the story of when he had a fight with a waiter over the absurd price of some food and ended up going home where he ended up cooking his own eloquent feast for them at half the price.

Love is clarity in this world of chaos and knowing that no matter how bad you screw up they'll be there to work through it. It is wanting the other person to be happy more than anything and them wanting the same thing for you. More importantly, love is something that can never really be defined, but it can be seen and felt. That is what made the love between Iris and Rob so special, it was a love that needed no definition as they felt it running through their bodies.

Rob remembered this particular walk because this was the day that he realized that he was going to propose to Iris one day. They had arrived at a wide-open field with nothing near them except one large rock and once they had entered the field Iris jabbed Rob in the arm and started running looking back and flashing her perfect come and get me smile. Rob, of course, was never one to refuse a good chase and this exchange had become quite common between them. Now they had each found the speed where he looked like he was truly trying, but would never catch her until she wanted him to despite his ability to do it at any moment. He would bask in her beauty as he chased her and lived for those small moments where she would peek back showing her sky-blue eyes. It was also at this time that the playful smile she always carried was most prominent. That smile of hers was perfect and would stretch from ear to ear.

As he chased her, he would think of all the things that he loved about her. First, he would always admit that he had a special weakness for blondes, but she was so much more than just another blonde with locks flowing in the wind. Her heart was the purest that he had ever met and just by being around her he felt as if he could be a better man than he was. He never knew anyone who had a bad word to say about her and she was impossible to hate. Now she may have been extremely intelligent, but she had a habit of indulging in "blonde moments" that always made him laugh. Between him and her friend Danielle they always kept her honest when she did something stupid. Maybe the thing she loved the most was that she could be a piece of work, but she was his piece of work that put up with his insanity every day.

When she finally let him catch her, he lifted her in the air with a firm and tender grasp. He spun her in the air a few times and set her down. Then she turned to look at him as if she expected something. He was never one to disappoint as he placed a kiss on her forehead and she embraced him. They both walked over to the rock in the field taking off their shoes so that they could feel connected with the earth below them. They sat against the rock letting the wind rush through their hair and the grass tickled their feet. It was calming feeling. There was a sweet innocence in those days before the War. As they sat, they continued to just talk as they usually did on their walks and like before there was no direction to the discussion they just talked. Even with all the talking they did there were still secrets between them. They knew that they were each keeping secrets but it was young love, so they would keep working until they could get close. Until that day they knew what they had was love because

***

In the midst of his dreaming, Rob was jerked awake. At first, he couldn't figure out what had awakened him, but then he heard his name being called and the sound of rushing footsteps. As the source got closer, he saw it was a woman and the noises she was making were turning into wails. The sadness in her shouts became more and more evident, eventually, he was able to make a face out. It was Kendra moving in a state of hysteria. Her face was filled with fear and she was crying uncontrollably. She ran into Rob's arms and he quickly tried to comfort her the best he could. She was falling apart having a complete breakdown.

"What happened Kendra," he asked with concern quickly taking over? He had spent many days with her and had heard many nasty stories, but nothing had ever drawn such a strong reaction. He knew that something had to be disastrously wrong for Kendra to be in this shape.

"Carly never came home last night Rob," she screamed as she looked up at him! Rob's grip grew tighter at this statement. Normally, people would think that in their line of work no show mornings would be common, but these girls knew the danger they faced and made a promise that every morning they had to return home before noon to insure nothing had happened the night prior. If none of the girls had seen Carly than things were looking deadly.

"Let's go find her then. Do you know who her first client was last night, we need to work this through from start to finish," he tried to say in a soothing voice knowing how fragile things were.

"Yeah, he is a regular. His name is Jim Horick and we usually find him on 3ʳᵈ street at that little bar," she said clearing the tears from her eyes. Rob picked her up and they rushed to the bar knowing time was now working against them.

Chapter 8
Bar Room Brawl

Third Street wasn't known for being an enjoyable sight anymore. The street had once been the bustling epicenter of downtown Despartian, but during the War, the people abandoned it. Then as things returned to normal post war the people slowly began returning to it. However, what they found was a mess. Instead of reinvesting in it they let it remain rough and it became the part of town that only a tougher crowd dared enter. Now given this fact most of the bars were rugged messes, but the one Kendra brought Rob to was something else. Calling the building a crumbling mess would have been kind. The building had survived the War, but given how heavily damaged it was it likely would have been better off crumbling. The walls were covered in burns from when the battle was its most intense and pieces of the walls had been blown away during the bombings. The sign that read 'The Leaking Glass' was broken and the lights that still worked were dim and flickering. The flickering lights now spelled something else now as the 'gl' portion was missing. Despite all of this, the most noticeable thing was the smell, it was intoxicating.

"Man, I don't know if I've seen a prettier bar," Rob muttered trying to make light of the site and situation. He may have been a perennial drunk, but he had always avoided this place due to its reputation. Besides, he was always a fan of drinking alone, less of a chance of him getting in a fight.

"Never seen this place? I'm surprised, I thought that the name alone would make you a regular," Kendra replied with a smirk as she finally managed to draw a smile.

"It's good to hear you joking around again," Rob replied pulling her close to him, "Now you know that I hate to do this, but please wait here. I don't need you to get hurt in a place like this." She wasn't happy with his decision, but knew he was right, so she allowed him to go on alone. He slowly opened the decayed entrance door to find a mass of people all drunk off their minds and ready to cause trouble. It did not take him long to realize that the crowd around him would not be an easy one to get information from. From the moment he stepped in he recognized that this crowd was not a favorable one. After the first few steps, he started to notice that several patrons wore jackets that had the symbol for the radicals that opposed him during the Civil War. If he caused trouble in the bar, he would have no help, but a friend was in danger so he moved ahead. There was no room for doubt in his convictions.

"Is there a man named Jim Horlick here," he called out arrogantly! He was trying his best to control the room and bolster his confidence. He couldn't let any of them know he was afraid that he was not as strong as he once was.

"He just went to the head. What do you want with him you damn Blite," replied the bartender? It would figure that the bartender would recognize Rob right away. During the Civil War, the radicals often called the other side Blites because it was often white men defending, the discriminated groups, most commonly the African American communities. The bartender was an intimidating presence and Rob knew that he would be best off avoiding him at all cost, as he was a girthy man with a scar straight across his face and three fewer fingers then he should have had.

"I'm looking for a friend of mine and I've heard Jim might know where to find her," Rob replied as he approached the bar refusing to be intimidated by the bartender. He could feel the eyes piercing through him from all directions. He did not intend to make a scene, but it was becoming more and more likely. He had a creeping feeling that everyone in this bar knew who Jim was and unfortunately, they all knew now that Rob had likely shot at them before.

"Jim knows lots of people and he ain't that friendly to people he never met before, especially damn Blites like yourself," the bartender snarled back in broken English. They were now staring each other down with only the bar top separating them. Now that Rob had a better look at the bartender, he saw that he was giving up over half a foot and at least a hundred pounds. Despite the overwhelming odds Rob still refused to back down the stakes were far too high. They continued their stare down until their concentration was broken by the bathroom door being thrust open.

"Oi, that be a good ole stinker right there! I'd say y'all should avoid that for a good hour or so. Now Carl serve-up the next round up! I got to rehydrate after something like that," a loud boisterous man yelled as he came stumbling out! He looked very similar to the bartender and Rob realized instantly he was in trouble but opened his mouth anyways.

"Well if it isn't old Jim-Bob himself and just by looking at you Carl here must be your brother, man momma must be proud," Rob joked as he slowly prepared himself for something to go wrong. Both of the men stared at Rob in shock, there were few men that would dare insult them, especially within the confines of Carl's bar. Jim started walking towards Rob with his chest puffed out to accentuate his size. There was no way that he was going to let Rob's mouth run for very long.

"Did you get hit in the head or something Small Fry cause ain't nobody talks to us like that? 38 years we've been around and no one has gotten away with insults, specially if they bring in Momma. Ya know, I should knock you out right now, but I won't yet. I gotta know what in the name of the Good Lord do you want," Jim replied as he grew angry! He began to roll-up his sleeves as he prepared to deliver on the threat he just made. The one thing Rob had going for him was the fact that Jim's movements were sporadic as the copious amount of alcohol he had consumed was disrupting him.

"I'm looking for a friend of mine named Carly. I heard you may have seen her last night," Rob said as he tried to hold back any detest that might be in his voice. He knew the situation was about to blow-up, but he at least wanted to get the info he needed first.

"Ah yes, Craving Carly, you'd be right to say I bent that lass over last night. Man, that woman knew how to work. She did just about anything for the right price and after you could throw her ass back on the street where it belonged. She should be lucky I let her put all her clothes back on first most times," he laughed. Jim's voice alone began to irritate Rob and as the man insulted his missing friend, he grew irate. His fist began to clench as he absorbed the words. "Now I don't know how you misplaced your little whore, but I got nothing for you. I would never hurt her and do you want to know why?" Rob shook his head and bit his tongue resisting the urge to lash out.

"It is simple really no other girl is able to do things with her tongue the way that girl did," the brothers began to laugh at Rob thinking they were untouchable in their bar. This was the final straw and when Jim finished laughing and turned back to face Rob dropped him with one punch. Enraged by the incident Carl leaped over the bar and started to attack Rob as his brother tried to regain his wits. The rest of the bar stood up ready to help their friends, but Jim waved them off as he regained his footing.

As Rob engaged Carl, he tried to figure out how he was going to take out the monster. He first tried using his speed, but he was out of shape and unable to sustain the pace plus the pure mass of Carl was overwhelming. Carl's mass of fat was absorbing all of Rob's blows and in the meantime, Carl was hitting haymakers that would have knocked out other men much sooner. The longer their fight drew on the stronger and fiercer Carl's blows became until one landed directly on Rob's rib cage cracking it instantly. Blood came spurting out of his mouth and sent him reeling for a moment. It had been a while since Rob had fought and it was clear that he was rusty. The fact that a man like this could outdo him was insulting and pathetic.

He had to rethink his strategy especially with the damaged rib. He re-engaged with Carl with a refined strategy, but still blinded with rage his fighting was sloppy. He tried to use quick blows to the ribs and kidneys to exhaust Carl while, avoiding as many strikes as he could. It may have been simple, but Rob was the better fighter and just needed simple strategies. It started to work, but before Rob could land a crucial blow Jim grabbed his arms from behind. The second brother had entered the fight and now Rob faced two disadvantages one in size and the other in numbers. Three years ago, this would have hardly been a challenge for Rob during the War, but peace along with tequila had dulled his technique and skill. Rob was defenseless and Carl was able to land haymaker after haymaker. Each blow robbed him of precious air, causing him to start to lose consciousness. All he could do was hope that they didn't break any more ribs as he grew limp.

After several minutes of beating, Jim picked the smaller man up and threw him through the bar, while the rest of the patrons cheered and laughed. The Radicals enjoyed the suffering of the Blites now that the War was over. They had been embarrassed and now enjoyed any bit of revenge that they could have. Rob had known that no one would come to his aid, but he had hoped that he wouldn't need anyone. Now Rob's nearly unconscious corpse was sprawled out, twisted in the rubble with an unknown amount of internal damage. He should have given-up. He had the information he needed and it was clear they had no intention of killing him otherwise they would have tried already. However, his stubborn pride wouldn't let him surrender. The warrior in him couldn't lay there while a couple of drunks gloated over his beating.

"Alright that was a nice little warm-up. Should we get the real fight started," Rob muttered as he rose in defiance of the brothers. Both of them looked at each other in bewilderment. They had thrown their best at him and yet he stood, be it a wobbly and uneasy stance. Not knowing what else to do Jim steadied Rob's body with his left hand and wound up for one final blow with his right. Rob smiled as the blood dripped down his cheek. A truly unnerving sight for the drunk Jim who hesitated. Then just before he let loose, he heard a loud crash. When he turned to see what it was, he saw Carl on the ground and a chair shattered around him. Jim couldn't believe his eyes and when he turned back to face Rob the old soldier had gathered enough strength to drop Jim again, this time for good. Now that both brothers were down, Rob could try and figure out what had happened. He had to wonder in a place like this who could have come to his aide. With a hazy glare, he scanned the room and found a short black man standing over Carl's unconscious body and next to him was Kendra with a worried look in her eyes.

"I see that you got in over your head again Rob," the man said just as Rob's body finally gave out and he collapsed to the floor.

It took several hours for Rob to regain his strength and when he finally woke-up he found himself in a stranger's bed. It was odd that he didn't recognize the bedroom as in some manner he had been in almost every house in the city. He had built most of them and 'visited' several others. He continued to scan the room trying to figure out where he could be, until he finally noticed the black silhouette that was sitting in the corner next to him.

"Adam, I haven't seen you in a minute, what brings you around these parts," Rob asked as he tried to sit-up? He instantly started to cough remembering the broken rib he had obtained in the fight earlier.

"Whoa bud, don't move too fast there. She'll kill you if you hurt yourself again," Adam replied as he stood up to calm the stirring man. Adam was a shorter man, but despite his small stature, he was built like a tank. Every inch of him was muscle and on top of his strength there was a terrifying amount of speed for his size. On the inside there was a man who cared deeply about his friends and would knock the teeth out of anyone who messed with them, as Carl discovered earlier. That being said he didn't really care for fighting and tried to find more peaceful routes. These qualities, along with his family history of police captains, are the reason that he was able to gather a group of men to act as the city's police force. The average citizen may be against the concept of organized government due to the War, but they appreciate Adam's work when things are going to dangerously.

"What do you mean by she? Where did you take me," he asked? Rob was clearly confused, there are only a few places Adam would take Rob in a situation as this, but he would recognize most of them.

"Well she is a mutual friend of ours and she also happened to have the closest home to the bar. Now before she comes in, I should warn you that she wasn't happy that you coughed blood all over her house, but I think she'll forgive you like she usually does. As long as you don't do anything else stupid," Adam answered with a small smile on his face. Rob's face turned to dismay as he started to figure out whose house, he was in. One by one he crossed names off a list in his head until one remained.

"Whose house am I in," he queried with an anxious look on his face? He knew whose house it had to be, but he kept hoping for a different answer.

"One of these days somebody is going to break you and I won't be able to put you back together," Anna's familiar voice called as she entered the bedroom holding a brace to wrap around his core.

"I must say your plan to get me in your bed was a bit convoluted. There are far easier ways to do it, Anna. My favorite being just asking me," the battered man smart-mouthed off as he tried to ignore her comments. It was clear that Anna was less amused by the whole ordeal than Rob and he stopped laughing immediately. He hadn't seen such a serious look on her face in quite some time, so he knew that he was about to receive a verbal lashing unlike any that he had experienced before.

"I'm just tired of this Rob. Yesterday, I have to fix some stitching work because you were shot and today Adam comes barging into my house as you're gasping for air and coughing up blood in his arms.

You have to understand that a sight like that is never easy, especially when the dying man is a friend of mine. You see I don't do this because it is easy, I do it because there are people that need my help, but I can't just keep patching you up so that you can go running off to create new scars. I don't want to play this game any longer and I really don't want to be the one holding your hand while you are dying. I'm not strong enough for that," she lectured as she tried to fit the brace around his body. He was resistant to the brace as he feared that it would hamper the search for Carly.

"I went in there for ans..." Rob started before she put her finger against his lips to shut him up.

"Save it, Rob. Kendra and Adam filled me in. I have always understood why you rush into situations guns blazing, but dammit Rob we both know that there is something else and that is what I'm tired of. You went in looking for answers, but you kept getting up despite having your answer. It was a stupid and rash decision especially given your surroundings! That bar was filled with people that hate your guts and even if you could have beat the two moronic brothers fifty other men would have taken your head off and you knew it! On top of that you smiled as the man prepared to knock you out for good, you would have died had Adam not showed up with some reinforcements," she started as her eyes began to tear, "Now I know what you want to say. You want to claim that I wouldn't understand, but newsflash Rob I know you better than you want to admit. I know what today is and I know that you are fully aware as well." She paused for a minute to sit on the bed and think about what she wanted to say.

"Eight years have passed since that fateful day when our worlds officially changed beyond recognition. Thinking about it now it is amazing how young we were and naive we were to be unaware of how long that war would last. You see those memories are why I didn't go to work today. I didn't want to be confronted by the ghost of the past and yet when I heard about Carly I was overwhelmed. That said, I can only imagine what went through your head upon hearing the news. I can only wonder what hidden scars resurfaced. I know that you feel guilty about letting Iris down and that's why you still refuse to see her. She has told me why you feel that way as well. I know about the promise to protect her and her sisters no matter what."

"Then we lost her during the razing of Despartian and it was a heartbreaking day when we found the body. You know that I miss her amazing smile and her personality, but Rob everyone lost somebody that day. Do you remember the total from the first day because I do, it was 350? 350 people that we knew of in that one day, I'm not even including the few soldiers that were there to help. Can you imagine how many of those 350 died in my hands while I told them they'd be alright? They thought the great healer Anna could save them, but it was nothing more than false hope. People I called friends and co-workers died horrible deaths staring into my eyes. It was horrific, our city was invaded and nearly obliterated. Now the difference between you and everybody else is the fact you never forgave yourself. In order for you to truly heal you'll have to move on and let your mind heal." As she finished, she began to weep. In the meantime, Adam had disappeared leaving the two of them to talk in peace.

"Yeah. yeah. I've heard this speech before and I'm getting tired of it too," Rob replied. He was snide and arrogant as he answered her. This did not sit well with Anna.

"Then let it sit in you arrogant ass and don't just go running back to the nearest bottle, leaving us to wonder about your safety! It isn't fair to those of us who actually give a damn about you," she yelled back upset over his answer!

"There you go lecturing again. You talk and say things like you know the whole story and yet you only know parts of the truth! You weren't in the war room leading up to that fateful day and will never understand what I failed to do," he answered as his head hung low remembering the truth.

"Then tell us and get it over with," she begged as she tried to look him in the eyes however, he avoided her gaze at all cost.

"I... I can't, not yet anyways. I have to make-up for my failures otherwise I'll never be able to look you in the eyes again," he informed her. Despite her desire for more she knew not to ask. "That is why no matter what the danger is I will always rush in. If someone I care about is in danger, I will do whatever is within my power to save them. You're right this path might kill me one day, but it is the only way I can redeem myself in my eyes." Now his response felt genuine and heroic, and for the most part it was. However, no one could ever understand because no one could know that it was his idea to leak information to the radicals. Granted there was real strategic value to his plan at the time, but using Despartian as bait to draw them away from Minneapolis was cold. Rob's eyes started to tear and Anna wiped the tears away even though she didn't know what they were for. She knew there was more, but she hadn't seen him this vulnerable in quite some time and didn't want to push him any further. She just accepted who he was and continued her work.

"Do me a favor then," Anna started as she grabbed his hands, "Kick their asses next time!" Rob smiled at this nodding his head in agreement. "And next time remember that all of us are here for you. Adam is still considered the closest thing this city has to law enforcement and I learned how to fight pretty well following your team." Now that the two were on the same page again he let her finish applying the brace and did one final examination of his wounds.

"The good news is the only major damage is the one rib, which is a minor miracle given the beating you took. Now what that means is that as long as you keep the brace on and avoid any forceful blows to the area it should be able to heal on its own within the next six weeks. However, I'm not going to be stupid enough to say take it easy because I know you better than that. As soon as I let you leave this bed, I have the feeling that you'll either be chasing down Carly or training to get back in shape after that butt-whopping," she remarked as she stood up. Then just before she left one of Adams co-workers entered the room with a saddened look on his face. Both knew the news was bad when he refused to make eye contact.

"While you two were talking Adam sent me with Kendra to go looking for Carly again. We found her...unfortunately she's no longer with us," he said with his head hanging low. Despite the pain, Rob quickly rose out of bed. He started heading towards the door, forcing Anna to follow him to ensure his safety. He was not surprised by the news, but he had to see for himself and wanted to check on Kendra.

Adam's officer led them to a nearby alley where Adam awaited them. As they continued towards their destination a sobbing sound could be heard in the distant and with each step the sobbing intensified forcing the broken man to clench his fist tighter and tighter. He knew what he was about to see and yet he couldn't prepare himself for it. No matter how many people he lost the next part never got easier, but he had to push on. He needed to see things for himself because he knew he had to see it for it to be real.

Eventually, Adam and his officer reached a point where they no longer wanted to proceed. At this point, Adam simply directed them the rest of the way with the movement of his hand. They marched forward but, even without the help, they could have easily followed the wails coming from in-front of them. Eventually, they found Kendra hunched over another body crying with her face in her hands as she fell apart. Her tears and shouts of anger were directed at a world that she had once thought fair, but in turn that same world put her through the most miserable of fates. Rob approached her to try and comfort her, and as soon as he got near her, she jumped to his arms. Her cries continued to ring loud as he held her tight. He dared not speak a word as he knew there was nothing that could be said that would help. He thought he had seen every part of Kendra during their talks, but this was different. This was something he couldn't make better and now all he could do for her was to let her express the emotions that were overflowing. She didn't need Rob the hero, she needed the man who could take her sorrows, and she needed the man that agreed to carry the weight of the world on his shoulders no matter the cost to him. This is what she needed now and he was more than happy to oblige.

After several heart-wrenching moments her sorrow eased up and Adam was able to come to pry her away so that Rob and Anna could investigate the scene. Her medical expertise was often crucial when Rob faced things of this nature. Over the last three years Rob had spent most of his time in a bottle or at least that is what most people believed. However, on numerous occasions Adam had asked for his help when people went missing and died. The respect Adam had for Rob despite the troubles he had was immense. In turn Rob often went to Anna whose expertise crucial in many of the cases.

He knelt over her body to do his full examination. The first thing he did was move her hair back into place so that he could see her face one last time. It was the least he could do for a friend who had been there for him on many occasions. As he looked over the body it looked like she had died quickly which was the only solace he could take from the situation.

"She was not killed here there isn't enough blood splatter to go along with the wound. She was moved," he spoke softly, "From what I can tell she was placed this close to your house to send a message and unfortunately, I have a hunch the message was for me. Now as for cause of death it is clearly the stab wound to the heart. Thankfully, that should have at least been a quick death. Do you have any thoughts, Anna?" At his command, she began her own inspection looking for any detail that was abnormal outside of the obvious ones.

"I'll have to get her to one of my tents for further inspection, but I think that you're right about the quick part. I'm trying to see what kind of blade it might have been, but with what I have I can't get a true sense. The edging is pristine with little jaggedness or tearing. It seemed to go through her body like butter and by the size of the wound, it was long blade, that is all I can say with certainty. Now looking at the exit wound on her back this was a single stroke I don't know of anyone in the area who could do this, but they were efficient. This is truly something else. Also based on the preliminaries such as body temperature she likely passed sometime around midnight. And hmm," she started pausing for a moment.

"What is it," Rob asked knowing she didn't like stopping when she was on a roll?

"Well there is something odd here at the entrance point. It looks like there is an extra piece of fabric that doesn't match her clothing. It must have been on the blade before she was stabbed," Anna said as she analyzed the body feeling for any sort of inconsistency. Before Rob rose, he went to shut Carly's eyes one last time, but to his disgust, he found that her eyelids were gone.

"That's disgusting," Anna said as she covered her mouth. She had seen many things, but never had they been so deliberate.

"Disgusting is putting it mildly, but now I have to question why. What could be the motivation for it? In order for the killer to do this they would have had to take an excessive amount of time. They had to expose themselves for a long period of time and I don't know what could be so important about her eyelids. On top of that I have to wonder who lives in this city that could have the skills to remove them without damaging the eyes. There are so many questions here, and now all that I need to do is find the answers. I promise I will find the answers Anna," Rob exclaimed!

"If you are really planning on searching for the killer you are going to need help. Hunting a murderer is beyond your capabilities right now. You are not in shape and you are torn apart. A hole in your shoulder and a cracked rib are not ideal for a killer with these kinds of skills. Now you don't have to like it, but the man who is responsible for the bullet is your only chance. To avenge Carly, you need to have a reunion with fewer shots being fired," Anna claimed as she finally stood up.

"You know I can't go to him. Not yet anyways, I mean for all I know he is responsible for this. This could just be him trying to coax me into partnering up with him. He has told me he has a plan and I can't make his life easier," he rejected her idea even though deep down he knew she was right. He knew that the only person with the resources to track a murderer down sat in his tower overlooking the city.

"God you are stubborn. Okay let's play this game. Imagine that this isn't part of his and he helps us find the killer and keeps you alive. Now let's think about what happens if he tricks you: you kick his ass. It is that plain and simple. I've known both of you for a long time and the one thing I know is you two were like brothers. Now I don't know what he said that night those many years ago, but you have to move on. This girl is dead and you talk about doing whatever is necessary to find out who did it, but then you can't ignore the one man who could actually help you! Now dammit go to him or I will," she shouted looking him sternly in the eyes!

"But Anna..."

"Don't you dare! I'm done with the excuses. You two are the icons of this city, whether you want to be or not and you need to get over your issues! Either you go or I'll do one worse and sell my soul to him and I go. If you think that is easy for me you couldn't be more wrong. Remember that I saw the aftermath of the things that he did during those secret missions. He is a nasty man, but for sweet Carly, I will get on my knees and beg," she explained! Rob couldn't say anything he didn't want to go to that man, but he couldn't stand the thought of Anna going to him. He picked Carly up to take her somewhere more respectable.

"I'm not going to like this, but I'll go. The two of us have had a rough stretch of encounters so I'm not going to promise you anything else," he begrudgingly stated.

Chapter 9
Reunion

The following morning Rob approached the front steps of Ascension Corporations main building and slowly tried to figure out what he would say to John. He had promised himself that he would never talk to John again, not after their separation, but now he had to walk into his office to grovel. He was still in pain from the shot he took and with each step he took towards the building the pain in his shoulder intensified. He entered the building and the first thing he saw was the peppy little redhead sitting behind the main desk.

"Hello, sir! Do you have an appointment, some form of business, or are you here in search of work," she voiced quickly? The response was clearly one that she had practiced a hundred times as it was nearly robotic. She spoke quickly, with a high-pitched frequency, and with little rest between each syllable. On top of that she had a draw that made understanding her a near impossible task.

"Well hello there beautiful. I must say that it is nice to see someone so friendly working at the front desk. You see I'm here to see Mr. Kore who is an old friend of mine. It is quite urgent and I'm sure that he'd love to see me," Rob replied with a grin. He hoped that he would not have to answer any more questions. However, he knew that it would not be that simple. John was far too important to just be seen without an appointment, but it was worth a shot anyway.

"That's nice, but I know Mr. Kore does not have any appointments scheduled for today which means you are not getting in," she smiled. Rob stood there trying to think of something, but she looked up at him dashing all his hopes, "that means you can go, leave, really I don't care where you go, but it's away from my desk. Bye-bye now." Despite her insistence, he didn't leave he just looked over her desk trying to find something he could use. As he scanned around the desk, he found a jar of suckers. Trying to buy some time he kept prodding her for one until she finally agreed so that she could get back to work as he reached for his prize, he saw something interesting. On her desk was a piece of paper with some man's name on it, but the name had been written and crossed out angrily multiple times. After he saw the note, he looked the young lady over and formulated his plan. He wasn't very proud of what he was about to try and do, but he had done far worse in his life.

While Rob was figuring out how to get past a small receptionist Anna was taking care of more pressing manners. Instead of her normal medical tent she was spending time in the makeshift morgue that Adam had created under her request. She was reviewing Carly's body along with a couple of bodies that had appeared over the last few days. As Anna walked throughout the warehouse acting as her morgue, she began to notice a disturbing trend emerge. The body count had been growing suddenly up until a few days ago when there was a mass killing found and then Carly. All of them had died by a similar blade as the one that had killed her. It was all connected she just didn't know how. As she examined one of them, she started to hear a knock at the door. She went to go see who it was and found Kendra standing there.

"I wanted to say good-bye to Carly one last time," she said sniveling. Anna guided her in and brought her to the body. It was clear that Kendra was barely holding together, meanwhile Anna did her best to comfort her. Kendra leaned in to whisper into Carly's ear.

"What did you tell her," Anna asked trying to allow Kendra to express freely?

"I told her I'm sorry," she whimpered.

"There is nothing that you could have done. This was a sick human being," Anna said as she pulled Kendra closer. Kendra tried to pull away and almost fight off Anna for some reason.

"It should have been me Anna. I was supposed to run the route she took, but I was having a bad night. She took it instead and ended up dead," she cried. Once again Anna hugged her. There was no answer to her troubles, guilt like that can kill a person, but there is no simple way to reconcile with yourself.

"Kendra, I'm going to make one plea. I want you to find Iris. She is the best psychologist in this city and you need someone to talk to. You need someone to help you move on. Your life has been a rough one and you need someone who can truly help you," Anna pleaded wiping the tears away from Kendra's eyes.

"I can't go see the woman who was going to marry the man I have been sleeping with on numerous occasions," she protested. The mere thought sounded outlandish to her.

"Yes, you can. If it was anyone else you are right, but this is Iris. She not only will forgive, but will help you," Anna persisted. Kendra knew that Anna was right and nodded slowly.

Back at Ascension Rob was walking out of the employee break room alone. He was buttoning up his shirt and zipping his pants while carrying some homemade donuts. The receptionist was no longer at her desk and he had a smirk on his face as he made his way to the elevator. The whole walk he continued to contemplate what he was going to say. No matter how hard he tried, he couldn't find the right words. John and him had a complex relationship to say the least. Given that fact there was no easy way of phrasing his plea for assistance that wouldn't backfire. He finally reached John's office and knew it was now or never regardless of whether he had a plan or not. He opened the door and found John sitting while chastising one of his employees.

"Well isn't this a surprise," John said as he recognized his new guest! Rob's appearance brought a grin to John's face. The employee looked at Rob with a sense of wonderment on his face. He knew the rules. There was no way someone could enter John's office unless he called them or they were important.

"That's a nice donut, it reminds me of the ones my girlfriend makes. You see the key is precise preparation and it is amazing the way she moves around the kitchen," he finally remarked trying to find something to say that would break the silence

"That reminds me actually. I had to inform her that you two have to end this relationship, it is doing harm to both of your work and you are too important of an employee to sacrifice," John informed his employee. The man's eyes grew large by what he had just heard.

"I'm sorry sir, I have to leave our appointment than. I can only imagine how devastated she is," he responded as he grew flustered. He flew out the door as fast as he could towards a situation that will be extremely awkward given Rob's actions. After the man had left the room, John turned to Rob with a wicked smile.

"I told her that he cheated on her so, this should be hilarious. To think he believed me when I said he does important work. What an idiot? I don't even know what he does here, I just needed some entertainment for the day," snickered John, "However, fate has apparently brought me something far better. Now what is it that you need? I hope this isn't an attempt to get compensation for your accident the other night." As he talked, there was this air of arrogance that irritate Rob and John began to rise so that he could meet his old friends gaze. While John smiled Rob kept his face neutral. He refused to show any emotion or weakness that John could use against him.

"Don't misunderstand the reason for this visit. I am not here to see you. I am here because you are the only one in this city who has what I need. I don't like or trust you, but I need your help," Rob admitted as he looked at the floor wishing there was something else to say.

"That hurts Rob, I thought that this would just be a social call between friends, but alas you just want to use me and to say so in such a backhanded manner is inappropriate for men of our stature. On the other hand, I feel like you are about to grovel and I enjoy watching you beg, so elaborate Rob. I need details in order to draw up a fair deal between us. And don't you were I will take into account our brotherhood when determining your payment," John answered as confidence slowly began to grow. He was aware that he held all the cards and that he could have anything he wanted. On top of that he knew how to push Rob and drive him to his own breaking point.

"I should have known that any favor would come with strings. Regardless this is too important to not pay the devil," Rob mumbled as he started his answer, "Alright, here is the simple facts one of my friends was stabbed and I think an employee of yours is involved. If that is the case, I will need to bring him down, if not then I may need your help again." John immediately perked up at the request. What he figured would be mundane and boring has turned into something worth his interest. Most importantly at all the real Rob was standing before him and making the request. His old partner had raised his gaze to meet eyes. The hesitation and sloppiness he had seen the other night were gone. He now had a problem that was interesting, but was a man worth caring about again.

"My, my what have you gotten yourself into Rob. I thought you were out of the game, but you just changed it. Instead of killing you are finding killers. That is an intriguing twist, so what is the name,"

John snapped? It was obvious that the wheels were beginning to turn, as his fingers began to twitch and eyes grew distant.

"Unfortunately, I don't have a name yet, but according to others involved your niece will know who I am talking about," Rob replied. John was shocked when he heard Rob refer to his niece. The conversation just grew more and more interesting.

"You are full of surprises and I'm not sure which one is most shocking. The fact you don't have the name already or that you know about my niece. I have worked hard to hide her from you and yet here you are talking about her as if I made it public knowledge," John grinned. It may have been a surprise, but John still looked like he was in full control.

"Nothing like that, just pure happenstance really. She ran into Kendra and her housemates, took a photo with them, and I saw it," Rob snapped back with earnest in his voice, "That actually brings me to my main point. Apparently when they met your niece she was being bothered by the suspect and they agreed to help her out. Now one of them is dead and she is in the middle of all of it." After hearing Rob's explanation John stood and mulled over his options. As he contemplated his options he walked over to his window and looked over his city. He was virtually the king of Despartian because he knew how to pull strings and move at the right time. This may have been what he always wanted, but he could not afford to rush and give Rob an opportunity to take his throne. Finally, his grin stretched across his face as he began to speak.

"Let me remind you of a lesson we were once taught Rob. Sun Tzu said: Know thy self, know thy enemy. A thousand battles, a thousand victories. Gene pounded that idea into our heads and because of that simple philosophy we rarely loss. Now I have continued to apply this as I have taken over Despartian, however I feel like you have lost this. You come here asking for a name and yet I feel like you don't know who you are. I feel like you need more than just my resources and I fear I cannot help you find you. After years of living in the bottle, your skills and abilities have been diminished as well as that reckless confidence you once had. If I jump into a partnership with you now it could end badly for me because you are not the warrior who would do whatever it takes to win that I thought I was coming to the other night. You are now just a blunt instrument," John began to lecture, but before he could finish Rob had grabbed him by the collar.

"Don't you dare lecture me you snake," Rob yelled gripping John's shirt tighter! John separated himself from Rob as his grin disappeared. He was no longer amused by his old teammate.

"I would keep your cool from now on if you want my help," John began as he straightened out his shirt, "Whether you like it or not you need me and you will do what I say and follow my plan. You are not going to play cowboy or go renegade here otherwise I will destroy what is left of you." John stared Rob down as he waited for confirmation. Finally, Rob nodded his head.

"So, what is this plan that you have," Rob asked?

"Well, it is need to know and the first part is knowing our enemy. I will call Trisha here and then we can proceed," John answered. He walked back to his desk where he pushed a button to presumably summon his niece.

As the two men waited for the young lady Rob began to look through the office. He was biding his time and avoiding extra and unnecessary contact. However, everything went out the window when his gaze suddenly fell upon a picture that sat tucked away on one of John's shelves. As he reached for the unframed photo his hatred for John all but vanished upon seeing the contents.

The picture was a rare one from the war when both of them were smiling and enjoying their victory. Things were brutal back then and given the nature of the missions they performed there was seldom time for reflection, but this photo caught a rare opportunity. The photo showed both men bruised and beaten, barely able to stand. Blood drenched their clothing, and Rob sporting a black eye on his right side.

"I still can't believe a picture exist where the two of us were smiling together," John murmured. John had crept up on Rob while he was distracted and his voice startled him. Despite the shock and his desire to hate John the photo had softened him. He could no longer summon the same contempt he once held. In that one moment he saw the other side of John again, he saw the man that fought with him side-by-side, and he saw his brother again.

"We had just gone through absolute hell and survived, why wouldn't we smile," Rob replied with some joy in his voice, "Do you remember what we told the photographer when he asked why we were smiling?"

"Yeah, we told him we were glad it had finally stopped raining," chuckled John, "It was amazing really ten days stuck behind enemy lines with no support, little food, and minimum ammo yet the first thing we complain about was the rain from the past four days. We really were something else."

"Did it really only rain for four days, it felt a lot longer than that. I'm pretty sure it took about a month for my shoes to fully dry out. I don't know if I've ever seen so much rain, but in the end, we destroyed the main factory for that heinous drug. Although I have heard rumors about it appearing in some areas south of here," Rob said as he reminisced about the past with his old war buddy.

"I've heard that too. It is a shame that some of the supply slipped through our fingers. Leopard Skin was a nasty drug and the side effects could not have been worth it," John started as he paused for a moment, "Speaking of side effects how long did it take for that shiner to heal?"

"If I remember I was putting ice on it for about a week and Anna was pretty sure you gave me a concussion," Rob said rubbing his hand across his face.

"Hey, you knew we were staging a fight. We had discussed the plan thoroughly and just because you decided not to brace yourself was not my fault," John retorted in his defense of the accusation.

"I will take some of the blame for it, I did forget that you were left-handed. When the hit came, I was not prepared at all. Still, you didn't have to come at me with everything you had! I could have sold a softer blow," both men began to laugh a little at this remark, but their joy was interrupted when the door to John's office flew open. Trisha had barged her way into the office disrupting the serenity the two men had enjoyed.

"What is it, Uncle? Did you miss me," she questioned as her eyes fell upon Rob, "Now hello handsome, who are you and what can I do for you?" She approached Rob and started to move her hand softly across his shoulders as she eyed up a man she had never seen before.

"Enough Trish, it's only Rob you don't need to keep up the act," John informed her causing what was once a cheery flirtatious face to transform into a deadpan gaze. She dropped her hand as quickly as she raised it and moved to a seat on top of John's desk. She had darkened her hair since the picture was taken and was in a much duller outfit than she was accustomed to.

"What am I doing here then? I was just starting to dye my hair when you summoned and would prefer to get back to it as soon as possible. I mean you usually only call me to loosen up some of your more stubborn clients, so I thought this would be important," she inquired. Rob placed the image of him and John back onto the shelves. While at the same time removed the photo of Carly, Kendra, and Trisha from his pocket to show to the confused girl.

"Her name was Carly. And a friend of mine informed me that you helped set her up with one of her clients, but no one has a name. I need your help to find him as quickly as possible," he calmly asserted as he pointed to the woman in the photo.

"You said her name *was* Carly. I take it that the girl isn't with us anymore," she quivered as she studied Rob, looking for some kind of reaction or confirmation to come over his face; however, he did not surrender any information as he had dealt with John's tactics many times before. "I do remember her. She was a kind woman it is a true loss, but I guess things like this should not be a surprise anymore especially when you consider her career choice. I mean a woman as intelligent and beautiful as that should have found something else to do with her life," she asserted before pausing to shrug her shoulders.

"Now if all you need is the name it was Stevens who is a real creep if you ask me, but I would never have guessed he was capable of something as horrendous as murder. To me he always seemed more like a closet pervert than a killer and trust me I know a killer when I see one. That said I doubt he is the guilty party, but give the perv a good beating anyways," she ordered as she twirled her hair around. Trisha was just like Rob expected. She was cold and calculated with every word just like her Uncle. He had trained her well, but she had the opportunity to be far more dangerous as womanly charm made her an unprecedented threat. Rob knew that she was being helpful however, he also knew that he had to be mindful of her.

"Interesting, I was just informed earlier today that Stevens never reported to work. You are dismissed Trish, but before you go, I want to remind you to get ahold of our media interest for tomorrow," John muttered as he stood rubbing his chin as he fell into deep thought.

"It is already done Uncle. Now I'm going to finish my hair and have a quick practice session with Gene if you need me again. Try not to need me," she explained walking out. As she passed Rob she smiled and pressed her hand against his ribs. The feeling sent a slight jolt through Rob's body. He did everything in his power to resist a reaction, but he had to wonder what she knew. There was no way that it could have been an accident, not with this family, but he couldn't dwell long on the thought as he still had to negotiate with John. He knew what he needed now he just had to hear the asking price for information.

"She reminds me a lot of her Uncle. She feels like the kind of person who is always manipulating and playing the situation towards her favor. You really outdid yourself with her," he clamored as he put the photo of Carly back into his pocket.

"I feel as if now you are trying to insult me, but I am going to take it as a compliment. I've learned that the world is on constant set of strings and if you want to rule it all you have to do is know when to pull the right one. You might call it manipulative I just see it as using the opportunities set before us. Trisha shares my view of the world. Granted my expert parenting played a role in that, but it also because of what the world did to her. You see her parents were killed right in front of her. She was traumatized by the experience and I have merely taught her how to take control of her own destiny."

"Over the last three years I have turned her into the perfect apprentice while at the same time using her as a flawless weapon. One day she will become greater than I am, she will use her cunning, beauty, and skills to rule the world. Now back to your problems. The man you are looking for is extremely important to this company and my ambitions. You see he holds a prominent role in our research and development teams, with a specialty in cell development. His hope was to clone cells in order to regrow damaged tissue for people affected by the war. A very noble cause, but if his mind falls into the wrong hands it will be a disaster. He must be found immediately," John proclaimed! There was a sudden urgency in his voice that Rob had not heard in some time. He could tell that John was truly worried about how this could affect his plans.

"Does this mean you need my help," Rob questioned hoping he had finally gained some form of leverage?

"Don't get ahead of yourself. You see I just need a body dead or alive which doesn't require your help. However, you need answers from him which means you still need my intel and that comes with a price. Though it will be cheaper. All I want from you is support tomorrow during my conference about Hope Tower. You carry a lot of weight in this community and the opening will go far smoother if you are not protesting it as some form of trap," John explained as his gaze turned to his tower again.

"That is, it," Rob questioned? It felt like a small price compared to what John was known for asking for.

"That is all I ask for. I will explain what supporting the tower means in two days, but for now I just want you to show up," John said extending his hand.

"A man who is not willing to sacrifice his stubborn pride for the truth is not worth calling a man. I'll do it, John, I don't want to, but I need to do it for her. I will find the man who killed her, be it your Stevens or someone else," Rob claimed as he shook hands with a man he had resisted on multiple occasions.

"Better the devil you know than the one you don't. Isn't that right Rob," John said as if he was reading Rob's thoughts. His classic grin covering his face again.

"I guess you could say that, but don't you dare cross me John. This agreement does not mean I trust you or forgive you it only means that I agree that I need you," Rob answered as he let go of John's hand.

"Never trust anyone and you will live much longer. The plan is simple: you will go to room 27B which contains the office of our psychologist. There you will find Stevens' personnel files. Here is a slip that will permit you access. Then, go to his house, find him and report to me by 10 o'clock sharp two days from now at Hope Tower," John explained as he handed a slip of paper to Rob, "And if you would be so kind as to give these letters to our psychologist it would save me some time partner."

As Rob walked through the halls he kept thinking about John. There had to be more to his plan than he was letting on. There was no way he only wanted Rob to show up at his tower. It just seemed too simple and ordinary. He looked at the letters John had given him, but they gave no great insight, they were merely postmarked for the other Ascension offices in Memphis and New Orleans. Nothing out of character for a man running the only multinational corporation left in the world. At this point there were more pressing matters and if John did pull anything, he knew that he could end the plots.

With his mind slowly freeing from John's mental clutches he began to truly notice the building he was in. It immediately reminded him of what it was like before the war as the whole interior was pristine. It was also clear that John kept the best things Ascension had to offer for himself. The electrical grid had only recently been restored, but his building was filled with automatic doors and electronic locks. This building was the greatest stronghold in Despartian. After a few minutes he reached his destination and tried opening the door, but found it to be jammed. Though a small jam couldn't stop him it was a nuisance that forced him to use excessive force.

After several attempts he finally burst into the room. As he started to scan the room, he was speechless upon seeing who the psychologist was, however knowing John he should have expected it. Sitting at the desk in front of him was the woman he had promised his life to, the woman he loved was only feet away now. She sat there waiting for him to say anything, but his mind was barren and unable to find a single syllable. He was captivated by her glistening blue eyes and the softness in her face. He had not talked to her and seen her in over five years, but the second he saw her every feeling he once had resurfaced. Then after a few minutes of silence she smiled and it nearly put him on the ground. His heartbeat went from 0 to 100 in a millisecond. He may have been ashamed to see her all these years, but it was clear that didn't matter to her, she still loved the fool standing in front of her.

"Do you still have it," Iris asked with a tenderness in her voice that made him shiver? The request was vague and non-descriptive, but without any other thought, he knew what she meant. Still lost for words all he could manage to do was nod his head in confirmation.

"Always! It brings me luck and more importantly it reminds me of the joy I once treasured. More importantly it reminds me of when I was better. That is why every morning I stare at it before I get out of bed, so I can remember you Iris," Rob finally proclaimed. Iris slowly rose from her chair and made her way to Rob maintaining eye contact the whole time. She placed her hand on his chest as she began to speak again.

"You have always had a way of saying sorry without using the word and it is what you were always best at. Maybe that is why we stuck together for so long," Iris whispered into his ear as she began to circle around him. She observed every part of him trying to reaffiliate herself with him. On the other hand, he stood tall merely following her with his eyes.

"Oh, there were far greater reasons than that," he smiled, "So, how have you been Iris?" As he spoke, he grazed his hand against her cheek stopping her in her tracks for a moment. Standing there with her, he finally felt peace that had eluded him. It was obvious that he did the same for her. Their love was special and they both needed this moment; they needed each other's presence.

"I've been well. Just trying to make it with the man of my dreams avoiding me and my best friend still missing after the War," she began. Her words and tone were sharp, she wanted them to pierce the thick skin he had developed and wanted him to understand the pain she had experienced.

"Despite all of that though I've found a comfortable position here at Ascension and I'm doing what makes me feel fulfilled in life. How about yourself Rob, doing anything groundbreaking," she asked as her hand swept across his brace? She paused to feel it, but knew that he had gotten himself into trouble again. It was clear to her that he was also in pain and despite their separation this hurt her soul. From then on, her touch grew even more gentle unsure of what else ailed him.

"I've been attempting to stay out of trouble. I've failed miserably at it, but I have tried," he replied cracking a small smile as he knew she could feel the damage. In turn she let out a small chuckle which helped him relax at last. He knew he had hurt her and the seriousness of their conversation had made him feel uncomfortable. That chuckle was all he needed.

"So, what you are saying is there isn't anything new," she replied, shaking her head a moment, "Now I want to believe you are solely here to catch-up, however, I'm not naïve enough to actually think that is true." She pushed herself away from him and made her way back to her desk. She had completed her evaluation and based on what she saw she wanted to get back to her work.

"I wish I wasn't so predictable, but you are right," he responded as he removed the note and letters from his pocket. First, he gave her the letters and then the note. She knew that he had business, but the note still disappointed her. She wanted this to be their moment, but it was not meant to be. She read the note carefully as she sat on top of her desk. While, she scanned the document he continued to be captivated by her. He had not seen her in years and somehow, she had grown more gorgeous while he felt he was deteriorating from the years of hard living.

"I see the note says there is a dead woman and that you have been granted access to the personnel files of Mr. Stevens. Definitely not the favor I expected when you walked into my office, I guess some things have changed," she claimed as she strolled into her back office to look for anything that might help him.

Meanwhile, he studied her small office hoping that more good memories would return. The first thing he noticed was the brightness, she had managed to block out the chaos that surrounded her by filling her life with art and happiness. He did not recognize the pieces, but she had several professionally made paintings hanging each screamed joy. Despite the liveliness of her walls her desk was mostly bare. She kept two singular photos on it surrounded by piles of work.

The first was her and her two sisters; Ali and Jenny. The second, was of her and her best friend/adopted sister Danielle who had gone missing during the war. As he picked up each photo, he started to picture the happy moment attached to each. The family picture was a candid piece where the three sisters were outside playing with their golden retriever. It looked like fall based on their outfits, but any coldness at the time meant nothing to them. The other was a staged photograph from their freshman year. It was taken during a Halloween party where Iris had dressed as Wonder Woman and Danielle was an NBA star. Both of them tried acting tough for it, but that only made him laugh harder as neither were the classic definition of tough during that period. They each had come a long way, but early on they were the sweetest, kindest women he had ever met.

After a few minutes Iris returned to the main office. She noticed that Rob was looking at her photos and she smiled. Then she noticed he was lost in a trance and took the opportunity to surprise him a bit. She took the large file she just retrieved and slammed it down as loud as she could in front of him. This quickly snapped him back to reality, she in turn laughed at his response.

"Were you forming some dirty thoughts like usual or just reminiscing," she chuckled as Rob placed the photo?

"If you are involved, they aren't dirty thoughts...they're called dirty memories," he laughed as he swished one of her hairs back that had fallen out of place.

"Whatever you say. Well here is your file! This is everything you could possibly need to know. Which includes an address and a psychological profile I created a month ago," she stated as she made her way back to behind her desk. She looked over the paperwork that filled it and grimaced at the sight of the piles. He had known her long enough that it was obvious that she had no interest in returning to her work. This cramped office was not her style, her preference would be outside as she walked around with her patients. Making them smile and helping them open up. However, she couldn't complain as this was the best opportunity she was given. Before John had offered her the position her and Ally were in a tough position. After the War Ally quickly took up a position as a teacher, but that wasn't enough to support them in the new world. Iris needed something as well, but she had mentally shut down after the War.

Iris rarely showed it, but in the days following the war, she was lost. Her sister had died, the city she lived in collapsed, her best friend had gone missing, and most importantly the man she loved had changed. She didn't understand it, but when he came back, he refused to see her anymore. Before the War Rob barely drank, but afterwards he loved the bottle more than her. She understood people she knew he was broken, but unfortunately, he hurt her in the process. Then things got worse, he started whoring around. She didn't judge him for that, but Rob was a public figure which meant rumors would swirl. She would try to move on, but here the stories about his escapades every day. All of Rob's idiocy was a distraction that ate her up inside and made it impossible to hold down solid work. She had a smile the whole time, but the sisters were in trouble until John gave her a job. Rob didn't know any of this and the idea of her owing John her life would kill him.

"You said you created a profile for him. Is that standard for all employees," Rob asked as he reengaged Iris in the conversation?

"No, there were extenuating circumstances that had arisen," she answered moving back to the table top.

"What kind of circumstances are we talking about," Rob asked as he flipped through the file marking his address and anything thing else that seemed important.

"Simply put his wife had recently passed and John was worried about some of his recent behavior. His fellow coworkers reported oddities that worried them so I began my interviews to assess whether he was a risk to himself or others. However, during my interviews I found nothing out of the ordinary for a man in grief. His wife had died suddenly and was left alone with his teenage daughter. Odd is normal in that case. Knowing that I still met with him weekly so we could work through any issues that arose. I honestly don't think he could be your killer Rob, but if that is what you and John are convinced of, I can't stop you," she explained as Rob flipped through her notes. As he flipped through the notes, he was happy he had found the one doctor with legible handwriting. She even highlighted and stick-noted things.

"I believe you, but there is too much circumstantial evidence to rule him out as of now. I promise you though if he is innocent and I find him I will bring him back to your care. Thanks, Iris," Rob told her as he started to make his way for the door.

"Before you go. Can I ask you something," Iris said stopping Rob in his tracks?

"Anything," he replied, turning back to look at her. Her gaze had fallen to the floor and she was holding her left arm with her right to shield her body. There was something uncomfortable about the question she was going to ask, he just didn't understand what it could be.

"This may be an odd question to ask, but since I never know how long it will be until the next time, we speak I have to ask it," Iris began as she began to rub her left arm.

"What is it, Iris? You know I've never kept anything from you that you asked me about," he answered as her eyes now turned to the side. He had never seen her avoid his eye contact like this and decided if her eyes would not rise to meet his he would lower to hers. He approached her and knelt slightly so he could look into her sparkling sapphires again.

"Was I your first choice," she asked blatantly shocking Rob? He clearly didn't understand the question or where it was coming from.

"What makes you ask that Iris," he asked trying to find clarification?

"There are numerous reasons why; anxiety, fear, time, fact, etc. As you know I've studied people for years now and as I've studied them, I started to think about us. More importantly I started thinking about you and how you've acted. I started to realize that either you were lying to me or yourself this whole time. You blamed your separation from me on the death of Jenny and the failure you associated with it. However, after that day you still wrote, and tried to contact me. I'd even argue you were a better fiancé after her death.

The true change came years later when Dani disappeared in that disaster of a mission she was on. It was when she vanished that you lost your light. You stopped talking to me and started avoiding us all. At first, I thought it was just losing another friend had finally shut you down. However, time went by and something was just off. It was as if a part of you died that day, a very similar thing happened to Stevens when his wife died. In fact, it reminded me of several widows and widowers who have seen me after the wars end. I know that you cared for her, you always said she was like a sister to you, but did you love her? I understand it, you met her before me and she was an incredible person who brought the best out of us, but I need the truth. Was she the first choice while I was just the rebound? Is that why you couldn't return to me because that person you loved was gone," Iris pleaded as tears formed in her eyes? Rob understood the question and yet the answer seemed distant to him as if it was one, he couldn't truly give her. Unable to find what she was looking for he did the best he could and wrapped his arms around her and placed a kiss on her forehead. Out of everything he had done to her recently this still felt like the biggest failure of them all.

"Iris I love you never doubt that for a second. And you are right I did care for Danielle and losing her hurt me more than the loss of Jenny. But Iris none of that matters, because it doesn't change what you mean to me. I was going to marry you because you were the greatest thing that ever happened to me, not because you were the backup. I would never do that to you because you deserve to be loved fully and if you want fully honesty you are still the best thing that ever happened to me. Even in my darkest days the thought of marrying you still remained. Unfortunately, for us during those dark days I saw the truth about myself and before I can think of coming back to you, I have to fix myself, because I can't make you responsible for fixing me. I promise that I will come back to you when I think that has happened. This will not be the last time you see me Iris, I promise," he guaranteed her as he held her tight in his arms again like he had so many times before that. After a few moments, he let go of her and made his way towards the exit.

Rob's journey for redemption and revenge was just finally beginning and couldn't spend any more time away from the case. Iris, on the other hand, returned to her work, at least physically, as her mental state was far away from that office. They were both gone from that office one was searching for Carly's killer, the other had returned to the night Rob proposed and the absolute disaster it had been. However, she said yes to that man despite the melted chocolates, the rain, the nearly lost ring, and raccoon that made its way into their apartment. Since that day he kept every promise he made that he was in control of and she felt confident about this one

Chapter 10
Not What We're Looking For

Rob left the office and followed the address in the profile to Stevens' house. The whole time he was running to the house he was bothered by the events unfolding. He felt like things were too easy for him. There was a suspect, a witness that could confirm the meeting should have taken place, and a recent profile that pointed towards him being in recent distress. The clues were there, but he couldn't shake the feeling he had that something was wrong. Once he arrived at the house, he found it to be boring and dull as it matched many of the neighbor houses. It was a cookie cutter house with no true individualism. The walls were all white, the door a plain oak, two windows, and a small flower patch, just like every single house around it. It wasn't a surprise as this was the neighborhood Ascension had taken full control of in order to house their employees away from the rest of the city. This also gave the company control over more of their workers' lives, it isolated them further away from the world around them. The monotony around Stevens' house, however, made it obvious that something was off. At first, he could not discern what was off so he moved to take a closer look. He gradually crept towards the house still wary of what he was getting himself into, this man could be dangerous or in danger. His fears were quickly answered when he saw the door was propped open ever so slightly. It was not flung open, instead, there was just a crack of distance between the door and its frame. It was left open, but necessarily intentionally.

Before the war began Rob would have run in the other direction, calling the police, during it, he would have barged through the door guns a blazing hoping to catch the inhabitants off guard. Now he was hesitant remembering the words that Anna had said to him. Feeling both his shoulder and rib he questioned if he should proceed, but there was no more time for him to go looking for aide. Along with this, he couldn't put any more people in harm's way he had lost more than enough allies for one lifetime.

He glanced around him checking for any snooping eyes and then slipped into the house silently to avoid detection if anyone happened to remain. Instantly, he was greeted with a horrific smell. He hadn't encountered it for some time, but it was unmistakable it was the stench of melted and decaying flesh. The smell should have turned him away, but he had experienced it several times before and was now determined to follow his current lead regardless of what his gut was telling him to do. Following his nose, he made his way to the bathroom of the house, and as he got closer, he started to notice something else there was an odor that he couldn't recognize. He opened the bathroom door and uncovered a skeletal corpse with most of the flesh dissolved in whatever acidic mixture it had been placed in.

Unsure of what mixture was used to dissolve the flesh he began searching the house for a way to pull the plug without getting anything on his hands. He headed towards the kitchen hoping something would be there while he looked for a tool, he kept his eyes open for any other clues that may have been left by the killer. He eventually did find a long pair of tongs but saw nothing else out of the ordinary. Everything was perfect and tidy barring the dead body in the bathtub. It was too clean, even the pictures had been removed as dust surrounded bare spots of tables that would have once been photographs. The house was empty. He knew there was nothing to find and returned to the bathroom, still unable to shake the unknown smell he had encountered earlier.

After he emptied the tub and found some cloth towels to use for gloves, and then he removed the body gently to avoid any more damage. Once it was secure, he started to examine the body looking for any kind of clue as to who this person was. He looked over each aspect of the body looking for anything and as he studied, he saw things were odd.

"It's not him," a familiar female voice cried out. Rob's face turned white as his mind processed who it could be. He turned quickly to see if he was correct and yet was disappointed by what he saw. No one was there, there was a voice, but no source. After rubbing his eyes, he turned back to the body to return to work. When he suddenly jumped backward after seeing Carly sitting next to the body.

"It... It can't be, you're dead. I saw your corpse there is no way that this is real," Rob stammered as he denied what he saw.

"You're right honey this old soul and I are playing together in the afterlife. And I'm afraid that the two of us won't be the only ones if you don't hurry, but I guess you already knew that didn't you," she mocked. She looked so lively for a pure figment of his imagination. He still couldn't understand what was happening.

"You're not real. That other smell, it was some kind of hallucinogen wasn't it. I remember something like this during the War. Now why are you here," Rob started to ask as if he was working through a puzzle?

"It is good that you are cute because when there is a beautiful woman around you can be extremely stupid. However, I'm not going to give this to you easy, so why with all your struggles would I be your hallucination? It could have been anyone, but you subconsciously decided on me," she commented as if she was having fun seeing him struggle. His subconscious was playing with him and the only way for him to get through this was to play along with.

"I must say you are an interesting choice, but you have been on my mind a lot, so it would make sense for you to be here. Plus, you are the person who actually saw your killer, so why not? It is better you than John," Rob answered as he began to regain his composure.

"If that's what you believe then it must be true. Maybe there is more to it than that, but it is your crazy brain you have to deal with. In the end, I'm just a manifestation and whatever you say goes. Truthfully, I'm just surprised that... oh, I guess we're going with the schoolgirl fantasy today. I should have known even when surrounded by death you are still you," she smirked as her outfit seemed to change. He even laughed at the change. Whatever this drug was it wasn't the worst he had ever been given.

"If you're going to help me. At least you can also lighten up the mood. Now can we get back to work," he explained with a grin on his face.

"Your choice Rob, but you are on a deadline remember. I recommend that you do something and fast," she answered back. He grabbed the file that he received from Iris and began to comb through it. Things just didn't make sense to him.

"You look disturbed Rob. Is there something wrong," she questioned as Rob's face grew more troubled.

"According to the file, Stevens was a taller man standing just over six feet. This body, on the other hand, is barely over five feet. Then look at the hips here they are far too wide for a man. Whoever this was she wasn't Stevens," Rob proclaimed. He kept fingering through the file and would turn the bones looking for clues.

"So how are they connected Rob? We have a dead girl in this man's tub and someone tried to melt her beyond recognition. Why? Can you find the link," Carly prodded as she tried to draw the answer out of him? He had to know if he terrorized another woman before Carly. His eyes grew large as he found his answer.

"It was his daughter," he started with a saddened look on his face, "I remember Iris mentioning her, but I didn't want to believe it could be her. According to the information here she was 5'1". She was the only person he had left, why would he do this to her? Like Iris said he was depressed, but he loved her according to this. He had even put in a request to have her join Ascension as part of his team." He bent down to take a look at her and Carly placed a hand on his shoulder.

"His daughter! That is some kind of sick monster. You need to find him Rob not just for me, but for her she didn't deserve to lose her mother and then have her father do this. I guess it's true you can't avoid your demons you can only pray that you have the strength to overcome them," Carly said as Rob seemingly ignored her. She was the unconscious anger he felt, but he had to be objective he had to look deeper. Things are rarely that clean. He became desperate trying to find something. Even though the evidence made him look like a monster, that was not what Iris found and she was too good at her job to be this off about a man. Just before he gave-up he found something wrong with the scapula that set him off.

"He didn't kill her," he proclaimed shocking Carly's embodiment.

"I think you're going to need an explanation for this one. I mean he killed me so we know he is capable of it! It is his daughter meaning he had an opportunity and was clearly going through some issues which aren't motive, but enough for a break," she stated in a shocked tone! He was fighting himself with her counters, but this is what he needed. He needed something to make him dig deeper. He had not thought this hard since the day before his fallout with John. It felt good to do this again.

"I need you; I mean me... us to follow my, our logic. There is no motive to do this now. Had he done this after his wife's death, it would make sense, but he was getting better. Iris and her were helping him cope. That being said there appears to be no sign of overloading going on with him. He was working hard and had just completed several big projects. Things were starting to go his way in multiple facets. On top of that this scene is too clean. The house is empty, pictures removed, and no sign of anyone besides me being here for some time. He only went missing in the last 24 hours. If we were to ignore the other facts and assume, he was on some kind of psychological break than he should not have been composed enough to clean this well," Rob explained.

"Okay so, that is all good and nice, but it isn't a guarantee. There is nothing substantial here to prove that he isn't our man. The bottom line is that it is his house and there isn't any evidence any one else was here. His daughter and him could have had an argument. It isn't the first man with depression to drink too much and do something stupid, then he started cleaning up when I arrived and boom now, he has two bodies to get rid of," Carly pointed out.

"Maybe, but my biggest question is why would someone who lives with her strike her in the back. He stabbed you through the heart and yet he beat his daughter, he broke her scapula," he explained as he held up the shattered bone.

"He's insane and sick," Carly protested! Rob merely smirked at this answer.

"Maybe you're right, but listen to me. As I told you he loved her and this just smells rotten both figuratively and literally. I think that there is something at play here. This feels like a setup to me. It is as if someone used her to get to Stevens. What if he was threatened to kill you and they used his daughter to make it happen, then they killed her anyways and likely disposed of him," Rob explained as he tried to figure out all the pieces. It wasn't unheard of for someone to do something like this, but to do it so cleanly. The new suspect had to be powerful, he had to have connections.

"That's a strong possibility, but right now you are standing in another man's home with a decaying corpse while talking to yourself. Regardless of what you think you have to get out of here before someone finds you or things are going to get sticky really quick," Carly explained. As she finished, they heard a creak coming from somewhere else in the house. They turned and looked at each other knowing that trouble was brewing. She was right, he had become so distracted trying to figure out the puzzle that he had become numb to his surroundings. Someone was in the house and he could be in trouble.

"It's not the first time you've crawled out a window Rob. I'd high-tail it before whoever is here finds you," she suggested as Rob headed for his exit. He jumped out of the window and ran as fast as he could to escape whatever had found him. Once he thought he was far enough away, he started to wander around planning out his next move. The fact that someone had returned to the house meant they were concerned it might be discovered.

Behind him, in the house, there was one man with a cloak that had found the scene in the bathroom. Though the cloak covered most of his body, it was clear that he was large and strong. He bent over to look at the body and picked up the skull to observe it. As he brought it closer to him his grip tightened around it crushing it into pieces.

"Keep following the maze. Deeper and deeper you go until you can't find your way out," the figure whispered as it rose to stare out the window Rob had just escaped through.

Unsure of how to proceed Rob started to make his way home, but before he left the Ascension Estates, he found the nicest bar in the city. It was in pristine condition. The windows were large and clear, the smell was fruity and lacked the odor of vomit he was accustomed to and every light that was on still worked. He was reminded fondly of the old wineries that Iris once dragged him to before the war had begun.

The inside was just as eloquent as the outside. He began to wonder who owned the place, but as he was gazing around the room, he saw John's picture hanging. John wanted to control every aspect of his employee's lives. He tried to make it superior to the rest of town, but in the end, it was just as much a slime hole like every other dump in the city. It was all a sham and it was more appalling than the buildings that were half burned down. At least the rest of the city was willing to admit its troubles, but this dump was pathetic. It cried out desperation and fakeness.

His broken rib and bad shoulder were catching up to him as he wobbled towards the bar, and it had been hours since he last ate. It had been a long day, he had discovered his friend was dead, saw his ex, and found another dead woman. All this was all catching-up to him at last and he just needed to breathe. As he sat at the bar his eyes began to glaze over and his heart felt heavy. The stress both mental and physical were beginning to overtake him. Two bodies and more questions than answers had left his mind churning. He grew depressed and angry knowing he was now at a dead end.

"You going to order something or you just going to sit there like a damn bum," the bartender barked harshly with a deep draw in his voice. Rob looked up to see an overweight bald man with a snarl on his face. "This here is a nice joint and if you think you can drag your dirty, worthless self here and loathe in your own self-pity without ordering something you are sadly mistaken my friend." Rob looked around the bar finally pulling himself out of his own head.

"I'll take a couple of shots of that and a plate of your cheapest grub," Rob finally said pointing at a jug of some clear drink with no label on it. The bartender quickly reached back and slammed a couple of glasses down. He then pulled a lever, which rang a bell off in the distance. It was mere moments after the bell rang that a short little man missing his left arm came rushing out with a plate of mush. Rob looked at the plate with disgust, but he was so starved that he began to dig in without much hesitation. Occasionally, he would stop to breathe or take a shot. The alcohol had a burning aftertaste, but it hit the spot. He finished the meal and started to pay when he knocked the photo of Stevens out of his pocket.

Before he could react, someone picked it up from behind him. Now with a few shots down Rob was irritated and turned to face whoever had taken his picture. What he saw could only be described as a monster of a man. His shoulders were broad enough to fill a doorway and he stood several inches taller than Rob. His face was scarred, but several features remained hidden behind the hood he wore.

"This man was a researcher at Ascension," the figure pointed out softly. Rob merely nodded his head in agreeance as he tried to make sense of what this man wanted, "If you're looking for him, I'd suggest looking around the oak tree that sits in the park on 7th and State. Ascension has been heavily connected to the area as of late."

After the explanation, he gave the photo back and started to walk away.

"Who are you? Why are you telling me these things," Rob yelled in a tone of anger and frustration? This man knew nothing of what was happening and yet he was giving advice and telling Rob what to do. The man ignored his questioning and continued to walk away. This only served to infuriate the slightly intoxicated Rob more. He charged to catch the man, but in an instant, he had been completely stopped and was being held in the air. The man had caught him with one hand and managed to lift him off the ground with it. Rob was lost for words not only was he in complete awe, but the man's hand had a firm grasp of Rob's throat. He couldn't believe the strength on display and it was only at this time of vulnerability Rob noticed that the mere presence of the man had managed to clear out the entire bar. No one remained that could help him and for the first time in years, Rob was powerless. The stranger had complete control and if he wanted to kill Rob at that moment there was no stopping it.

"Information is a man's greatest ally, but it is also his greatest foe. You do not need to know my name nor my purpose for neither will help you in your journey. When the information becomes important it will all be revealed, but for now, you must trust that I am here to assist you and my intentions are to save this city in any manner I see fit. We are on the same side my friend," the stranger explained as he simultaneously threw Rob back to the bar. He was in complete shock no one had ever manhandled him like that and there was something about the right hand he was held with that didn't feel human. The pure strength was astronomical.

Embarrassed Rob hurried out of the bar with his tail between his legs. It was time for a full retreat. He needed to sober up and rest the injuries that were nagging him. His body was failing and his death would not help anyone. With this new lead, he had a purpose but needed the energy to pursue it again.

Chapter 11
Connected by Him

While Rob was running around town Iris was still sitting at her desk back at Ascension. She tended to go home mid-afternoon, but she had too much on her mind to go home tonight. Seeing Rob again threw off her whole day and now she just wanted to get back to her routine, but every time she finished a few pages he would crawl back into her brain. He was a distraction, but not one she minded having. He was the man she loved more than anything in life and despite how much of an idiot he could be, he was still her idiot. Just as she was coming out of another daze there was a knocking at her door.

"Come in," she called unsure who would be knocking at such a late hour. Most people tended to evacuate the building after five. She was surprised by the man who slinked in, but not at the same time as it was the only one that made sense for the current hour.

"Do you mind if I join you for a while," John asked as he entered the room holding a bottle by his side.

"Of course, boss. All of this is because of you," she answered as she cleared a spot off on her desk and placed two glasses in place of the clutter. He placed a bottle of red wine down on the desk and pulled a chair up from the back of the room. It was clear by his ease of movement that this wasn't his first time exploring the room. He moved with precision as he prepared a spot for himself.

"How is the work coming today," he asked as he uncorked the wine and began to fill the glasses?

"To be honest things are moving a lot slower than I'd like given how busy tomorrow is going to be," she answered regretfully as she took a sip of the wine. As she swirled her glass around in her hand, she looked at the mountain of papers still calling her name.

"If you need a little more time please take it Iris. I know that today has been quite the ordeal. First you had your private practice patients to deal with then a couple of ghosts came rattling through these halls," he responded taking a drink himself, though his sip was much larger than hers. There was something heavy on his mind that he clearly wanted to forget at this point.

"Thanks for the offer John, but I'll get it done. Besides, it helps me keep my mind off of all the other things going on in my life," she explained as she nearly finished off her first glass.

"I take it you are referring to Rob when you are talking about 'all the other things'", John pointed out as he looked at her.

"Yes, yes I am. These days he is a bit more difficult," Iris explained bowing her head slightly.

"Difficult is one word for him. I believe he is more like a hurricane that leaves a trail of ruin whether it means to or not," he began as he filled his glass back to the top, "Speaking of him, I've always been curious to hear your professional take on him. I mean I met him fairly early in that contest, but even at that point there seemed to be something going on and as the weeks turned into months, which in turn became years he got worse." Iris did not react to his comments, instead she just stared into her glass. Her eyes grew distant as she began to turn an answer over in her head. She had something, but she wanted to phrase it carefully. She was well aware of the relationship they had and didn't want to give away something that could be used to hurt Rob. However, John was the only other person that could probably help Rob in her mind.

"I guess I probably don't have to tell you this, I mean you are probably the one person that knows Rob as well as I do, but to understand Rob is to know loneliness. Looking at him sometimes is like looking into a void and yet there are days that you see a light rising from the darkness. In those moments you feel hope only to see it disappear again when something else happens," Iris started to explain as she swirls her drink again, "Most people think that void started during the war, but in truth it has existed since his childhood. Then the war cultivated it and helped it consume him.

As I'm sure you know he is an only child, and since then his life has been filled with isolation, loss, and rejection. It started early when his grandparents died early in life. Making things worse was the separation and lack of connection to the rest of his extended family. There was nobody for him except his parents and as you know that is an important relationship, but not enough. Then he continued to struggle making connections at school. He felt like every time he got close to people, they hurt him and eventually he learned that if he pushed them away first, they couldn't hurt him. A very destructive model of development. He explained to me once how love was a great struggle. He felt like love interest were rejecting him and making him feel unworthy at every turn no matter what he did. He yearned for connection, but at every step it seemed to reject him.

He began to feel like the world didn't want him. Then in his third year of college, just a couple years before the war started, he met my best friend Danielle. He told me stories of how she reminded him of what he wanted to be. She was young and had her own troubles, but seeing her happy made him happy, for the first time in a long time. Whether she knew it or not early on in their friendship he adopted her as his little sister and he promised to help her however, he could because she had helped him more than he could admit. That small flicker was all he needed to escape the void for a moment. A moment just long enough for him to meet others to make deeper connections unlike anything before. Then we met and I guess the rest is history with us.

Unfortunately, the horror movie that is life kicked in. He was happy until that war. Things got worse for him. He started to lose people left and right. All the connections he made were dying in front of him and he was helpless again. It brought back the darkness that had plagued his childhood and I think he lost himself, but at least he still had Danielle and me. After the city fell, he felt he failed me which was as bad as losing me. Then to make things even worse Danielle went missing. His rock was gone and at that point nothing else mattered to him. He was alone and became what you see now," she explained as if she was reading off a psychological profile. She chugged her glass down after the story. It hurt coming out, but she told the whole truth. Even the parts about Danielle that made her doubt her relationship. It was up to John now. She could only wait for his response.

"That is an interesting take on the man you loved," John chuckled as he leaned back in his chair. It was clear that the response was not what she expected and she blushed. She was hoping that his response would bring her some form of clarity, but that was just a fairytale.

"Yeah, I guess you're right. Maybe it is a little harsh calling him a void," she answered trying to take back what she had laid bare. John finished off his glass and leaned in again.

"Sorry, for the laughter earlier. I didn't mean to insult your diagnosis. It was just funny to hear you talk about him so frankly. In truth, I agree with you to a point, but I see the phrasing a bit differently. He is not a void, but a blank space. When I see him, I see unlimited possibility and the fate of the world hanging in the balance. Most people have a path in life a destiny that has been traced on their souls. It is as if we are all tied together by strings that are just waiting to be pulled at the perfect moment. On the other hand, he exists outside of this framework. He appears capable of doing whatever he likes, unattached to the rest of the world. He is the one who has cut the ties holding him, yet we are all connected to him. He is the lynchpin that can either destroy or save this ruined world of ours. I think that is why he is my closest friend. He is either my foil or perfect compliment. That is why, I missed him," John explained as his eyes moved to the ceiling. He began to daze as he remembered the good times and bad with Rob.

"That is an intriguing way of putting things, but I think that is enough talk about Rob. How are you doing ahead of tomorrow's speech," Iris asked as the psychologist finally came out? John returned from his daydreaming upon hearing her inquiries.

"Well, I'm here talking to you instead of preparing am I not," he responded filling his glass up one more time and topping hers off with the remainder of the bottle?

"So, what has you so nervous that you come to my dingy little office," Iris asked as she pushed for more truths.

"Tomorrow has to be perfect and if they are not everything that comes after is pointless. My whole legacy, and the plans I have been making for years a waste, it is the most important day of my life," he responded chugging his glass down and slamming it on the desk. It is not often that people saw John like this. He made it a point to always be in control and the thought of something unnerving him was unheard of. Yet, Iris did not bat an eye at the sight.

"I thought we had made a breakthrough last time. Control is an illusion and I thought you would have realized by now that no matter what you do, things are going to happen that are out of your control. I mean how many times has life given you the middle finger," Iris probed as she swirled her glass around.

"That is maybe the best thing a psychologist has ever said to me. I mean really professional," he replied as he grew defensive to her comments.

"We've tried the nice routine before and you just tried to control me then, so this is the slightly tipsy, made me think about my ex irritated approach," Iris yelled at him as she finished off her drink! John just smiled at the fire Iris was showing.

"I do enjoy this side of you Iris. This is the therapist I need in my life, if I wanted to work through my countless issues. However, at this point I need to be in control here and I will be the one pulling the strings! I have accounted for a hundred possible outcomes and possibilities! I have figured out everything and thanks to Rob finally coming back into the picture things will be perfect! This will not be like the rest of my life where others used me! This time I AM the one in control and after my plans are done there will be no more chaos, the world will be back to how it should be! No one controlling anyone else just themselves," John proclaimed as he stood up from his chair and began to stumble away from her desk!

"John things don't go as we plan, especially when Rob is involved trust me. I know from experience," Iris explained as she leaned back in her chair. John just waved his hand as he closed the door behind him. She looked at all the papers on her desk and leaned back with a sigh.

"I'm not going to get anything done am I," she said putting her hands to her face. It was then that she felt her engagement ring. All this trouble was because of him and though she wanted to hate him for it. She did love him.

Chapter 12
Trying to Get Ahead

After resting a few hours in an abandoned home near the bar Rob finally rose to the glimmer of sunrise. His body moved slowly as he struggled through the pain. His poor rib was agitated the night before when he was thrown into the bar. If Anna had found out she would likely lose her mind, but there was no going back now. The slow progress he was making in getting up was accelerated when he realized that it was almost time for John's speech and he refused to go there empty handed. He composed himself quickly and made his move to the park that the mysterious man had told him of.

The park was very peculiar as most of it was brown, dying, or dead. There was no beauty to it however, somehow in the center of it all stood a majestic oak. The leaves were lush and thriving, the trunk hardy and impenetrable. Rob began to search around the tree just as the man suggested, but nothing seemed odd besides the tree's resilience. Then instead of focusing on the area around he turned his search to the tree itself. He began to knock on the tree listening for hollow spots that may contain some form of hidden treasure, but found little luck at first. With each failure he began to lose hope wondering if the man had lied to him and sent him on a wild goose chase. Worse yet he began to wonder if it was all a dream like Carly had been. He wondered what kind of sane person listens to some stranger he meets in a bar and follows their suggestions? This is how people get killed not how they find killers he thought to himself. Just before he surrendered to the tree, he hit one last spot and heard an echo that should not have been there. He had found his hollow spot.

He rushed to find a way into the tree. There had to be a hole. There would be no other reason in his mind for such a sound. When he finally found the hole, he became frightened by its contents. It was the most grotesque and unimaginable sight he could find. It was one that would haunt him long after this case was closed. Inside the tree he had found Stevens' severed head resting in the trunk. On top of it being severed his eyelids had been removed like Carly's and there was more. A symbol had been carved into his forehead. The Ascension logo, a famous star rising in the sky, had been flipped upside down. There were now three bodies and all were connected by something, yet there was no obvious reason they should be. On top of that the only lead Rob had acquired was dead and nothing was obvious anymore to him. With no options left Rob made his way to Hope Tower.

He knew that he was running late and made haste to the tower. He arrived at the tower completely out of breath and forced to search for John. He stumbled upon a meeting between John and Adam. He could not tell what it was about, but attempted to get his attention anyway. He was then met with John's gentle left hand to Rob's lips to silence him. While he kept Rob at bay with one hand, he finished signing documents that Adam had drawn up.

"Ah, if it isn't my favorite soldier. Did you find anything boy," John hollered with some excitement at the sight of Rob?

"Stevens is dead John," Rob explained with regret in his eyes.

"Well, that sure does save my H.R. Department a substantial amount of work," John answered with a cold smirk, "I take it that you have no more leads as to who killed him or stabbed Carly." John's face had turned from joy to nothingness in mere moments. There was no compassion in his words. He knew that Rob was in a weakened state and that he could break Rob, yet he hesitated to do what he had done many times in the past.

"Well I have good news for you. That document I just signed was a lease in some senses and I guarantee you that it will make our city safer. This day shall mark a new era of peace and safety that will soon spread across the world again. This Hell of a world started with a single gunshot, but now with the flick of a pen we shall bring peace. Now if you would be so kind, I need to make some final preparations before I make this city love me some more, go to the stage and find the seat directly to my right. I want the world to see you and I unified for a common goal," John explained as he guided Rob to the stage.

While Rob waited out front of the tower, he scanned the crowd out of habit. He had never felt comfortable in large crowds as they had brought great pain to him through the years. However, this time he was able to find comfort in the front row. There he found Iris sitting with Ali and a few other folks he had known, yet he could only focus on her. The woman he loved was so close, but he couldn't go to her it was not the right time. It was amazing how she still brought him comfort and even if he couldn't have her that is all he truly needed. His concentration was suddenly broke when the applause rang through the tower's plaza.

He turned to his left where John was dancing his way onto the stage, per usual John was basking in the glory and making sure everyone appreciated him. Its astonished Rob how this one man that he knew for causing havoc could bring so much hope back to this city. As he listened to the applause and saw the smiles, he had a moment where he regretted all his decisions to resist John. He began to wonder if had been wrong about John all along. Maybe it was all a misunderstanding that led to their break-up after all. At last John hushed the crowd and began his speech.

"For Seven long years' war ravaged this world. It rewrote the history books and it damn near burned everything to the ground. The United States called itself the greatest country on the planet and yet it turned on itself. It ripped itself apart over a single gunshot. You see I still remember that man who stood against the terror that plagued this country he was our last true hero.

Jeffery Irons stood for peace, he preached love, and acted as a savior. The people began to rally behind him and his messages of love. It seemed as if all the dissension that was tearing the world apart would come to an end. Then that day it all changed. As many remember he organized the largest gun collection program in history down in New Orleans. He wanted to take them off the streets to prevent the violence he saw coming. His idea was if less people had weapons there was a lesser chance of someone using one recklessly.

Irony it was, that the man who was collecting guns was shot down during his largest rally. A lone sniper that no one could ever identify brought this world to its knees and as far as any of us know was never forced to pay for his crimes. I was at the rally that day and I saw our hero fall. That day I experienced emotions I never knew I had and to this day I have never felt anything like it. I remember the crowd which had been in a near frenzy fell silent and all you could hear were the dreams of peace shattering around us. I cried that day to such a magnitude that I was unable to cry again until the final peace was declared and it all ended," John began taking time to wipe tears from his eyes. The crowd had fallen quiet with everyone of age remembering the tragedy of that day.

"No one knew what would happen after the last pillar of hope fell. At first it was just the riots in Carolina and the rest of the south, but they seemed manageable. It wasn't the first-time angry protest turned into riots. What came next was the greatest single day massacre in the history of mankind when Los Angeles was nearly erased by our own navy ships killing over 90% of the city's population. That was the first battle of this country's second Civil War. After that we fell into disarray. Soon after the rest of the world noticed and took advantage of our weakness leading to the break out of World War III, or as it is better known as finis temporis.

Amazing that a dead language such as Latin would define the greatest loss of life to plague our planet. Maybe it is also fitting that the dead would define death. It was an odd phrase that we chose, many believe it means something along the lines of end of time, but it more loosely translates to the end of the season. The world did not end, but we are not in the same world we were before. The leaves fell and the world grew colder, but as every season has passed this will pass as well. We shall rise and spring shall come," John paused at this sentiment allowing the crowd to cheer and holler at this strand of hope! Even Rob began to smile as he saw the city's spirits rise. John raised his hand to silence the crowd once more. Then he began again:

"I believe now is the time for this world to finally thaw and begin again. I believe that we have made it through the coldest of nights and I am beginning to see hope in this world again. Hell, I saw it when we were still marching through despair. When you are at war you see the utmost tragedies, but you also see mankind at its most basic and pure. How can you say this world is doomed? If you saw the things I have you would understand that man is greater than the plagues of humanity. I've seen twelve-year-old children stand against whole battalions because they are willing to give everything to protect their younger siblings after their parents died. I've seen soldiers kill ten men in a battle and an hour later were comforting an unknown child who felt unsafe in their village. We can persevere through anything.

Now I'd like to tell you all a story from my battle days. I was stationed in Taiwan near the end of the war and we were on a salvation mission. We attempted to help rebuild a town decimated by many battles. You see several of the citizens embraced our help, but there was this stubborn old man around 60 years old who was less embracing. He didn't want any help despite his age so one day I asked him why. 'You see son this is the third time I have rebuilt this house and I don't think anyone can do it quite like me,' he replied. Naturally I was shocked three times he had built the same house, I pushed further into why he stayed, 'What would moving do? It sounds like a great idea until you really look at the world. The town just a few miles north has rebuilt five times and the one to the south seven.

Soldiers may not understand this as they live their life on the move, but you can't run from your troubles. All running does is make you tired, eventually it catches up to you and often it comes stronger than if you would have stood your ground in the first place. All you can really do is stand proud and fight. You may lose, but you embraced it all head on and can die an honorable man with no scars on your back," John paused again to catch his breath and he looked over at Rob who was laughing despite the seriousness of the story. Rob remembered that old man he was wise, but crazy as well. The old man was known for talking to the moon bears native to the region, but he agreed with John's decision to leave that out of the story.

"The old man was right and I have grown tired of running. I am here to rebuild this city. I am here to bring it back into prosperity. If I fail or die before we are finished, I die with honor for I gave everything to this city. I fought the urge to cower like many of our leaders chose to embrace. This Hope Tower will be a beacon for our world. It will symbolize a new-found hope and guide the rest of the world to a similar fate. This city may have never been large, but it has the potential to be the fire to spark change. It has been a large undertaking and in order to protect this new world, our dear friend Adam Justus here shall head a reborn law enforcement agency to protect the flame. I have faith in this world like never before and I'd like to thank all of you for standing at my side and fighting for this. Thank you all, may peace find you soon!"

The crowd erupted in cheers for the last time as John basked in it for a moment, but he knew work still had to be done. Despite the cheers he exited the stage allowing for Adam to take over the mic to explain his role. Rob and Trisha followed John to congratulate him on his speech. The three made their way out of sight. John had exerted himself during the speech and moved gingerly, but managed to crack several jokes making both his niece and Rob ecstatic. Suddenly, a thump deafened the laughter. It was a sound Rob was far too familiar with, and the shade of red he saw in the air was one he could never forget.

Chapter 13
Loss

He had walked through hordes of dead bodies, burned entire villages to the ground, and lost hundreds of allies yet, he still felt overwhelming horror. Rob had seen the worst parts of this world, but seeing the man he had known as a friend and once viewed as unstoppable force laying on the ground dying was too much even for him. He was covered in John's blood only able to watch as John gasped for air and struggled to fight the imminent darkness. John's body wanted to give-up, but his mind refused to leave this world. Stubborn to the end and it was no surprise to either Trish or Rob. As John's life started to slip away neither of his compatriots could leave his side. They knew nothing could be done for him now and they understood that the best course of action was to comfort him in his final moments.

Trisha was hunched over his body as she bawled uncontrollably. He was all the family she had left and soon she would be all alone. As her cries grew louder Rob grew more surprised. When he had first met her, he had the impression she was an emotionless void like her Uncle, but now he saw her as she truly was. Despite her appearance, she was still a young vulnerable girl who had yet to figure out her place in the world. She was a girl who had lost her parents and now the man who had looked after her for years was bleeding out. The saddest part was that no one else could hear her tears except for the two men next to her. Her tears were being drowned out by thunderous applause going on just feet away from them. The crowd was still completely unaware that the source of their joy was nearly dead.

After a few moments Rob placed a hand on Trisha's back to comfort her and knelt down to fallen friend. He wasn't sure what he could say, he just knew he had to say something. After moments of soul searching, he attempted a fake smile and spoke.

"No way that a single bullet takes you down you stubborn ass. Not with everything you've survived," mumbled Rob with a quiver in his voice. He tried to stay positive and strong, but they both knew his words were untrue. The bullet had pierced his heart and nothing could save him, especially given the current technological standards. At this point he was starting to bleed heavily and he would not last much longer. In all truthfulness he shouldn't had lasted as long as he did. All that was left for him was to see how much time he had left. His last few moments were going to be miserable, yet as he coughed up blood and began to cry a wide smile stretched from ear to ear.

"I never imagined...I never imagined that when I died there would be people who cared for me, nor could I ever imagine that those same people I cared about would be standing next to me," he started pausing to take air, "I have been alone for so much of my life...I thought I would be in some jungle cut in half wondering what I did with my life..." His eyes were tearing as the blood dripped out of his mouth, "At least I get to hear my applause...At least I know I accomplished something...My plans were so close to being finished. I ask you Trisha please don't let it end...And Rob I never thought I would be asking you this, but take care of her. Trisha is young and needs your help... I see it now. The light people always talk about it really is glorious especially after years of nothing but darkness. I am sorry Rob that another loved one had to take a bullet...I know you want to join me...don't rush though we will soon see each other again. Now let me rest." John placed his hand on Trisha's face one last time to wipe a tear from her eye and with that took his last breath.

Rob grew angry as he clenched his fist and fought back the tears that were building up inside of him. With her Uncle's passing, Trisha became a wreck wailing violently. Her tears turned into an immoderate cry that pierced through the remaining cheers from the crowd. This disturbing sound brought the newly appointed Chief Adam to them in a rush. He was immediately taken aback by what he saw. Mere moments ago, this man was spreading a message of peace and hope yet, here he was lying cold and motionless. If that was not bad enough the man kneeling next to him was a decorated war hero who had seen all forms of horror was visibly shaken and unable to speak. He had four bodies in just over 24 hours and his mind was breaking. He thought by running to the drink and scantily clad women he could avoid all this, but it found him.

First, he lost a friend of his to a brutal stabbing, he had found a body in a bathtub, then he lost his prime suspect, and now the man who had been both an enemy and a friend died in a pool of his own blood. Despite not being able to make sense of the world Rob did the thing that came naturally. He held Trisha in his arms bringing her head to his chest in an attempt to comfort her. At first, she refused the help, but as he persisted, she finally gave in and allowed herself to be weak in his arms. She let all her anger and sadness out on him as the crowd surrounded them Rob held her tighter and covered her eyes so that she could not see the people around them. He had learned all too often people feel ashamed of emotion when in the presence of others and he knew the best thing for her was to release it all.

After some time, Philip made his way through the crowd and arrived at the scene. He took Trisha off Rob's hands so that he could do what needed to be done. Rob whispered to Philip about their new-found custody of the girl. With the caring affection of a mother bear, Philip took the girl away from the bloody scene to help her clean-up. Meanwhile, Rob took Adam and rushed through the crowd.

"Where are we off to," Adam called as he was being whisked away?

"Congratulations chief this is your first case and I'm going to help you. Based on how the bullet entered John the shooter had to be somewhere up in that building. Now I doubt that he is going to be there, but we have to pray that they left some clue," Ron answered as he pointed up to an old flat top building overlooking their position. Adam was initially shocked by the answer, but after he processed what was going on, he picked up the pace he was trotting at.

Disappointment. That was what came to both of their minds when they saw the roof they ran to. It was barren. Nothing on the roof seemed out of the ordinary, the only decoration was the Ascension electrical boxes that littered the city filling it with power. Despite the initial disappointment they still searched for some time, but nothing jumped at them. It was just like Stevens' house, the park, and the alley where Carly was found. It looked like it had been sterilized. Every trace of anyone's presence had been removed. Every bit of the kills was methodically planned and executed with a precision he had not seen in years. Whoever this killer was he was not just some thug he was organized and skilled beyond measure.

"Not a damn thing! The most important man in the world is dead and there isn't a single clue! How the hell is that even possible? There should be a footprint, cigarette butt, shell casing something, but no he cleaned everything up," Adam yelled in frustration! He began to kick the dirt and grow angry at his own incompetence. He had not been the chief of police for more than a half hour and his first case was cold. He then looked down at the mob of people who were in mass morning and a tear came to his eye. He felt like a failure and the case had merely just begun.

Meanwhile Rob became fixated on something that seemed meaningless. There was one electrical box where the cover was turned upside down. John was the type of employer that something like that would be sacrilegious. A mistake like that would never pass him. He was instantly reminded of the symbol carved in Stevens earlier and began to creep closer to it. Regaining his composure Adam noticed the interest Rob had showed and decided to follow him. Inside the box was a small slip of paper.

"How the hell did you know something was going to be in there," Adam queried as he tried to deduct Rob's reasoning? The question was ignored as he slowly began to look at the note. The note read as follows:

***

"People like to say that the conflict is between good and evil. The real conflict is between truth and lies," Don Ruiz once said. You would think after years of war that the world would learn to see through the smoke of deceit and yet it still plods along in constant ignorance. Even the world's great heroes fall for the deceit and they refuse to believe what is right, but I am that truth Rob, I am the answer Chief Justus. I've seen the world you created and the death you have left in your wake with no true consequence Rob. Jenny was not enough, not for all you did. Hear this you can't drink me away Rob for I am the gravest threat you have ever faced, but I will offer you an end Rob, actually I'll offer you two. The first is the way you want it to end, I left a bullet matching the one I just put through

John. When it is in your head this ends. The second, requires honesty. Not of your own sins, but those of your friend. You knew that Ascension was rampant with corruption and you ignored it. Now if you want it to end find the truth and ruin the dead man's name. You won't catch me Rob, when we meet it will be on my terms. Now make your decision quick for everyday more bodies will drop and they will sit on your conscious.

~See ya Bud - Bam, Bam

***

"Not going to lie that was a bit creepy. How the hell does he know so much," Adam asked as Rob reached for the bullet in the box, "Hey, don't you dare consider it Rob! Every criminal thinks they are untouchable we will find him!" Despite Adam's worry Ron was not planning on using the bullet, he was angry at what it symbolizes. He crumpled the note, placed the bullet in his pocket, and rose to look over his city.

"This man calls himself the truth and yet hides in the shadows not willing to show his face! He wants me to show the world the truth, I will! I will drag him out of whatever hole in the ground he is hiding in and show the world that this monster is merely human! I don't know who this is, but he made this personal and he will pay for it. He will rot in that tower as its first inmate this I promise," Rob stated coldly with an emotionless glare. Adam smiled at Rob's comments and the spirit he saw before him. He had not seen this kind of drive in Rob in many years and had wondered if it was all gone.

"Rob, I'll take care of the scene below and have any findings reported to you immediately. Meanwhile, I'd suggest going home and comforting that girl who just lost the only person in the world that mattered to her," Adam suggested as they both looked at the city below them. Rob nodded in agreement. As of now, there was nothing, he could do that wasn't already being done. For now, he needed to be patient and wait for the next move rushing would merely get more people killed.

He wandered down the streets as he thought through all the possibilities in front of him. He was forced to wonder how everything was connected and why it was happening now. It felt convenient and planned, yet there was so much chaos surrounding events, there would be no way to control it without manipulating every variable. There was no one left in the city with that kind of power. He had grown suspicious of John, but killing himself seemed a bit far even for him. Plus, the killer wanted him to investigate what John did at Ascension. Every time he thought he was on track for some answers he only seemed to find more questions. He was frustrated by everything, and once again was left unable to do anything.

Approaching his home, he paused before entering. He hoped that inside he would find Philip had already put Trisha to bed. It was not late, but after the trauma, she just witnessed it would not be a bad idea. On top of that, he didn't want to deal with the tears again. He could handle it out in the streets, but now he would likely be expected to provide more comfort. He didn't know how to do that, however. He was good with Kendra because they handled their issues in a different manner. With Trisha, he would need to be more empathetic and that was something he struggled with. In fact, he had a habit of making things worse. Upon entering his hopes were dashed as Philip had other plans.

"Rob why don't you come join Trisha and me for dinner. Now that we are a family, I think it would be appropriate if we sat down for a meal," he ordered. Rob looked at the two of them and his heart sank. He knew that Philip was right. It would be healthy if they were all together, but the pain written across her face was more than he could bear. When Rob had first met her, she boasted as a strong confident woman which made him quickly forget how young she really was, but now he saw the child in her. That look he had seen a thousand times over the course of the war was staring at him again. The loss of that paternal figure can damage a person, it can change them forever. He wanted to help her, he wanted to be the one to fill that void, but with his own issues, he couldn't find the strength to do it.

Out of desperation, he did the only thing that came naturally, he tried to raise his arm out to comfort her. He stopped when he noticed his own hand. For the first time since the incident, Rob took a look at his hands and then the rest of his body. Blood covered him, the dried remains of his friend, of her uncle, stained his body and clothes. Unsure of how to respond he ran to his room to hide. She didn't deserve this; she didn't deserve to see her Uncle's blood all over again after she had just been cleaned. As he closed his door, he could hear the wailing start again.

"It's funny, isn't it? You would think that with all the death this world has seen over the last ten years we would all be desensitized to it. I guess this is the first hero we have lost in some time, maybe he held a special place in their hearts," a somber voice said from the corner of Rob's room. He raised his gaze to find the source. It was met by the mysterious stranger he had encountered the night prior. Rob slowly began to reach for one of his books as the stranger began to speak again.

"The gun is gone. Hiding it in a book is a very old school trick, I also took the one from underneath your desk, inside the ceiling fan, and still one of my personal favorites the one under your pillow. At this point isn't that a bit of a cliché," the figure claimed as he began to approach Rob.

"What do you want," Rob asked cautiously? He kept his guard raised at all times. He had never met this man in his life and now within a 24-hour period, they had come into contact twice the subject of those meetings being new dead bodies.

"I wanted to clear my name before you start your investigation so that you do not waste too much time. I'm not a fool. I know that Stevens was dead when you found him and that makes me a suspect. I assure you though I have not killed anyone since the war ended," the figure proclaimed as he bowed his head out of respect. Rob returned the kindness but kept an eye on him at all times.

"The thought may have crossed my mind. I mean knowing the location of a severed head never bodes well, nor does the fact that your arm is different than most people's, and if that wasn't enough you spoke of Ascension as if you knew about some dirty secret. You might have some form of explanation, but it better be a damn good one otherwise I am taking you down," Rob explained. This time he was sober and aware of what the stranger was capable of. He was no longer the injured dog that could be surprised by him. More importantly, he had thought of the stranger as a suspect earlier, but with so little to go on, he had moved past it for the moment.

"You are right I do know things about Ascension, but that is because John hired me to work there. I was indebted to that man as he gave me the resources to create this new bionic arm. Now granted it was your squadron's fault that I lost it in the first place, but how can I be angry with a soldier who was merely following orders. It was war after all and at the end, we were doing horrific things as a species," the stranger explained as he removed the sleeve that covered his arm. It was made of some metal that Rob could not identify, but it shined in the dim light of his room. It was a sterling silver color with little damage to be seen.

"How is the war connected to this," Rob queried with both confusion and frustration swelling?

"The war is the link that connects everything Rob. It is not a coincidence that two of the most famous men are now in the middle of another great struggle," the stranger explained.

"Great struggle this is just one mad man killing more people. They were doing this long before the war began," Rob defended curious of what this new man was trying to say.

"You don't understand it yet. This isn't an isolated incident. This isn't just a random attack on you. Everything feels convenient doesn't it," the stranger asked. This caused Rob to hesitate for a moment, the stranger was right. Every time Rob became stuck something would happen to point him in the right direction.

"What are you trying to say," Rob asked trying not to let the stranger know about his doubts?

"Since the very beginning, we have all been part of some plan. I don't know whose plan it is, but they are toying with you, John, myself, all of us. I don't know how they are doing it, but they have some connection to the war as that is all we share. Everything has been cleaned because someone is pulling strings and making sure it looks that way," the stranger explained with worry in his voice. It was the first time Rob had seen this stranger in a sense of panic. Whether what he was saying was true or not didn't matter, he believed it.

"Why are you telling me this and what the hell is your part in this," Rob asked?

"For now, all you need to know is that I am your ally. If you must know more read the section in your journal titled 'Cambodian Regret'. I must have left some form of impression for you to write about it," the figure explained as he paused for a moment to throw Rob one of his old war journals, "Now I am asking for your help as well. Whatever is going on must be stopped and if you wish for the same thing meet me at the clock tower at 8 o'clock." He didn't wait for an answer from Rob and instead dropped a few smoke pellets to hide his disappearance. Once the man was gone Rob flipped through his journal to one of his darkest moments.

***

I've never seen a village burn like this one. We never imagined that there was enough material for it to burn for three days straight and grow during that time. I wish I could say that the reason I didn't sleep those days was due to the light that the fire created, but it wasn't. It was the smell and screams coming from the inferno we rested near. We had been told that it was a critical military encampment. One of the last ones in the area and if we could destroy it Southeast Asia would be ours. The village had barricaded itself in and left us with few options. A straight up fight would lead to a heavy death toll on our side so we burned it to the ground with all of the inhabitants inside, ALL OF THEM. They either died in the fire or by our bullets when they ran. I thought we had hit a low in humanity long ago, but this was new this was terrifying. What came next was the worst part and it was the moment I knew my team had finally lost touch with the reasons we were fighting.

Once the fire had run out of fuel we had to proceed. We marched through the village of ash and burnt corpses. I thought that the screams were terrifying, but the sound of bones crunching beneath your steps that is something you don't forget. One of the men got their foot stuck in one it was nauseating to remove. Taking lives had become routine, but this was completely obliterating them from existence. Many of them had become nothing more than smoldering piles of flesh and no one would ever know who was who. All I could think about was the families that would never have closure as they would never be able to tell if their loved one was one of the piles.

As we continued to move through the graveyard, we began to hear rustling from the ash piles. We figured that there would be at least a survivor or two there always is and at that point, it is often more merciful to put an end to the nightmare they now lived every time they closed their eyes. Dave started to fire at the sound knowing that even in a shambled state a sole survivor would be capable of injuring us gravely, however it didn't appear that he hit anything which was a rare occurrence for him. As I have recounted many times before Dave's ability to hit a perfect bullseye every time made him infamous within enemy ranks. Like most of our small team, the enemy had given 'do not engage' orders if found alone. After the misses, we started to search for the source of the sound. What we found was a man was holding two children who were no more than 8 years old. His right arm hung dead as he clutched the children with the one good one. He begged for their lives.

All I could think was that there wasn't supposed to be children here. This was supposed to be strictly a military target. The children were all supposed to be evacuated from the area according to our intelligence. Then the looming thought came to my mind. If there were two there were likely many more. How many did we kill; how many children had their last breath be a gasp for oxygen? In their last moment how many had to watch their mother or father burning to a crisp in front of them? What had we become?

"Rifles up," Gene ordered. Upon hearing this I turned to see the cold-eyes that he and the rest of my team had. Seeing no other option, I threw myself between the barrel and kids.

"We can't do this we are not monsters who slaughter children in cold blood. We are supposed to be the good guys remember. When this war began all those years ago, we promised to take a stand against the injustice of the world. At some point our ideals became twisted and instead of fighting hate we incited it. Gentleman if we do this right now there is no going back for us, so I ask you guys reconsider what you are thinking," I pleaded as I looked at each of them.

"You've grown weak Rob. When this thing started you would have just followed an order and been a smart soldier, but then you lose your edge. Don't you see killing these three is more merciful than letting them live? Those children are damaged beyond repair. Even the best psychologist couldn't save them, can't you see that. Worse yet they are damaged enough to be dangerous. If you let them live who do you think they will come after when they grow big enough. You talk about inciting hate yet you want it to fester in these kids," John yelled as he grabbed me by the collar! It had been some time since John and I had a dispute like this and the rest of the team backed down knowing only we could handle our issues.

"You may be right John. Maybe they are damaged beyond repair, but they deserve the chance to be fixed and live a life of beauty. If

you want to kill them than you have to go through me John and I don't think that is a fight you want to have," I replied back swatting his hand away from me. I looked him in the eye and for the first time saw the darkness I thought I had pulled him out of. At the time I wasn't sure if we were going to come to blows.

"I thought I taught you better than that. I thought when you gave the order to abandon Despartian that you had learned that your heart only gets in the way and the only way to achieve a true victory is to cut all ties," John said as he had calmed down. His mentioning of my failure at Despartian was a clear attempt to incite a reaction. He didn't want to throw the first punch, but it was clear that he was ready for a fight.

"Enough we are moving out," Gene ordered at last just as I prepared my fist.

"Fine let the little waste live, I didn't want to waste bullets anyways," John stated coldly. The war was still raging and we had a new target. As we left the three all I could think about were the man's eyes as he begged for help, I will never forget them.

***

Rob wasn't sure what to make of all this, but he knew that nothing good was going to come from wasting his time awake. He put the book down and went to his bed. Before he fell asleep, he remembered the bullet in his pocket and pulled it out. He turned the bullet over in his hand a few times when his sleepy eyes finally noticed something that was off. Engraved on the bullet was an "I" with a smiley face dotting it.

Chapter 14
Where There is One

While Rob was dozing off a storm began to brew on the other side of town, the shadow that had cast itself over the city was growing larger. This time it would consume the lives of innocent people that had no business being caught up in a mess such as this.

A young couple was strolling down a deserted road after finishing a wonderful date. They were laughing, and having a good time when they were suddenly approached by a figure wearing a colorful mask. The figure started to dance and act like some sort of fool as he tripped over himself, made weird motions, and began to juggle. Their laughter grew stronger than it was before and the fool took a bow out of appreciation. Out of nowhere a loud clapping began from behind them. Startled by the sound the couple turned and were greeted by another cloaked figure.

"Did you enjoy my friend's performance," the figure asked in a deep muffled tone? Uneasy of the new character they shook their heads and slowly began to back up. The first man had greeted them with joy and made them feel comfortable. This man however was an intimidating force that replaced their laughter with terror. Both of them figured that this was a mugging and the man began to reach for his wallet. He figured that if he was proactive about it maybe they could survive the encounter.

"My...my you two seem a tad bit worried. I assure you that I didn't mean to scare you," he assured as he waved the man's hand off, "This is not a mugging. We are merely street performers, but I do understand the confusion. Maybe names will set us all at ease. He simply goes by the name Fool and myself Eye. What are yours?" Despite the assurance of the strange man the couple still felt uneasy. There was something about these two that wasn't right, but eventually the woman gave in.

"My name is Jenny Malone and this is my husband Evan," the woman replied with a shaky voice.

"My those are wonderful names and just perfect for sending a message," Eye responded with a chuckle.

"What do you mean by tha-," Evan began before a knife had punctured his throat. The couple had made a fatal error turning their backs on the Fool. Before Jenny could scream the cloaked man had her by the throat and threw her to the ground. She tried to escape fighting for her life, but his grip was too tight. The more she struggled the harder he gripped. All she could do was mouth the words "why". The two figures laughed at the innocence and futility.

"It is simple my dear girl," he began as he slowly removed his hood, to reveal a blood orange mask with a black eye turned vertical resting on the forehead, "this eye that rests on my head is known as the Eye of Truth. The Eye places a great burden on me as it allows me to see what others have tried to ignore and removes desire and emotion from my actions. It sees through false Gods and heroes that made a name in the shadows. With that ability, it has tasked me with revealing the truth of those false beings and gave me wisdom beyond my peers. The Eye wants the world to know that truth is the only option and if we want to survive, we must realize this false hope that the world possesses has, is nothing more than that, false! I need to send a message to someone and unfortunately, your husband and you have the perfect names to send the message. I want you to know this isn't personal and we are going to make this as painless as possible, but to send the message we need you living through a very gruesome process. I assure you that my friend is the best in the world at this so you are in good hands." The man then flipped Jenny on her stomach, removed the knife in Evan's throat and gave it to the Fool. He took the knife to her back and started his work.

Chapter 15
Explanation

The clock tower was bustling early in the morning. Like the times before the war people are always in a hurry despite the fact the world all but ended a few years ago. Rob had always hoped that people would learn to live in the moment as they now knew the fragility of life, but alas they returned to their old ways when peace finally returned. There always seemed to be somewhere to go and something to do, yet despite all the hurrying nothing is finished. In the meantime, Rob took pleasure watching everyone. He would watch the oddities and mysterious actions made by people in a hurry. Rob found some habits to be quite comical as he waited for the mystery man to arrive. Fifteen minutes passed from when they were supposed to meet and he grew agitated. Then another fifteen go by causing his anger to grow, yet he stayed. A full hour went by and Rob never moved. There was something about this stranger and the words he said he had to know more.

"I must have caught your attention Rob. It is not often that a man will sit for an hour after the time of a meeting," a voice called out causing Rob to whip around in anger and storm towards the source.

"Don't you understand what is at stake here?! A man is killing people and you decide to waste my time! This better be damn important," Rob yelled as he approached the man! Despite the hostile environment the stranger stayed calm quietly sitting himself down.

"I realize now that I never told you my name, did I? How rude of me I hope you accept my apology. My name is Ponleak, but you can call me Pon for short," he replied calmly as he lifted his hand to shake Rob's. Rob just shook his head at the man, took a few deep breaths, and accepted the handshake. While he calmed down, he decided to take a seat next to Pon.

"What do you have to say Pon," Rob asked with agitation still in his voice?

"As I said I am looking for some assistance," Pon began, "I came to this city a little while after the War ended after hearing that it was where the great hero Rob Doran lived along with where John Kore had established his foothold. I wasn't sure if it was revenge or gratitude that drew me to you two, but regardless this became home. That is when I started to see the corruption plaguing the city at night, I had to do something. It was my obligation to use this life you spared. However, I was helpless without my arm. At least until John hired me and I was able to build this new one.

It was after this point that I started to fight back. I started off small and had a moderate level of success. It wasn't much, but it helped people. Then I started to notice a pattern. The crime was growing at a rapid rate, unlike anything the city has seen since before the War. I couldn't understand it until finally one of the small timers revealed that a gang was reorganizing in the city and with-it armed thugs.

At first, I thought it was an isolated incident, I mean one crime boss was bound to appear then I noticed different symbols on the thugs. We were headed towards gang wars and somebody was supplying them with heavy artillery which should not exist. I started to dig some more and found that someone was Ascension. Someone within the company was having weapons shipped in from somewhere south of here. It was a major find, but as I got closer to what I believe to be the truth I was fired," Pon explained. Rob was growing curious about where this was going. He had seen signs of organized crime's reemergence, but he never guessed it would be as rampant as Pon was describing. Then to accuse Ascension to have a hand in it was just preposterous enough to be true.

"Now that I was unemployed, I had few options and even fewer resources, so I intensified my fight and became a one-man army. You see I had always loved the old superhero stories and I chose to become one. The hunt for the truth continued for a few days with my simple solution of hitting people with my new bionic arm until someone finally talked. As the days passed, I continued to take out the small-timers but wasn't getting any closer to the top. Then just before I gave up someone finally squealed. They told me about a group that went by the name 'The Silencers'. According to my rat this was the gang that must have been operating as Ascension's underground arm. They were the ones making the deals for weapons and 'taking care of people' of interest. They were led by a man simply referred to as the Broker due to what he was doing as part of the underground. I went searching for these men and it was amazing now that I had a target their competition was more than willing to sell them out. The idea of honor among thieves had died with the last generation, I guess.

I found their facility on the southwest side of town in an old box store that still stood. Now the building wasn't good for much, but there was enough there for them to turn it into a fortified hideout. I took my time to scout out the facility and manufactured a plan, but upon execution I found it much easier to enter than I would have guessed. At first, I thought this was due to them expecting their competition, not a one-man army, but in reality, it was the first sign that something was wrong. I continued to search the building, yet I found nothing. Not a single guard was wondering the halls. I began to wonder if I had been lied to. That is what I believed until I finally came to the main corridor.

The main walkway was littered with Silencer bodies. There had to be at least thirty of them and the strangest thing was that not a single one of them was shot. Every person was either beat or butchered. That kind of efficiency terrified me. Even during the War something that clean seemed impossible, but regardless of my fear I kept going. When I finally found the Broker, I saw that he had faced the same fate. However, for some reason, the killer had removed his eyelids. Along with this, I found a note attached to him that read: 'The Eye of Truth sees all.' From that point on I wanted to hunt Eye down. I needed to know why he killed all those men. I had to see whose side he was on," Pon paused for a moment as he recalled the events from that day. Rob refused to say anything as he tried to process everything that was told to him so far. Rob had wondered if Carly's death and John's were connected, but based on what Pon was saying he was almost certain now.

"The more I tracked him down the more bodies I found. At first, I thought he may be a vigilante like myself or just some hitman, that was until the other night. I was doing my rounds around the city when I saw Stevens who I had worked with back at Ascension and your friend Carly. Unfortunately, I was already too late to help her as he was standing over her dead body and with them was a third person. It was a cloaked figure who without much hesitation removed Stevens head with a single blow from his blade. Unsure of what I just witnessed I chased the cloaked man to the river.

Upon arriving at the park adjacent he decided to face me one-on-one and to my displeasure, he made quick work of me. His weapon of choice was a form of staff that he handled with such precision. He is highly skilled as it only took him seven moves to take me out. He moved better than any fighter I had seen before. I knew at that time that he had to be specially trained. I thought this information would go to waste as I was certain he would kill me. Instead, he decided to kneel next to me. With him so close I tried to get a good look, but all I could see was this orange mask and a black eye on his forehead staring directly into my soul. He looked away for a moment and gazed upon the bridge where two people were sitting on its edge. Then he brought himself back to me to utter four words, 'Let the game begin.' Since then I have been gathering leads on the two dead people, I found Eye next to which led me to you, and this moment. I may not know what is behind that mask, but I know I need help. The rest is up to you Rob, so what do you think," Pon finished? Rob was amazed by the story he had just heard. He wondered if it all could be true and if it wasn't it was a tale unlike any he had heard. Unsure of what to do he looked to the sky where he saw two small sparrows fighting off an ebony colored crow of incredible size. If they would have been alone, they would have been dead long ago he thought, but when they worked as one, they could hold off the imposing foe.

"I'll help you Pon," Rob finally answered as he broke the trance that the birds held over him. He held out his hand and they shook on their new partnership. It was nice not being alone anymore, but neither of them had any more leads. All they could do was wait, and just as they figured trouble found them. Just before they left the square, a young man came rushing towards them. They both looked at the boy rushing them as they tried to figure him out, he couldn't be much older than 19 but wore a navy-blue uniform and a shiny new silver badge.

"I'm sorry if I'm interrupting you gentlemen, but Chief Justus sent me to find you Rob. There seems to be a great amount of trouble," the boy exclaimed as he tried to gasp for air from his long run!

"What is it boy," Rob questioned wondering what his old friend could need so early in the morning?

"Two more bodies have turned up and the Chief thinks that you may be interested in them," answered the young officer.

"Please lead the way," Rob ordered as both he and Pon hurried off to find the source of this new incident. They both were well aware that whatever was happening was connected to Eye. Above them, two more crows had joined the fight and ended the sparrows with little effort.

Chapter 16
Face-to-...Mask?

Not wasting much time, the trio arrived upon a mass of people circled around some kind of disturbance. Considering recent events and the urgency of the young man this could only mean one thing. Another day has come and another body had been found. This body was the mystery man fulfilling his promise from the note.

"Rob, at last, you're here. I was beginning to get worried that you had disappeared given all that has occurred over the last few days," Adam excitedly pointed out!

"I promise you, Adam, that I have no intention of ever leaving again. This place needs me especially now," Rob replied with a certain calmness in his voice that Adam had not heard in a long time.

"Before we get to our current situation, I wanted to give you the shell we extracted from John," Adam explained as he searched his pocket, "Now normally I wouldn't do this, but there is a strange marking on it I wanted you to see." Adam handed Rob the bullet at last and turned it over to show the letter "D" engraved in it.

"Strange. I will look into it further after we handle whatever this is. So, Adam what is this," Rob asked as Pon had already made his way towards the scene without him?

"I must warn you Rob. I am fairly confident that this was targeted at you and I guarantee this will strike a chord," warned Adam as they made their way through the crowd. Rob approached the scene with hesitation but knew he needed to face whatever was in front of him. The body of the man was covered by a blanket, but the woman's back was fully exposed as a message had been etched into it:

You Failed Again
Jenny ♥ Kyle
Eye

"Their names are Kyle and Jenny Malone. According to our files they were only married for about a month now. It appears that they were on their way home from date night when our killer jumped them," Adam explained as he flipped through his notebook, "Finally, the medical examiner was here and told us that the woman was alive during the carving process." Adam's voice trailed off as he finished the debrief. As Adam finished Rob grew angry. These were innocent kids and Eye used them to get under his skin.

"Who the Hell is this guy? And how does he know so much about my life," Rob muttered to himself? Confused Pon stayed silent as he let things work out, but he knew this was more than just a random killing.

"I promise you that this guy is going to pay. If the death of John and Carly weren't personnel, now it definitely is. Using the names of the dead to spell out my ex-fiancé's dead sister's name is a whole new level of twisted. This requires an exceptional amount of planning. They had to know about me, had to follow couples to get it right, and then execute. The improbability is unlike anything I have seen before," Rob was physically shaking as he uttered the words. He tried to collect himself, but his emotions were overflowing giving Pon some time to examine the body. He found nothing as he searched her person, but soon turned his attention to Evan. It seemed like a lost cause at first, however, there was something odd about the wound to his throat. The wound had been folded in on itself as if it was trying to hide something. He unfolded the area to expose a set of numbers etched faintly on the skin.

"650 10, now what could that mean," he asked out loud? No one seemed to have an answer. In truth, they were all surprised that some stranger was digging into the throat of the dead man in the first place. Rob's face slowly began to turn colors as if he was remembering something dastardly.

"650 10th street is Anna's address," Rob muttered. Anna was well known in town and the news shocked the crowd surrounding them.

"You heard him men, 650 10th street on the double. We have no idea how big of a lead he has on us. We'll meet you there Rob and whoever the Hell you are sir," Adam barked. Several of the people in the crowd dispersed and headed to the address. After the officers had left Pon placed his hand on Rob's shoulder to comfort him. They said nothing and unbeknownst to Pon Rob had reached into his pocket to feel for the bullet he was given the day before. He had to wonder if he had used it would these people still be alive or would the killer still have committed the act. He knew he couldn't focus on the guilt, but it filled his thoughts at the sight of the bodies. Eventually, he was able to shake his thoughts they went to help Anna.

The front door of her house was busted in and no one could hear a sound coming from inside. The newly formed police corps surrounded the building as they waited for orders. Meanwhile, Rob and Pon stood in front of them all preparing to enter the building unsure of what would be inside. As they entered, they noticed clear signs of a struggle. Regardless of the outcome, it was clear that Anna had given the intruder Hell. Most of her furniture had been broken and several holes were scattered across the wall. During her time as a war medic she had been taught how to fight by both Rob and John knowing that if she was going to follow them on some missions, she would have to be ready. Along with the training, she had worked hard during her collegiate days to be strong for sport, so she was no pushover especially if Eye was not prepared for her to fight back.

Rob made his way slowly to her room with Pon close behind him. As they finally heard something, a tap. Then they heard it again as they came closer to the room. It was a hauntingly loud tap...tap...tap. It was the sound of metal bouncing off the wood floors over and over again. The sound grew louder and louder as they got closer to her room. It was not a call for help it was methodical. It was a challenge being laid out in front of them. They knew Eye was inside and was challenging them to come to get him. They entered the door slowly and there they saw him. The Eye sat at the edge of the bed and he was slowly hitting his staff on the ground. He lifted his head showing Rob the infamous mask for the first time. The hazy orange mask and the pure black eye that seemed to pierce the soul. The chin of the mask was heavily scarred by burn marks that it had acquired over the years. He wore what looked like a bulletproof vest and plated clothing that shined with its mixes of grays and blacks. He was a man ready for a war and began to chuckle ominously.

"I was wondering how long it would take you two monkeys to show-up. I must say you did not disappoint me. But I do question your decision to bring that excuse for a police force into the fray. Once I get past you, they will barely be worth calling a cool-down," he taunted as he implied that he would make it to them. The pair stood in silence as they surveyed the room their nemesis resided in.

"Where is she," yelled Rob as he finally broke his silence and halted Eye's laugh?

"I think you should be more worried about your own life Rob," he replied chuckling at Rob's futility.

"I'm not worried I just want to make sure I don't hurt her when I bring this house down on you," Rob grinned as he prepared himself for battle.

"Bring the house down on me, huh? Can't wait to see it you punk, but in order to put your mind at ease I'll tell you that she is safe. I told you I would kill someone every day, so I'm saving her for the finale," Eye responded as he twirled his staff around. The arrogance on display angered Rob, but he knew he had to be careful. In order for him to take down Anna he had to be stronger than he appeared.

"Finale? What is this all about," he questioned as he looked upon his foe? Rob couldn't figure out this man's motive. If he was purely just a psychopath, things wouldn't be this planned out, if it was riches there were less messy ways of going about things, and if it was a target on Rob's back a poisoned glass of tequila would have sufficed.

"I was bored," he answered without hesitation causing shock to fill the room. The answer was so candid that Rob and Pon could not understand "You seem shocked by that, but why do I need a reason to kill people. During the War people made-up reasons to kill each other. They just did it because they were ordered to. On the other hand, I embrace the monster I am and enjoy the hunt. Maybe that is confusing to you, but it is reality that is void of the lies that society has taught us to tell."

"Why me then," Rob asked as he tried to hide the frustration?

"Simply put you are the only opponent worth having in this city and no game is worth playing without stakes," Eye explained.

"I don't understand," Rob replied dumbfounded by the remarks made. This man talked as if this was just some type of game. People were losing their lives and yet he treated it like a videogame where one person would win and the collateral didn't matter.

"I'm not surprised...you do look a lot dumber than I expected," he laughed as he tried to agitate Rob, "But I should expect that sort of answer from someone like you. You see you keep pretending that things are going to go back to normal. You think we survived the worst, but we are merely in a break between near extinction and extinction. Worst yet you spread the lie to the rest of the survivors which has forced them back into a meaningless existence, but not me I know the truth. I know the end is near and that the only sane way to live now is however you want!" As he finished his rant he began to slowly rise from his bedside. The time for talking was drawing to a close.

"You're crazy, aren't you," Rob accused as he tried to buy a little more time?

"Such harsh words kid. It hurts me deep down," he began pointing towards his heart, "You see calling a man crazy is to dismiss his ideas and stance on life without understanding him. I'm not crazy Rob I've just seen the truth and the truth is that you and John were fooling these people while leading them to a miserable end." As Eye spoke Rob could feel his gaze cutting straight through him. This man hated Rob and couldn't understand any of the madness he was trying to explain.

"If that is what you believe then why am I alive? The day that you shot John you could have ended me just as easily so, why not," queried Rob? It was clear to him that the continued questioning was irritating the man, which is just what Rob was hoping for. If he could get the man off his game, he could take him far easier.

"Your questions are growing repetitive and are just making you look dumber. I told you why I spared you in the note I left. I'm using you to destroy what is left of Rob. You will show the world John was the villain of this story and in doing so you will shed light on the truth," he claimed as he prepared his weapon.

"And what is that truth," Rob asked as him and Pon prepared themselves for a fight?

"That we are all just living to die," Eye finished as the Fool jumped Pon from behind. The confusion startled Rob and he was quickly overtaken by Eye. Eye had immediately honed in on Rob's bad shoulder and kept pressing the attack from that side. He moved with technical efficiency that Rob hadn't seen since the War. Rob tried to fight back and avoid critical strikes, but this man might have been on Rob's level as a fighter.

Rob was forced to stay on the defensive longer than he desired, but it allowed him to analysis Eye's fighting style. Throughout the course of the War Rob had seen hundreds of men fight and studied them so he could fight any opponent. This man was unique though, he had a plethora of styles that he switched between which kept Rob on his toes until Rob saw an opportunity to disarm his opponent. Eye seemed to brush off the counter, and quickly moved into hand-to-hand grappling. This was a realm of fighting Rob was more confident in. There were few opponents that could best him when he had his hands on them.

Meanwhile Pon was slowly able to turn the table on Fool. Fool had used small knives to dig at Pon, but nothing was deeper than superficial. Once Pon had regained his senses after the ambush he started to use his metal arm to overcome his opponent. It was clear by the way he moved that Fool had not anticipated Pon or his metal arm. The two men expected Rob to be alone and this extra figure was not part of the plan. Pon slowly gained an advantage over his foe while Rob began to notice a gimp in Eye's movements. He had an injury and Rob used it as an opening to reach for the gun Eye had in a holster. In what seemed like a flash Rob used the injury to flip Eye, steal his gun, and place it against his temple.

"Come on now shoot me kid! I know it is what you want to do more than anything! I've heard rumors you haven't killed since the end of the War, must be tough for an addict like yourself to avoid the thing that once brought you joy! It must be difficult to hide who you really are under gallons of liquor and an endless line of whores, so shoot me and become the monster you know you are," Eye challenged Rob! The words he said felt familiar. Since the War ended Rob had refused to kill because he was afraid of himself. It was this conflict that kept him away from Iris and he was on this journey to forgive himself, but if he pulled the trigger the monster would become real and he would never be able to return. On the other hand, the man kneeling before him was too dangerous to let live. The turmoil caused Rob to hesitate.

"I shot the wrong partner I guess, because John would have had the guts to sacrifice himself for the city," he shouted as he grabbed the gun from Rob's distracted hand and struck his ribs! The blow dropped him instantly with blood launching from his mouth. This sudden change in fortune distracted Pon enough that Fool was able to drop him as well. Both men laid on the ground defenseless as Eye pointed the gun at both of them. He didn't pull the trigger though. He just stood there taunting them. Until he finally, knelt down beside them and spoke.

"You know how to end all of this Rob. Show the world what kind of monster John is or put that bullet that's in your pocket through your skull. If you don't do either Anna dies and then maybe I move on to Iris," he said as he left the room laughing with the Fool. The blows they suffered rendered them immobilized and all they could do was listen to the screams coming from outside. The young officers were no match for the pair and the screams were over in mere moments. Rob laid there in pain thinking about his inability to act. He could have ended everything right there, but he had waited and because of it; Anna was in grave danger, a group of young officers might very well be dead, and the man who killed John was running lose. He had the killer in his grasp, but all he had to show for it was a further damaged rib.

Pon was the first to rise as he had only been stunned by the Fool and had little true damage. Rob, on the other hand, was not only physically damaged, but mentally broken as well. The man he had fought was better than him and likely only let Rob get an advantage to test his will and Rob had failed. He couldn't help but wonder what he was going to do if he met Eye again or how he was going to beat him.

Pon helped Rob rise gingerly as he spat up a little more blood from the internal damage. Once they were both back to their feet, they headed outside to investigate the damage done by Eye and Fool. They found the officers all unconscious, but they were breathing. All of them were bloody and close to death but would live to fight another day even if that day wouldn't be for a while. As they observed the scene, they were both disappointed, not in the officers, but in themselves. They felt responsible not only for this but all the pain that had befallen the city. Pon felt that if he could have been stronger and smarter, he could have stopped this from ever beginning. He had the leads; he could have asked for help earlier maybe this would have ended before it began. Rob on the other hand only felt more guilt. More people were being hurt because of him, just like during the War.

"Where to now," Pon asked as he looked at Rob? He only shook his head to indicate he didn't know. The failure was eating at him and in truth, he just wanted it all to end.

"Does it really matter? He knows every play and as we saw in there, they are better than us Pon," Rob finally answered as he knelt down next to one of the officers who looked like he should still be in school and not fighting dangerous men like Eye.

"Man up," Pon yelled at Rob! Rob had never seen this form of emotion from his usually quiet partner.

"Why, so I can watch more people die? Sorry, I'd much rather be curled up with a bottle of tequila," Rob responded as he looked Pon in the eyes!

"Why?!? Because you are the only one who can save Anna and protect Iris from that nut case," Pon exclaimed as the passion grew in his eyes! At first, Rob did not respond. Instead, he fell into deep thought.

"Iris that's it. I know where we need to go, come on," Rob ordered as he turned and began to run. Pon was dumbfounded by the sudden change in expression, but he was happy to see it and decided to follow his ally. It could be a trap Rob thought, but that had to be why Eye mentioned Iris. He knows about their connection and more importantly knows that Iris could get Rob into Ascension to find whatever secret Eye wanted him to see.

Chapter 17
Building Trust

On the other side of town, Trisha and Philip sat around Rob's house having a meal that he had prepared. She had spent most of her morning crying and it was the first time she had truly left the room that day. It was understandable given the circumstances and Philip did whatever he could to make her comfortable. It was odd to her; she had not been taken care of this well in some time. During the few years, she had been with John he had always been very strict and demanding, so it was quite a change coming to Philip's loving care. They had been eating in silence for a few moments when she finally raised her head up to talk.

"Why are you taking such good care of me? We just met yesterday," she asked Philip as she placed her fork down. He chuckled for a moment and stopped eating to respond to her.

"It is quite simple. You see you are a guest of Rob's and once you enter this house you become family," Philip explained as he looked the girl in the eyes.

"Okay. Well why do you serve that drunk and good for nothing anyways," she insisted as if she was trying to make Philip feel idiotic for following Rob.

"That is an even easier question to answer. When I was at my worst, he saved my life not once, but twice," Philip said as he continued to eat his meal.

"What did he do," she asked him?

"The first time he saved me was during the War. The enemy had been driven from the city by a force led by Rob. With the threat, gone people began to look for survivors in the rubble that was once a city. I was one of those survivors though as I laid trapped in a building near collapse, I wasn't confident that I would be. Just as I began to give-up, I began to hear shouts from a search crew looking for people, I began to call for help as I prayed, they could hear me.

As they grew closer to me, I could hear them arguing about the safety of entering the building I was in. I couldn't blame them; I was one man and there was a risk more of them could die if they entered. Then one man rushed past them all to come to save me, it was Rob. He pulled me out of the rubble and took me to safety. Once safe I informed him my wife could still be inside, but I did also tell him I hadn't heard her voice in some time and feared she had died. He didn't care and rushed back inside without any hesitation. As the building grew more unstable, I saw him walking back with her body in his arms. She was dead as I had feared and when I asked him why he still brought her out, he explained that he wanted me to have a chance to say good-bye and bury the woman I loved. He could have left her as any sensible person would have, but he refused and went the extra mile for me.

The second time was in a bar after the War had ended. After I lost my wife whiskey became my best friend and it caused a lot of trouble. I had been thrown out of multiple bars and was close to wasting the life that Rob had saved. Then one day thought it was all over. I had picked a fight with a large man who ended up pulling out a knife during our fight. I should have run away, but I had nothing and was ready to die and join my love. Just before he plunged the knife into my gut another man smashed a glass over his head. Once again it was Rob coming to my aide. He was able to settle the man down and kept me safe.

After the incident, Rob took me back to his place to sober up. The next morning with a clearer head we had a discussion about my future. He gave me a job looking after the house here and helping him when he needed. I was surprised by this kindness and gratefully accepted as you can see. Now that I had a purpose again, I went stone-cold sober with his support and I haven't had a drink since that day. He has had many, but that is beside the point," Philip explained as he pushed the food around with his fork thinking about their past. Trisha had become enthralled by the story and listened intently to how Philip came to working for Rob.

"So, Rob really is the hero that people claim he is," she said smiling as she thought of the man now in charge of looking after her.

"Rob isn't a hero. That is something we have argued about before, but now I understand his viewpoint on the subject. People use that term hero to describe someone and it gives them a certain air and a mythos about their actions. He hates this and always argues that he is just a man. He is filled with flaws and scars. He believes the only thing different about him is that when faced with a decision he always chooses the path of helping others and if that makes him a hero than we are all heroes in hiding. We are all capable of choosing love, compassion, and selflessness it just so happens we are also capable of choosing hate, anger, and selfishness. Hopefully, now that the world has restarted, we can all start picking the former over the later," Philip explained, "Now that I have gone on may I ask you how you came into John's care? What happened to your parents?" Philip hoped that now that he had revealed so much, his new guest would do the same. At first, she was hesitant. The story she had to tell was not an easy one, but one she felt like she owed him.

"He saved me, as Rob saved you," she began as her eyes fell to the table remembering the pain from her past, "Both of my parents were murdered in front of me and after that my Uncle took me under his wing and helped me work through the loss." Philip reached his hand across the table to hold hers knowing this could not be easy, but it was then he noticed something was off. She was not crying nor was there sadness in her voice.

"Don't worry too much about it. My father had it coming. It was roughly about this time of year, three years ago. I remember because it was just before my 15th birthday. I hated my father, he hit my mother consistently and she just acted like she didn't care. She took it and accepted the monster for what he was. You see he had ties to some illegal operations in Florida where I was born and Mom was petrified of him.

Things turned for the worse after I turned 14 and started noticing my father liked playing with my friends more than I did. At first, I didn't understand it, but when it became clear I grew to hate him even more. I just wanted him to die, I wanted him to stop hurting the women in my life. Then one night my wish was granted. I don't remember the night to well, Iris says it is a form of dissociative amnesia, but according to Uncle John who found me: Two men entered our house and dragged me into their bedroom where they forced me to watch my parents die a painful death. According to Uncle John the two men were connected to the gang my father ran with and he had betrayed them or something, but I don't remember.

All I know is I was covered in their blood when my Uncle brought me out here to take care of me," she told Philip. Her eyes were cold and not a single tear could be found. Philip was worried about her but knew that trauma like that can destroy a kid even if she hated her father as she claimed. She stood up and started walking towards one of the windows where she saw kids playing outside. There were four girls playing games including Alex. They were kicking a ball around and having fun. Philip walked over to Trisha and placed a hand on her shoulder.

"You don't have to worry any more girl. Rob and I will take care of you. You are part of the family now and Rob will just about anything to protect you," Philip started as he looked through the window, "Besides I think he has always wanted a daughter to look after. You should see how kind he is to that girl over there, but I wish he could know the truth." Philip pointed at Alex as his voice trailed off.

"What do you mean by that," Trisha asked looked at her caretaker?

"Oh, never mind that. It is something that Iris and him have to talk about one day," Philip said trying to backtrack on his earlier comments.

Rob and Pon made their way back to Ascension's neighborhoods. The house they arrived at was a small two-person home. Like every other house on the block it was painted white and had been maintained perfectly. The uniformity of it all sickened Rob, but at least he didn't have to live there. Rob went to knock on the door and each knock seemed to enervate him. Despite his urgency to be greeted, he did not want to see who would be on the other end of the door. When it was finally opened, he was met by a surprise. Kendra was the one that had answered it. Saying he was speechless would be an understatement. He had no response to her appearance. She was the last person he expected to see at this time.

"Wh... What are you doing here," he finally asked when he could find words again?

"After Carly passed, I went to see the body at the morgue and met Anna there. After a short conversation I came to the conclusion that I needed to change. I was heading towards a dead end and that flash of mortality made me realize it is now or never to change," she said in the most eloquent tone he had heard her speak in. He had always hoped that one day she could find peace in her life, but now that he was seeing it in front of him, he couldn't believe it. Most importantly he realized he was alone now, there was no going back to the old ways of how they dealt with their issues.

"Happy to hear that," Rob smiled. He was trying to find the right words, but there wasn't a whole lot for him to say. She was in the process of truly healing while he was running in circles letting his damage fester.

"Now I take it by your surprise you aren't here to see me, so what is it that you want," she asked?

"I'm here to see Iris. Is she here Kendra," Rob asked?

"Oh, she's here, but if you want to get to her you'll have to take your verbal lashing from Ali first," Kendra answered with a smirk on her face.

"Please Kendra I need to speak to Iris and I'll take whatever whooping I have coming," he begged. There was sincerity in his eyes that she hadn't seen in a long time. Whatever this was, it was important and she turned to go find Iris. Pon looked at Rob with a smirk of his own.

"Let me get this straight now. The call girl you fool around with is seeing a psychologist. The psychologist she is going to just so happens to be your ex-fiancé who you ended things with poorly. Topping it all off they are doing the sessions in the older sister's house and she really doesn't like you," Pon clarified as he began to laugh at Rob's misfortune. When Pon finished laughing Rob turned to see Ali coming down the hall. He wasn't sure what to say and she appeared furious so he turned back to Pon for help, but he had disappeared.

"Heeeyyyy," was the only thing he could think of which was not enough. After his lack of words, he took a slap across the face that nearly dropped him.

"I must say you are a piece of work and I am glad that you and my sister broke things off," she began as she tried to regain composure, "I feel so sorry for Kendra and it is clear that you really did nothing to help her. All you did was continue to use her vulnerability as a way for you to cope with your own."

"It wasn't like that Ali. I did care for Kendra and appreciated the moments we spent talking and working through our feelings. In all honesty, I think that our moments on the bridge were more important than any of the sex. Now I wish I could sit here and justify some of the other stories you may have heard, but there are more pressing matters to take care of. Anna is in danger and the only way to help her might be Iris," he explained to her! He knew regardless of how angry Ali may have been the thought of Anna in danger was enough for her to move on. She quickly called for her sister and went back inside the house to be with Kendra.

When Iris appeared, she was dressed in a simple pair of blue jeans and a white button-up blouse. There was nothing special to that wardrobe, and yet even now the simplest looks still took his breath away. She leaned against the doorway with her arms crossed and he was defenseless. He could not let the distraction last for long, however as Anna was still in danger and needed his help.

"Iris, I need you I.D. to get into Ascension's main building," he ordered. He could see that his tone upset her as her brow crinkled a bit as she prepared her response.

"You could at least say hi this time," she replied in a snarky tone as she waited for him to slow down.

"I'm sorry Iris. This time I do not have time for this. I would love to take another trip down memory lane with you, but this time I'm not just searching for a killer. I'm looking for a nutcase who could threaten the whole city. I said it last time and I'll say it again I still care for you, but today isn't the day to get into our relationship," Rob replied as he begged for Iris to understand. He knew if she had heard all the stories Kendra had to share, she couldn't possibly see him the same way as before, but he needed her to get past it for now.

"Say sorry one more time and tell me what this is about," she ordered not budging at his demands.

"I'll say it a thousand times. I'm sorry for what I did to you, to Ali, to Kendra, to a hundred people, but now there are more important stakes. The man who killed Carly has Anna hostage and if I can't sneak into Ascension, I might not be able to find her," he explained as he nearly got down on his knees to beg. He was desperate and she could see it.

"Alright, I will help you for now because of all the history we shared, but when this is all over, I hope we can have a talk," Iris said as she began searching the coat next to the door for her I.D. card.

"Iris, if I survive this, I promise you we will have the chat that you deserve," he guaranteed her as he rose up a step to meet her in the doorway. She handed him the key card at last.

"Now one more thing," she began as she moved closer, "bring her back alive!" She ordered and with a final kiss on the cheek. With that he flew to Ascension grabbing Pon out of the bush he hid in during Ali's confrontation. Meanwhile, Iris just stood in the doorway and watched him run.

Chapter 18
Uncovering the Truth

It had only been two days since Rob last stood next to the great Ascension building, but in that short time, it had gone through a massive transformation. The building had turned into a fortress in the hours after John's murder. Jefferies had the front door heavily guarded and made sure the only way in was through the employee's entrance. It was unclear whether the attack on John would be isolated, so Jefferies did everything in his power to protect his master's baby.

The two men stood in front of the building as they looked to confirm each other's feelings. They didn't need to say a word as they knew what was at stake. If they didn't discover the truth a woman would die, but at the same time, that truth could change the world around them. Whatever happened inside they had to be willing to make a tough decision. They walked to the security checkpoint and used Iris's credentials to ring themselves in. That aspect seemed to go smooth, but it was a dangerous game carrying only one set. Even before John died Ascension was known for harsh treatment of intruders and spies. It made sense as the work they did was critical and if anyone tried to interfere, the world would suffer.

It did not take the vaunted security force long to find them after their entry. They quickly became tense knowing that they would need to think fast or risk having an army come crashing in if things went poorly. It was only two, so they could just take them both out, but that would be a great risk as it could bring the whole building crashing in on them before their mission even got started.

"Identification boys," one of them asked with an authoritative voice! Rob handed him the set of credentials he had hoping that they would be alright with just one. He looked over the card multiple times looking for any signs of forgery and finally gave them the nod of approval.

"Everything seems to be in order with this one, now how about you," the guard asked? Pon prepared himself for a fight without those second credentials he figured there would be no other option. He had worked for Ascension too long to believe that things could go smoothly. Before he could act, however, Rob had placed his hands on both guards' shoulders and leaned in close to speak with them.

"I have to tell you guys something. My partner here is an incredible machinist and scientist, but he has a lot of airhead moments. When he has these moments, he can be quite forgetful you see. It appears this morning he had one of those moments and forgot his damn card. I mean I even had to let his dumb ass into the building this morning. I swear if it wasn't for me, he wouldn't be able to put his shoes on the right feet those days. Now, gentlemen, he is working on several important projects and I'm begging you guys to let him go just this one time. If he is delayed at all it would set the projects back weeks," Rob pleaded. As they processed, he readied himself for them to see through his tale. He tightened his grip on their shoulders so that he could place them both on the ground. However, the one who had been quiet had taken an interest in Pon. Something seemed familiar. He leaned over to his buddy and whispered something. Neither could hear what was being said, but the two guards began to smile. Finally, he spoke in a high-pitched squeaking tone.

"I remember you your name is Ponleak. I don't recall meeting you in person, but I have seen your face. You helped invent those new bionic parts that gave my daughter her legs back. I do appreciate that and normally I wouldn't do this, but in your case, I'll let you go," he explained. The other man just shrugged his shoulders and they started to make their rounds. Rob and Pon breathed a sigh of relief. Even in the relief, however, something did feel right. There was no further questioning. They just let them go far too easily. They could not waste time focusing on it so when the guards were out of earshot, they began to formulate their plans.

"Well since you were an employee at one time any ideas on what we may need to look for," Rob asked?

"Well when I was doing my investigations, I had started to look into the disappearance of the four old board members that were let go when John took over. They reportedly refused his offer to stay with the company and were never seen again. Now when I say never, I mean no one even saw them leave the building that day. I was going to check out the main conference room where the meeting was held, but before I had a chance, I lost my job and clearance. Given that I suggest we start there," Pon replied.

"Alright. Show me the way and if I may suggest we go the way with the fewest guards and security points," Rob whispered as they began the journey. The pair made it through the first floor without any more incidents, but they found several guards checking I.D.s at the staircase. They knew that the same story would not work twice, so they attempted to come up with a new plan.

"My old office is here on the first floor. I'm not sure if they destroyed everything yet, but we can see if there is anything left that is useful," Pon said as he began to walk in a new direction. They made their way to a dim corner on the bottom floor. The heavy metal door was not locked like many of the rooms on the floor allowing for Pon and Rob to sneak their way in. The room was mostly empty with very little left, however Pon still seemed excited. Rob was obviously confused by his partner's enthusiasm, but if he had learned anything it was that things were not as they appeared.

"Why are you so happy Pon? The room is empty," Rob asked as his partner was feeling the bottom of one of the workstations.

"It is simple my new friend. I customized everything in this room. Most things were for simple convenience, but this table was for emergencies," Pon explained as he pressed a button causing the workbench to open up. When Rob approached, he saw an impressive display of equipment sprawled in the secret drawer. Pon grabbed most of it and placed them in his arm's inner compartment. After most of the goods were removed, he handed Rob a strand of cable and a hook.

"What do you want me to do with this," Rob asked as he was curious about his equipment?

"Easy at some point we may need to tie people up and that cable is long enough to be cut up multiple times. It is also strong enough to hold up to 500 lbs. It was something that I perfected just before I was kicked out of here," Pon explained with a smile on his face. He appeared to be impressed by his own work. However, before they could enjoy the new bounty the door behind them shut and they heard the cracking of knuckles. The two guards from before had followed them.

"Ponleak was fired quite some time ago. I remember because I helped throw his traitorous ass out of the building. Now, do we have to get rough or are you going to explain...uh," just before he could finish his partner and him were struck by two darts. Rob turned to see Pon's fingers smoking on his metal hand.

"What was that," Rob asked trying to figure out what had happened?

"Hopefully they were my last two sleeping darts, otherwise they are not waking up from that," Pon said with a slight grin on his face. It appeared that the gadgets he placed in his arm were quite useful.

"Man, we really could have used that earlier," Rob joked as a plan started to form, "More importantly, I think we found our way past the checkpoint. Grab the uniforms and let's go." The pair stripped the unconscious men and changed as quickly as they could muster. Using the uniforms and the cards from the guards they made it into the stairwell and past any other inspections that came their way.

Upon arriving at the conference room, they found fortune was in their favor. Someone had left the electronic lock undone making it possible to enter without knocking the door down. Still, they were hesitant at first knowing that everything up until then had been a trap including Pon's office.

They snuck into the office staying as silent as possible, but it appeared as if their worries were needless as the room was empty. All their precautions were for naught. The inside was nothing spectacular. It was just a corner office with two sides made completely of glass. Rob made his way over to the windows and looked upon the world outside. It was so quiet. The city was moving on just as it had now for years. Despite all the tragedy it had faced recently nothing seemed to stop it, even now only a day after John's death there had been no real mourning, instead, it just kept moving forward, hiding the pain with progress.

"Amazing isn't it. The city has seen death after death. Tragedy after tragedy, and yet it can keep moving forward. I marvel at its resilience and yet I can't help but wonder if the way it acts is healthy. I wonder if running from our problems is the best way to handle things," Pon stated as he began searching the room. Rob bowed his head, he knew that last line was about him as well as the city, but he could not deny it.

"What are you looking for exactly Pon," Rob queried?

"I've been in the room next to this one and I don't remember it being quite this deep. The dimensions of this room just don't fit and this wall is just wrong," answered Pon as he continued to search the empty room. Through his efforts, he finally hit a spot that was out of place. The plaster wall felt like metal. As soon as they found a starting point, they began prodding the area around looking for a way past whatever was there. Finally, Rob was able to find a slit with air passing through it.

"Here I think I found our way in Pon. I need you to use that metal arm of yours to pull this open," he ordered. The two of them began yanking on the metal frame and after several minutes they were able to lift the metal door. An empty hallway greeted them and they entered slowly. Immediately upon entrance the wall shut behind them and overhead lights flickered on. They crept their way down the hallway to a crimson red elevator and looked at it knowing it could easily be a one-way ticket. Given their knowledge of John, if this was his secret it would be protected heavily.

"This is a trap isn't it," questioned Pon as he stood looking at the empty carriage?

"Who knows maybe this was just John's 'fun' room. There is no reason to think its a trap," Rob answered as they entered the elevator. It began its descent and the song 'Highway to Hell' began to play causing Rob's grin to fade.

"Yeah, it's a trap," Rob eventually muttered just loud enough for Pon to hear.

Chapter 19
Way Down They Go

The two men stood in silence as the elevator made its low plummet into the earth. There was no joking around or lightness to the journey as they both knew the severity of the situation. They stood in silence knowing that there was not a thing that could be said that would make a difference. Silence is often feared by people as they hate the awkwardness, but words can be nothing more than verbal distractions and with what awaited them neither man need a distraction.

At last the elevator stopped and dinged in recognition that they had arrived. The doors slid open with an eerie creek as they were greeted by the most gruesome of stenches. Wherever they were now it reeked of burnt hair and rotted flesh. Both men covered their noses as the smell stung. If the pits of Hell had a smell it would be that basement. Whatever awaited them would not be for the faint of heart.

The room they had entered was poorly lit, but there were several things that were clear. It was far larger than Rob or Pon could have anticipated. They had to be at least thirty feet below the surface. Despite how far under the ground it was, it was fully furnished with metal walls plating every surface. Wires and pipes crisscrossed every direction as a slight humming could be heard in the darkness.

"Secret lab under the building? A bit of a cliché, even for John," Rob suggested as he looked around for what it was used for, "And I'm sure everything down here was ethical and not a violation of human rights." It was not long after his comments that a clicking came from the walls.

"Ethics my old friend are nothing but hurdles that the ignorant put up to slow the progress of true genius. People talk about the War crimes scientist commit, yet they have no issue dropping bombs on innocent cities! My science can save and improve lives at the sacrifice of a few, while governments sacrifice millions for the improvement of none! Yet it is my science people have an issue with! Luckily John never had that hypocritical moral standard that you have so he let me work down here. He let me change the world without any of you knowing about it. One day people will respect my genius," remarked a familiar voice over a set of speakers!

"I'd recognize that condescending voice anywhere," Rob whispered as he looked for the source, "I should have known that you would be the skeleton in John's closet, Rick, considering that you haven't come out of your own yet!" Rob couldn't find his old teammate and instead was trying to antagonize him.

"You know what you are implying is false! I am not gay in any fashion Rob," angrily replied Rick the team's old scientist and expert in deceit! Rick was also known for having the shortest fuse during the War, especially when it came to his sexuality.

"I wasn't calling you gay Rick. You're what people would call a necrophiliac. You are only willing to touch them if they are dead," Rob smirked as he continued to prod his old squad mate.

"Those townspeople were liars and dirt! They deserved every bullet hole we put in them. Although it was a waste of some good specimens when YOU had us burn the bodies," Rick responded as he tried to dig up Rob's own ghost!

"We didn't have time to bury them and they didn't deserve to just rot there in the jungle," Rob answered as he justified his past decisions.

"Sure, pretend that you aren't a monster like the rest of us, it doesn't matter to me. All I know is that you two failures have stumbled into my forbidden lab and that means neither of you will leave alive. You will both play by the rules of my fun house," Rick explained as he calmed back down. As he finished a wall rose behind the pair blocking their exit, followed by a smoke cloud rising from the ground. On top of that Rick dimmed the already sparse lights. He wanted the men confused and lost as they stumbled through his lab.

Rob knew his old friend well; he was a master of traps and deception especially when he had time to prepare. This lab was likely one big booby trap and if they were not cautious it would be disastrous. As the two men treaded warily, they began to realize why Eye had sent them to uncover John's secrets. If he knew Rick was involved, he knew that this would be a suicide mission to infiltrate. It was better to sacrifice Rob and Pon then risk his own twisted life.

The two continued to tread until Rob stepped on something wet and squishy. Before he could react to the substance fans began to blow the smoke away and the lights flashed on. The sudden increase of light nearly blinded the men as their eyes tried to adjust to the increase in stimulation.

After blinking several times, they were finally able to see what was around them. Rob was standing on a dissected leg while the rest of the body hung in front of him. As the body swung Rob saw the intestines that were ripped out and the parts hacked off. Adding to the horrific sight was what surrounded the body in front of them. More bodies were scattered across tables in front of them along with shelves of different organs and parts. As they studied the bodies, they saw each had something removed and stitched on from other bodies. They looked like real Frankenstein monsters. It was the most gruesome sight the men had seen as the dried blood plastered the walls and had puddled around them. Pon nearly threw-up in his mouth.

"Isn't it beautiful boys," Rick asked as the men took in the sights around them?

"It's sick," Pon yelled as he tried to overcome what he saw!

"This is doing whatever is necessary for science! This is what is meant when we talk about breaking eggs for an omelet and let me tell you this omelet is beautiful! It is just a few breakthroughs away from me creating life! In a world where death reigned, I am creating change," he boasted in a haunting tone! He began to laugh and it echoed throughout the metal caverns. It was a screeching sound that sent a shiver down Pon's spine. Pon had fashioned himself a scientist as well, but what Rick was saying was different. It was clear that he was on a level only with the infamous Josef Mengle.

"What is this...what have you done Rick," replied Rob with a horrified look on his face? He had seen Rick perform some horrific acts, however this one was something straight from horror stories.

"I did whatever John asked me to do and worked on some of my own dreams. He was the only one that ever believed in me and I was not going to disappoint him. He had me creating doubles to protect him and they were almost perfect. Every aspect was near perfection, but there were still some mental lapses where the subject would return to its natural tendencies and he was very hesitant about that. The plasticity of the brain is incredible, but hard to manipulate by outside forces. The mind isn't like the body that can be rebuilt and changed. The mind needs to maintain some individuality as you slowly take control. You have to train it and it is a slow progress to overcome hand dominance and other quirks. I was so close, but then he was struck down. That is why I finished my work and will build an army in his image. I will complete his dreams. The first soldiers are ready and you will be their perfect test," he cackled as four figures creeped their way closer to Rob and Pon.

"What the hell is this? Who...What are these things," Rob yelled as he braced himself?

"I know them," Pon uttered in shock, "Those are the four board members that went missing, but he has turned them into something unrecognizable." The four men limped into the light and into full view of Rob and Pon. The men were old and looked like corpses years ago, but now they were nothing but husks. It was unclear how much Rick experimented on them, but it was obvious that they had been enhanced. They were weaponized zombies at this point.

A few of them had metal limbs like Pon, others just patches of skin grafted over metal plates. One had obviously been torn and stretched as he had different shades of skin stitched across key junctions. Another one had extra fingers attached and several ribs removed. Finally, all of them were shaven with stitches across their scalps where the tops of their heads had been opened and a mechanical eye in place of their left one. All of it was sickening, but the eyes were by far the most unsettling as they continued to scan the room.

"I can tell by your expressions that you two are impressed by my work, but you haven't seen anything yet. Attack boys," ordered Rick! The former board members moved with agility that far surpassed what they would have normally been capable of. They were merciless with their strikes, but their fighting style was sloppy and the technique was poor. Most importantly they moved with no fear or care for their own safety. They threw gigantic blow after blow, but each swing would leave the assailants open for counters. Rob managed to grab hold of one of them during their wild attacks and managed to break his human arm. Yet he wasn't even fazed by it. Instead he started attacking harder and used the broken arm as a club. He swung it wildly at Rob with no regard for any possible continued damage. After seeing that the pair knew this fight was not being fought under the same rules, the men made a tactical withdrawal.

"They're like zombies. They just keep moving despite our best efforts. Right now, all we're doing is wearing ourselves out and getting nowhere," panted Pon. The pair were exhausted while the four opponents had only continued to move forward. Up until then all their efforts had been futile and they couldn't keep this battle up for long. Rob's cracked rib was far from healed and every time he locked up with one of the monsters it strained him greatly. On top of that, his shoulder was still bothering him from the gunshot he sustained the other day and the battle with Eye. They had to find a way to end things quickly.

"I bet you boys are wondering what I did to make these frail old men into perfect soldiers," Rick began as he listened for a response despite knowing Rob was in no mood to talk, "It was quite tricky, but nothing that a genius like me couldn't overcome. You see I started out thinking the brain was just a computer that I needed to overwrite, but it is far greater than that. The brain is an organism that is continually changing and morphing into a greater or worse form of itself depending on how we use it. That means it can't be overwritten as it will always adapt. That stumped me for months, until I decided to use its plasticity against itself. I created that eye of theirs as an illusion for the brain. I wired it to the brain in multiple regions in order to control electrical impulses. Neurons that fire together wire together and if you can control that firing and fool it you can control the person. That is what I have done, but don't worry Rob this was not a painless process for them or the throwaway test subjects I used.

Now you may think you can beat them by removing the eyes, but it would break your moral code. If the eye is removed their brains will melt. I wonder what you are going to do Rob. These men are the perfect soldiers, by controlling impulses I can override pain and force them to move forward no matter what. That means this ends one of two ways: either you die or you kill them. Can your conscious handle more bodies," taunted Rick over his speaker system as the two men attempted to complete their strategy? Rob sat for a moment as he slowly began to realize what Rick's words meant.

"When we faced Eye, I hesitated and it may very well cost Anna her life. I couldn't kill him then because of a promise I had made to never kill again. I was afraid that I would become the monster John was, I was afraid of becoming something that I couldn't control, but it is time to make my choice. It is time to put myself on the line to save the people I love," Rob muttered to Pon as he made sure Rick couldn't hear him.

"I may not have known you for long, but you are not a monster Rob and you will not become one. People like Rick, Eye, and John kill without compassion or thought. You did it for duty, but it killed you on the inside. You feel pain and empathy, you should not have to kill, but unfortunately in our world we have to do what we can to survive. That is all I ask you to do now, survive. Now what is the plan," Pon said as he placed a hand on Rob's shoulder?

"You say I am not a monster Pon, but the plan is to become one," Rob said as he rose to look the men in the eyes. Rob's eyes had grown dark and shallow much like those of the men in front of him. Rob launched himself at the group of men and started to fight with the intensity of a trapped animal. He struck whatever came close to him trying to place crippling blows on his targets. Pon quickly came to Rob's aide and they stood back to back fighting off the creatures in front of them. The fight continued to drag-on and though the two men had far more intensity than before, they were still running on fumes. That was until Rob finally had his hands around the neck of one of them. In that moment he thought of the danger that Anna was likely in and twisted the man's neck as ferociously as he could ending his existence. Rob let out of feral yell as loud as he could as the beast fell to the floor. All of his frustration over the people he had lost was released in that moment.

The scream forced the other three to stop for a minute so they could analyze what had occurred. Both Rob and Pon noticed in that moment that Rick's override was not as perfect as Rick thought. In that moment the three men looked afraid and unwilling to continue, but Rick was able to regain control and started moving them closer again.

Just before combat resume Rob noticed that in the final moment the man he had killed had smiled. The figure laid on the ground and embraced the death that had come because it was a release from the pain Rick had put him through. Rob had never truly believed in the idea of mercy killing as he always wanted to give people a chance to become greater than they were, but at that moment he needed something to save him from the guilt of murder.

This smile energized Rob and Pon as they began to fight harder knowing that there was a way to stop the creatures and it was a way that was approved by the men inside the husks. They fought carefully as they avoided any unnecessary blows and killed one board member at a time. Each one had a smile on their face as they fell to the cold ground below them. The pain and the experimentation were over at last. They were finally free of the world they were enslaved by.

Once they were all dead Rob and Pon stood over the corpses. They were exhausted. Their bodies and minds had been drained from the battle. Even for trained soldiers like they were killing still wasn't easy. They felt empathy and loved life which meant that with every kill they carried a certain burden around with them. This one was easier to carry as it was assisted by the idea of mercy, but in the end innocent men were dead by their hands. Even if they had been forced by Rick to do it. On top of that they had each absorbed massive amounts of damage as during the fights and the pain was starting to become a nuisance.

Their 'victory' was short lived as a slow clap began to echo through the laboratory. They still had at least one more battle to fight. The pair began to walk towards the clapping sound knowing that they may very well be walking into another trap. As they came closer to the source it stopped. It was then that they noticed a metal staircase and sitting on top of it was Rick smiling at the sights below him. He appeared to be impressed that the pair had managed to beat his monsters. The arrogance on display enraged Pon and without thought he rushed after Rick only to be met with a severe electrical shock upon contact with the staircase. The shock was strong enough to send him flying and rendering him unconscious. Rob attempted to attend to his partner, but there was little he could do once he found the heartbeat to be stable. Rick had remained in the same spot during all the excitement. Suspicious of what had just happened Rob found an old rock on the ground and tossed it at Rick. To no surprise it passed right through what turned out to be a projection.

"Nothing gets past you, does it Rob? I guess you are a bit smarter than the other fellow," Rick taunted. His voice was different this time. It no longer sounded like it was coming over the speaker system. This time it was his natural voice.

The room fell pitch black again and before Rob could move his exhausted body, he was sprayed with some form of gas and dropped to his knees. His head grew dizzy and images started to flash in front of his eyes. Then someone cranked the lights back-up and all Rob could see was jungle.

"I'm curious Rob where did the mixture take you? I designed it to take the victims to a nightmare scenario," Rick chuckled. Rob began to walk around, but his movements were slowed by whatever gas he had inhaled. He wobbled around for some time as he tried to figure out where he was. The sights, the sounds, and smells around him were false, he knew that, yet they seemed familiar.

***

As Rob stumbled through the forest, he heard a scream call out for him and he ran to it. Several more would call out before he reached a village that was burning. Before he had fully slipped into the dissociative state, he had heard Rick mention a nightmare reality. Little did Rick realize that Rob faced no greater nightmare than his own past. Rob recognized this memory was from the campaign in South America. His squad had been forced to retreat after a failed assault on the enemy fortress. He also remembered that it wasn't the first battle that brought him nightmares it was what happened during the enemy's retaliation.

Rob remembered the battle clearly as it was one of the squads most ill-advised. It was early into the second part of the War when it went worldwide and they thought they could capture a critical outpost in South America, so like many times before they infiltrated the main base. However, the intel they had was leaked straight from the enemy and was used to set a trap for the legendary team. The group had managed to escape by the skin of their teeth. Unfortunately, the enemy knew it would be their only chance to catch the team in retreat and they had to capitalize on the opportunity to remove a major key in the War. This was not a memory he wanted to remember especially with whatever drug concoction Rick had sprayed him with adding the chance of surprises.

Rob slowly walked into the village his men had retreated to. It was dangerously quiet. Not a single sound could be heard outside of the wind hitting the trees. He entered one of the huts and found dead bodies stacked on top of each other. They were part of the local reinforcements that had assisted the squad in the attack. The men that assisted them didn't last long once the enemy brought the full force of their base on the small village. As he observed the mangled bodies of his comrades, he heard another sudden screech. He exited the hut to see the infantry rushing the village. Bottles of fire were being thrown at the huts, gunshots filled the once silent air, and men were rushing into the buildings and dragging out any survivors just to kill them in the dirt. Rob had to continuously remind himself that what he was seeing wasn't real anymore it was all in the past, but it felt just as it once did. It is one thing to live a made-up nightmare, but to relive what has already happened is far more painful. As he stood watching the world around him four men with knives surrounded him and began to assault him. At first, he took the fight easy knowing everything was in his mind, but then one of their strikes landed and drew blood from his side. Before he could retaliate the men were gone.

It was in that moment, Rob realized Rick wasn't just playing mind games he was using the hallucination to cover his movements. It was a simple game of cat and mouse, but deadly, nonetheless. He now knew he had to focus as one slip-up could mean his end. He couldn't just let the world happen he had to be an active participant. He strolled through the village again, it was now littered with death and fire after the enemy had left. He kept walking until he came across John standing over one of the enemies as he brutally beat him to a pulp. Whoever the enemy was no one could make out the face anymore. The man was clearly dead, but John just kept going. John looked up to see Rob and spoke.

"This isn't how I remember it Rob," John began, "If I recall the scenario was actually reverse wasn't it. Even as I attempted to pull you off of him you just continued to throw punch after punch until brain covered your knuckles. Before that you were always my friend, but it was at that moment that I realized you were just like me. Whether you want to believe it or not you and I are two sides of the same coin. The only thing that separates us are a few decisions here and there, including one final push. Look around you. There is

nothing but death and you are alone just like me." The next thing Rob heard was John's laugh echoing around him as he now stood alone in a field. He was now wearing his uniform from that day. It was torn and stained with the blood of both friend and foe. His knuckles had blood dripping from them and around him saw fifteen dead bodies. Each one had been brutally destroyed. One had his eyes gouged out, another an ear bitten off, one had been stabbed over thirty times, and another had his face beaten to the point where it nearly caved in. Rob had done it all these were the sins he regretted more than anything. He had finally lost control and unleashed the monster that slept inside him.

He began to run again as he tried to escape what he was. He continued until he ran into more figures. This time they were the ones he recognized. Carly, Stevens, Stevens' daughter, John, Trisha, and even Anna in front of him.

"You failed us Rob," they all said in unison as they approached him. Then they kept repeating the phrase as they grew closer.

"You are alone, just as you should be," John started to say as the rest continued the chant. He drew a blade from his hip and prepared to strike Rob. Could it be Rick? Rob had no idea and despite telling himself that it wasn't real all he could hear was the voices of people he had let down. The sound intensified as he saw behind John a crowd of his allies that had died in the war. John started the descent of his blade and Rob had accepted his fate. As he closed his eyes, he heard John's blade make contact with something metal. He opened his eyes to see a beautiful brunette standing in front of him holding off John and besides him was Iris.

"You are never alone Rob. We are always with you," she said as he kissed him awake.

***

The kiss from the woman he loved brought Rob back to reality. It was there he found himself on his knees holding Rick's wrist in his hand. Rick was holding a butcher's knife and had tried to thrust it into his old friend, but the man who should have been a mental wreck had fought back. Somehow Rob had resisted the compound and Rick was astonished. What should have been an easy kill was now a battle he would surely lose. He struggled as he freed himself from Rob's grasp and backed away in awe.

"How? How did you break through? I had perfected those drugs on over twenty patients without a single problem, yet in a state of complete exhaustion you did what no one else could. This should be impossible, but now for the sake of science I must ask what did you see," Rick asked as his surprise turned into a look of curiosity? However, Rick found the answer unimportant as he began to creep away from Rob as quickly as he could. He knew that even in a state of utter exhaustion Rob could still defeat him without excessive strain.

"You are right that serum does create a nightmare scenario, but you forget that I live my nightmare every day. I was able to overcome your serum because I understand my failures and face them every time, I look in a mirror," Rob responded, "You see Rick I am nothing like you or John. I have a monster who is capable of unspeakable acts, but I am not the monster I am a man who at the heart of all his actions has good intentions. And most importantly there are people who care for me and count on me. I promised them that I would come back to them and you are not going to stop me!" Rick didn't understand what he had just done. He thought he was pushing Rob over the edge at last, but in reality, he had forced him to finally face the demons he had been running from for so long and could at last see clearly again.

Being thee coward he was Rick began to run, there really was no other options at this point. Rob pushed through the pain he was in and gave chase. He refused to let his last possible lead get away and more importantly he refused to fail Anna like he had failed the others. He eventually caught up to Rick who stood with a knife pointing to his gut. He refused to be caught at this point. He knew what he had done in that lab couldn't be exposed and was willing to choose death over capture and exposure.

As he began to plunge the knife towards himself a recently awoken Pon caught and stopped his arm from behind. He took the knife from Rick's hand and knocked him out. As the two of them dragged Rick back to the elevator Rob felt the unused bullet Eye had given him earlier. He no longer wanted to use it on himself, now he used it as a reminder of how far he had come. He now knew he didn't have to run from the monster he carried, he just had to keep being the man people knew he could be.

Chapter 20
It is Him

"So, do you want to tell the world what you've been up to Rick or do you want me to," Rob asked as the trio of men ascended in the elevator? Rick refused to answer as he stood silent and still. They had used rope from his own lad to tie his hands and secure their prisoner. He was a beaten man and yet the look in his eye was not that of surrender, no it held a glimmer of despair. Rob and Pon were both smiling as they waited to reach the top. Their bodies had been beaten by the controlled board members, but they had emerged victorious. Rob had finally secured a lead and he was one step closer to finding Anna. The only issue now was what was he was going to do with Rick. He knew that Rick's work was atrocious, but it had been stopped and revealing what was happening would be a step back for Ascension and its good work. People would lose faith again and that was something he couldn't allow. On the other hand, he needed to find out more about the Eye and Rick had to know something.

"How did Eye know about your work," Rob asked him as they continued to make the climb? The question made Rick perk-up and smile.

"It is still so cute how you can be so clueless. I understand why John always enjoyed messing with your mind. Your answer will reveal itself soon enough boy," he answered as his smile continued to stretch. Rob wanted to press him harder, but they were near the top and it was time to move on and get him to Adam. That meant they had to somehow sneak him out of the building without a fight.

Once the elevator reached the top floor the men entered the hallway, but for some reason the lights that had once been automatic before did not turn on. They had been shut-off. Given past events the pair of men grew suspicious, but became distracted when Rick made futile attempts to escape. They subdued him again as they stumbled their way through the darkness to the doorway. When the door opened, they were met with a sword being thrust toward and piercing Rick, followed by two kicks that sent them back into the hallway. Somehow, Eye had made his way to the secret entrance and chose to impede their path. Startled and unsure of what he was about to do Rob and Pon braced themselves, but instead of attacking again he closed the door in front of them and locked it. They were all stunned by the sudden turn of events and Rick in the confusion had grabbed ahold of his captors. The sword had no only pierced his gut, but sliced the rope that had restrained him.

"Why did he stab you," Rob screamed as he attempted to free himself from Rick's dying hands? At first Rick did not answer, but then another smile grew on his face.

"You are naïve Rob. You did everything a crazy man asked you to and didn't think that there would be a plan for when I got caught," he cackled. As the dying man laughed Rob noticed that the blood coming out of Rick was not a normal crimson but instead was glowing.

"What the hell is this Rick," he questioned as he became mystified by the sight in front of him? Whatever was occurring was unlike anything that Rob had ever seen before.

"It is the plan Rob. If I were to ever be caught, one of my greatest experiments would be tested. I injected myself with a serum that once inside my body begins to duplicate and attach itself to red blood cells. Once most of my cells are coated with the serum it lays dormant until ignited. Now as you can imagine I wouldn't want something that explodes easily so the serum only reacts when it comes into contact with extreme amounts of iron. An amount far beyond what is in a normal blood cell, an amount very similar to what is used in steel construction. Originally, I was supposed to take out the whole lab with that knife I had, but things happen," he laughed as he began to cough up blood. His insides were already beginning to ignite with micro explosions taking out his critical organs. Unaware of how much time they had Pon and Rob started to pry the door open again.

They were unable to open it at first, especially given their state, but they kept pushing trying to open some kind of space. As soon as they had a small opening they ducked under and took cover in the conference room. The blast behind them blew the metal door flying through the windows opposite it and ruined the walkway they had just been in. As far as either of them knew there was no way back to the lab. Both men were disappointed again to come this far only to be met by more failure.

"I thought your old squad's specialty was stealth," joked Pon as he attempted to lighten the mood. Rob was not amused in the slightest, his anger only grew as he was ready to snap at any moment. Several guards came rushing to investigate the noise. In a fit of rage Rob lashed out at the guards striking recklessly. They were caught off-guard and man handled by him at first. As time went on however, his adrenaline wore off and his stamina would give out so in order to protect his comrade Pon joined in. It took several minutes, but the anger had made it so Rob felt nothing anymore. He was ready to unleash the monster he had been forced to face again, then Jefferies made the mistake of coming in.

"What is going on here," demanded the former butler? He was unaware of how out of his depth he was. Rob lunged at him without hesitation picking Jefferies up and then slammed the old man on the table. His eyes were filled with murderous intent.

"Where is that son-of-a-bitch," yelled Rob as he pushed the old man harder into the table? Rob was moving like a possessed man. The calm and collected individual was gone and nothing was there, but passion. Pon was taken aback by this sudden anger, he understood the guards as they would have hampered their ability to escape, but Jefferies was a helpless old man.

"Who? Who are you talking about Rob? I know nothing, I'm just a simple butler," the old man muttered. Despite how frail he seemed to be Rob returned his remarks with a quick strike to the face as he tightened his grip with the other hand.

"Where is Gene," Rob yelled giving a name to his question? The old man continued to squirm until Rob struck him again. This time he opened a gash above Jefferies' eye.

"Why do you need him, you bloody psychopath," he answered? Unhappy with the reply Rob threw him down the table crashing into the chairs on the other end. Having seen enough Pon grabbed Rob and tried to calm him down. The old man used this moment to crawl under the table and try to regain his wits.

"Have you lost it Rob? I know that you're mad another lead is now dead, but beating up an old man isn't the right way to do things.

Besides we need Eye not your old commander," Pon said gripping Rob tight in order to keep him off Jefferies!

"Eye is Gene! I can prove it too I just need a location out of this rat," screamed Rob! This answer shocked the other two men and Pon released his hold on Rob.

"What do you mean you can prove it," Pon asked weary of this revelation?

"I wasn't sure, but I've been suspicious ever since we crossed one another at Anna's house. You see the style of fighting he used is called bojutsu and the specific moves he used are unique to a set of monks in southern Japan. The same monks that taught Gene, John, and myself how to staff fight during the War. The monks were very selective with who they taught, but it could have been a mistake on my part. There are several forms of fighting and his could have just been too similar for me to distinguish. The next problem was that he also knew way too much about me. Since the War I have been very discreet with most of my actions and besides my tendency to sleep around very few people know about my personal life, except for the people in it. This means to know all he knew he would have been following me, doubtful since even when I am drunk, I take several precautions to not be followed. That means that he had to have known me to have the information he did and out of all the people in my life there are only three that could have known everything John is dead, Iris isn't going to do it, and the last person was my mentor who was like a father during the War. Lastly, I keep my circle small, but John's is even smaller. Of those people fewer would have a close enough relationship to know about that lab. That attack was no accident, he knew about Rick's serum and used the whole thing as a trap to get to me. On top of that Gene would have had no issue entering and leaving since he was a close associate of John before his death.

The only problem I have is the motive Gene would have for all this. I mean I understand turning on John if John pushed him too far on day, but me. I just don't understand, but he is the only person that fits. He is a tactical genius, has connections from his time with John, and is a skilled enough fighter to pull this off," Rob explained. As he spoke Pon's face was relaxing as everything started to make sense. Jefferies on the other had growing concern coming over his face, he knew something and it was becoming obvious to the other men in the room.

"I must say I thought you were the one that finally snapped, but really you were just upset upon realizing what was going on," Pon said filling in the blanks left to be explained.

"I never thought that the day would come where Gene would be my opponent, but it is the only thing that makes sense. The other man I am not sure about yet, but Gene is the one we should concern ourselves with. Now like I said I know I am right and based on Jefferies expression he knows it is the truth as well. Gene was working for John. John told me that himself and if that is the case than he knows where he is and either you help me force the location out of him or I go through you," explained Rob as he pulled Jefferies out from under the table!

"I hope that you are right for all our sakes. I'll try to keep the rest of the guards out as long as possible. If they are allowed in here with us, I fear that in our weakened states we won't be able to stop them," Pon stated as he began to search the room for ways to barricade the door. With his partner supporting him Rob grabbed the old man and held him, dangling from the shattered window.

"I'd guess that from this height you have about a 15% chance of surviving the fall. Unfortunately, that survival might be a fate worse than death," threatened Rob, "Now do you want to chance it and keep playing dumb or are you going to give me my answers!" Jefferies hesitated for a moment as he looked at the city below him and as he did Rob began to slowly loosen his grip. It was unclear if he would truly let go, but his grip loosened enough to scare the old man.

"It is amazing how similar you and John are. I can't tell you how many times he threatened to throw me out a window, yet he never did and neither will because you both need me," he mocked. Rob tightened his grip as he hesitated. He wanted to throw Jefferies out the window, but the old man was right he couldn't. There was too much on the line along with the fact that he still had no intent to truly kill. The board member he came to peace with because of their state, but as far as Rob knew Jefferies was innocent and would look that way to the people of the city.

"Now I'm not saying I won't tell you where Gene is, but it is not because of your threats," the old man boldly stated.

"Why tell me than," Rob asked as he continued to dangle the old man?

"Simple Gene is going to put you out of your misery just like he did John. He promised to show the world the truth and I am not going to stop him instead I am going to help him by giving him you. Gene is hold-up in an old farmhouse in the bluffs. It is on the highest peak and I can tell you that he will be waiting," Jefferies proclaimed as Rob decided what to with him. He could still drop him, but adding more bloodshed to the buckets already poured was senseless, so instead he threw him at the conference table knocking him out and more importantly shutting him up. He tied him to the table with one of the guard's belts and left to help Pon with the door.

During the interrogation Pon had managed to barricade the door well using all the scraps from the explosion, but with half the building likely on the other side they had to find a new way out. Regardless of whether or not they would win the fight it would take too much time and delay their chances of saving Anna.

"Rob do you remember that rope and hook I gave you," Pon started and Rob shook his head knowing where this is going, "Well it is time to use it. The table should be bolted to the floor, so hook the rope on and pray that it holds us." Rob did as Pon ordered and then grabbed it as he prepared to repel down a few floors. Given the fact that the whole security force was outside the door if they could make it a few flights they could escape before the guards knew any better. The men grabbed the rope and jumped. It was long enough to make it down two flights before crashing through the floor's window. From there they hobbled out of the building pulling glass from their bodies. Thankfully, the explosion caused most of the building besides the guards to evacuate which meant the escape went unnoticed until the guards finally busted through the barricade. The next stop for the pair was the farmhouse Jefferies had described.

Across town, in the basement of an old farmhouse Eye was removing his mask and equipment. He placed his mask on a shelf and his blades hung from hooks next to it. He stood there staring at the items, he was admiring the fresh blood still dripping from the blade. His stance was that of a proud man, but there was still a weakness in it. His body had endured decades of hardship and it ached for the day it could finally stop or at least slow down.

"Gene that damn women bit me, again! She nearly took off my finger this time," hollered a voice breaking his concentration! A door opened and Jackson came wandering into the room where Gene stood.

"I told you killing her isn't part of the plan. We need her alive, at least until Rob kills himself or we do it. That is the plan and trust me you don't want to fail," Gene responded with a soothing tone. His partner stood irate, but he did not dare cross his old commander. Despite the decades Gene was still a superior warrior to almost everyone he met.

"Well next time you feed her. I'm going to need stitches for this," he complained as he looked over his hand. Gene brushed him off as he walked into the connected room. He made his way towards the center of the room where a chair sat facing Anna. She was tied to the floor and had her whole body immobilized by her restraints. He sat in the chair and stared at the woman as she continued to struggle and fight. All he could do was chuckle at her resistance.

"You never were one for the damsel in distress role. I guess that was one of the many things I admired about you, so why we chose you as the target is beyond me. Iris would have made my life so much easier and she still would have made Rob move with urgency. I mean that fight you put up almost ruined the plan entirely. We may have had numbers and the element of surprise, but you were still able to weaken me to the point that Rob could capitalize. If Rob had a little more mental fortitude, a healthy shoulder, and had pulled that trigger this would all be over. Now I don't think you understand if that was the case some powerful people would have become extraordinarily upset," with that he paused for a moment and looked her in the eyes as she remained quiet, "I guess you're not much of a talker today, huh. No matter this will all be over soon. Rob will be dead and this city will burn. In the meantime, I ask that the next time just take the food we give you or I'll let you starve," Gene stated as he began to laugh. She tried to fight one more time, but it was useless as he laughed himself out of the room. Outside Gene looked around as he started to talk.

"Do you think he's coming," he asked the dark room? A moment passed with no answer then from one of the dark corners a devilish smile grew and a syringe was thrown to him. Gene understood what it all meant and laughed at his ignorance to even ask the question.

"I guess I should make the preparations then," he said.

Chapter 21
Mercy

As Pon and Rob made their ways to the old farmhouse all Rob could think about was how he never wanted to be in this situation. John was the only person that Rob was closer to than Gene and he was the only one that did not side with John during their split. Gene was like a father to all the men in the squad and he had taken each one under his wing so that they could perfect whatever skills he saw as their greatest. Before him Dave the feared marksman missed everything because he couldn't handle the kickback of his weapon. Rick was always overcomplicating his traps and often getting himself caught in them. Chen was the type of character who could drive fast when relaxed, but as soon as pressure grabbed hold, he would look like a grandmother driving blind. Jackson was far to gentle and though his hands were quick when defending himself, he couldn't force himself to attack. Though John came to the team later Gene still helped lessen his arrogance and made him a more competent leader. Lastly, there was Rob who he turned from a weak, confidence lacking guppy to a super soldier that could turn the tide of a battle. The legend behind the squad all began with Gene. He was the greatest teacher a man could have and he was loyal to them. He did everything in his power to protect them. The men loved Gene as much as he loved them, however given the current circumstances there was a day that Rob regretted. The day he saved Gene's life for the first time.

***

It was during the second year of the War and the squad which had yet to include John was searching for a threat in what was then North Dakota. If being in North Dakota wasn't bad enough a winter storm had rolled through making travel difficult and on top of the heavy snowfall the temperatures had fallen drastically beyond what the men were prepared for at the time. The mission was considered top secret and everything was considered need to know which created large amounts of uncertainty within the squad. However, the men still trusted Gene and very few people would consider doubting him. The only details that were given about the mission were that a small squad was to use an incoming storm to cover their movements into enemy territory where they would find a facility and destroy it. The higher-ranking officials knew that the mission would likely be suicidal, but failed to mention that to Gene when he was given control of picking the squad he would be leading. The mission was a success as the facility, which was a weapon manufacturing plant as well as research facility were destroyed, however, the success did not come easy as twenty of the original twenty-six men lost their lives during the mission. All that remained was six of the soon to be mythical seven; Dave, Rick, Chen, Jackson, Gene, and Rob.

The ferocity of the enemy caught Gene off-guard since he was unaware of the suicide designation the mission had and because of this he took a massive amount of the blame for the loses. Making matters worse the return voyage home was when nature showed its own firepower. The storm stalled over the region causing what should have only been a foot of snow into 20in or more in some areas. If that wasn't bad enough the wind had average gusts of nearly 45 MPH. The storm had broken them all. They were injured, freezing, and just generally miserable from days in enemy territory. The unity of them all began to fracture and it came to a head inside of a cave that they were forced into during the storm.

"Gentlemen, I failed you on this mission and I am sorry. I didn't get enough intel beforehand and I cannot express to you how much I regret I feel," Gene said as he shivered in the cave. The other five men looked at him. Rick was treating one of Rob's earliest gun wounds. It was merely a flesh wound grazing his left rib cage, but with the severe weather leaving it untreated for long could have cost him gravely.

"Oh, you are sorry Gene! I'll go tell everybody else. Never mind we're all that's left, that's right. Sorry is not going to cut it anymore boss! We lost twenty brothers and sisters out there and you were the one who led us into that slaughter! Then you had us march right back home in this storm and look at us. We are not making it out of here," Rick responded with distaste! It was clear he no longer

trusted the man that had trained him. Gene's head fell as he recognized that fact. He had lost the rest of his squad regardless of the fact that they were still breathing.

"What do you want me to say," Gene asked as he threw his hands in the air? He was clearly frustrated by the events that had unfolded. His was given orders himself and followed them. There is no way he could have known what he was in store for when his superiors refused to give him any more details.

"There really isn't anything you can say except the truth. Did you know that this was suicide," Dave responded from the corner of the cave?

"No! I had no idea that the mission would play out like this," Gene responded trying to defend himself! He was right he didn't officially know, but given the secrecy he should have assumed something was wrong.

"Then what did you know," Chen asked from his curled position he had taken against the wall? Telling them the truth would have been worse than saying it was suicide. It would have shown him as incompetent. Any good leader should collect as much intel as possible and he didn't. He leaned against the wall opposite them and slouched to the floor. He had no response and that told them everything, he didn't need to say anything else. The man that had trained them was responsible for nearly killing them. He could have done more research, but failed and in doing so all but guaranteed their deaths. Everyone had fallen quiet as reality began to set in. The only sound that could be heard anymore was the wind howling outside and their equipment shaking from the fits of shivering they experienced. The will of these men had been broken and the only thing left was rescue or death.

Several hours had passed the tension had not decreased and Gene had to do something. He couldn't stand sitting in a room full of men he had let down. He was too old for that, so he rose from the corner he was slouched in and made his way out of the cave. Rob watched as he left the cave. He was mystified by the sight as the storm was only intensifying and night was coming causing the temperature to drop rapidly. He couldn't comprehend what the old man was thinking. He couldn't do any good out there.

"I guess he finally made his decision," Dave said as he looked up from the guns, he had been cleaning for the last few hours. The rest *of the room stayed silent, they were all older and had an idea of what Dave met, but Rob was still young.*

"What are you talking about Dave? What is Gene doing going out there all by himself," Rob asked unsure of what the rest of the world knew that he didn't?

"It is easy kid, he is going to end it," Chen answered coldly.

"Why would he do that? Sure, we almost died, but without him we would not have made it as far as we did. You know as well as I do that anyone else leads that mission given the circumstance all of us die and the mission fails," Rob explained as he attempted to argue the point.

"Kid I was born American, but my Chinese heritage has always been strong. I was told stories of the old country by my grandfather. Some of his stories included run ins with some old time Japanese fellas who would describe the old samurai tradition of seppuku. These fellas were big into honor you see and when they felt they did something to lose it they would take their own life. I don't know all the details about it as I am neither Japanese nor have, I heard the stories for years, but I think Gene is feeling that need. I don't blame him he has lived a long life filled with war and this failure was quite substantial," Chen explained. The rest of the men did not need to say anything they just nodded their heads agreeing. Rob couldn't believe that they all accepted that the man who had taught them was ready to go and kill himself. He couldn't believe they had lost that much faith in him.

"The Chinaman is right Rob. If you didn't notice the only thing that old Gene took with him was his revolver. The end is near kid," Dave said pulling a cigarette carton out of his pocket. He lit it up and offered one to Rob.

"You might as well take a cigarette of your own kid. If you think this is bad wait till the rest of the War comes," Jackson added as he grabbed one of Dave's cigarettes. Unwilling to accept their words and apathy any longer Rob ran out of the cave after Gene. The storm had nearly wiped his footprints clear, but there was just enough left for him to follow. He wasn't sure what he was going to say to the Gene, but he needed to do something. He didn't want to lose another comrade due to that mission. Eventually he came across the rock where Gene was sitting with his gun in his hand. Rob could see that Gene was falling apart and a tear was strolling down his face.

"You don't have to do that Gene," stated Rob as he attempted to comfort Gene. The old man just shook his head.

"Kid you don't understand this world, do you? I was once an expert at strategy and this whole war thing. I had top tier generals eating out of the palm of my hand because they knew I could not only train the best soldiers, but make them weapons of destruction that walked on two feet. In my prime I had battalions of my men winning wars, but then war changed and they didn't need my men. The age of technology was here and we were fighting with drones. I was obsolete, I had nothing left after that. I was a man without a purpose and a man without purpose isn't really worth keeping around. I was going to end things.

I wanted the darkness to go away, but it was at that time I realized I was afraid to die. As a soldier you know death can come at any time, but when the gun is in your hand and the target is yourself you realize how terrifying the unknown is. Then one day I got a call. There was a new war and they needed men like me to train boys like you. I was so happy again, with the country tearing itself apart the modern techniques were less effective. You needed the old school ways of looking each other in the eye. I jumped at the opportunity, but what did I do with the chance? I fail and lead all of you to death. I've grown old kid, I think I have just outlived my usefulness," Gene told Rob as he twisted the revolver around in his hand. The snow kept blowing in each man's face, but they had already gone through hell this was nothing anymore. The cold didn't bother them anymore not with the gravity of the situation.

"Gene I never met you before the War and I doubt we would have ever really gotten a chance in any other circumstance. We are different, I know that, however I know that you have done good work. You may look at this day as a failure, but without you twenty-six of twenty-six would have died. This was a mission with suicide written all over it and yet your superiors sent you out here. They are to blame not you," Rob proclaimed trying to defend Gene and talk him down from the proverbial edge.

"It doesn't matter whose fault it was; I should have seen this coming and done better. We always have a choice Rob. It may have seemed like there was none, I mean I was the one who taught all of you that when you are given an order you follow it. The truth is you don't, yes there are consequences like being court martialed, but in

the end, you can still turn it down. I chose to lead you all to death despite reservations to do so. A man who cannot stand for what he believes in anymore is not worth the life he has. It is at that point he becomes a cog in a machine and that I can't live with this. The fear of death is no longer there and I just want this to end," Gene yelled as he raised his gun at last, but just before he could pull the trigger Rob grabbed the gun away from him and he began to point it at his own head.

"Sir I say this with all respect, but cut the crap. You are not the only one with darkness in their heart and mind. You have to fight it sir. I know it isn't easy, I've fought my own battles, but you have to keep pushing forward for us. You know as well as I do that you are the only one who is capable of getting us home safe. The rest of the men may not see that right now, but give them time they are angry. I beg you to help us and I can tell you if you walk back into that cave with conviction and show them you have learned from your mistakes; they will eventually forgive you. If you help get us out of here, I guarantee they will forgive you and follow you to hell and back. If you chose to end it though I won't blame you, but I will follow your lead because I am not going to die in that cave. I am not going to freeze to death, that is not how I'm going out," Rob finished as he handed the gun back to Gene. He wasn't sure if the boy was right, but now he was curious what was next for them.

"Maybe you do know something about this world boy. I don't know if you're right or not, but if there is someone willing to die with me or for me that means that I must still be needed. I think I'm going to stick around a little longer, so let's get out of here kid," Gene finally remarked as the men made their way back to warmth.

***

Rob turned out to be right that day, the two of them had a lot of fight left in them and without either of them the rest of the crew would not have made it out of that cave nor would they have survived that war. When Gene returned it shocked and inspired the rest of them and never again did, they question Gene's leadership. Unfortunately, Rob was now left wondering if that was a good thing. As him and Pon were climbing the hills to the farmhouse Rob tears began to form in his eyes because that day he could have let everyone die and maybe the world would have been better off. He had made a choice and now the world felt his consequences. He wondered what would he do today? What would he do when he found Gene?

Chapter 22
Life

It had been a long day, but the tired men finally arrived at the farmhouse just prior to sunset. As they huffed after the long trek, they reflected on the day they went through and took inventory on how their bodies were doing. They had been beaten and pushed to their limits, but they still had a long way to go. Mere feet away from them was a pair of men that had already beaten them once that day and now they would have to redeem themselves. It wouldn't be easy, but they couldn't afford to lick their wounds when the enemy was so close. Rob took several deep breaths and finally collected himself both physically and mentally.

Now focused the men looked at what awaited them, the first obstacle was a giant stone gate that guarded the property from intrusion. The gate felt out of place as the rest of the surrounding area was flat and quiet. The land around the farmhouse had been cleared and transformed into a prairie. Except for a singular line of trees that went from the fence line to the back of the house. The grass inside the fence line had grown above knee height and the farmhouse inside the property seemed to be abandoned. The house had the appearance of a property that had been beaten and destroyed years prior with the only reason it still stood being its own stubbornness. Holes littered the roof and siding of the building making it inefficient for protection. Along with the holes in the walls several windows lacked glass panes. It didn't feel right to the men. It did not appear to be the hideout of a master criminal. Instead it felt more like an abandoned shack that was lost in time.

"I guess the old man lied to you Rob," Pon pointed out as he scanned the estate. He was not impressed by the things he saw and was fully expecting another lie. However, Rob was not buying it. Something didn't feel right to him as he ignored his partner's comments.

"No, he's here. I can feel it. This would be his ideal battlefield," Rob replied, "The property may look abandoned, but it is a trick.

The grass has been grown this tall, so that he could set traps within it. Then those trees over there are his path in and out of the estate. You see besides being an explosive expert Gene was also excellent at jungle combat. He loved climbing trees and hiding in them. He knew the importance of having leverage and vantage points. On top of that I want you to look at those holes in the walls. They are in places where it is easy for him to slip muzzles through. He could drop us both without ever knowing it.

Gene is an expert strategist and he has set this building up to be the ultimate fortress. It uses smoke and mirrors to lead his prey in and then makes it impossible for them to escape. When you are at war the first rule is to control as many variables as you can and right now, he has the advantage." After he finished his explanation, Rob reached down and picked up some rocks that were on the ground. He tossed them into the grass one-by-one with no particular pattern and after a few tries he finally hit something and a small explosion went off.

"It isn't much, but something like that will take your leg off and knowing Gene it was filled with nails and other debris. You might not have died from the blast, but the shrapnel will render you obsolete before you hit the ground," Rob pointed out as he figured out their plan.

"Well what do you suggest because I really enjoy the three limbs I have left," Pon exclaimed!

"Well I have an idea and I hope you enjoy jumping around because from what I know of him there is only one way in and it's that tree line. The problem is that he knows we are coming and will have set a trap. I'm not sure yet what it will be, but he is waiting and nothing about this will be easy," Rob explained.

"To be honest with you, I have never been the most limber fella, but I prefer it over walking through a minefield plus why would we want things to be easy at this point," Pon said as they made their way. They began to ascend the first tree cautious of what might be waiting. As they did Pon was impressed by how easily Rob moved in them. There was an unforced ease in his movement as he flowed from one branch to the next, especially compared to himself. He had found himself nearly falling several times as he tried to match Rob's pace.

"You look like you've practiced this before. Did you do a lot of climbing as a child," Pon questioned his partner?

"No, I use to hate climbing as it seemed pointless at the time. However, when I entered boot camp Gene made this a central element of our conditioning. He was a unique drill sergeant compared to the rest of them. He believed in a training style that he thought would be more applicable," stated Rob as he took a moment to allow Pon to catch up, "His biggest belief was that we rarely fight on our own terms in war and in order to win we have to be comfortable in any environment. Thus, he trained us in forest, lakes, and took us to deserts as well. He wanted to simulate any possible circumstances. His other objective was to make us masters of moving without being seen. When you are infiltrating enemy territory, you have to be a ghost to be effective. I would be lying if I said it didn't work wonders for us. We won countless battles that should have been lost because of the things he taught us. He was an amazing teacher regardless of how much of an ass he could be at times. He became an extra father to many of us and I wish things could have been different." The reminiscing affected Rob as he began to slow down substantially. Pon began searching for words to say, but before he could utter a sound a shot rang out. Then a bullet came flying towards them and managed to hit the tree just missing them both. Without hesitation they moved to cover in the canopy.

"I see your aim hasn't improved," Rob taunted as he tried to coax his enemy out of hiding! This was followed by another shot which cut through the branches next to him.

"I see that loud mouth of yours still works kid," Gene replied from his fortress! While Gene was yelling, Pon attempted to advance a few trees. However, Rob's distraction was not great enough as Gene still saw the movement and shot. The bullet caught Pon's metal arm and nearly knocked him off the tree. Luckily, it merely ricochets down to the ground.

The pair knew that Gene was honed in on them, but they were not far from the safety of the building itself. The odds were not in their favor and a rush seemed like suicide, but there was a zero percent chance if they stood still. Gene was not the greatest marksman, but with them trapped if they stood still, he would eventually take them out. Given the choices the men rushed through the rest of the trees and managed to avoid bullet after bullet. Rob found it odd that it was so easy to avoid the shots, but he was not about to wait and take a chance that his fortune would change. After they finally reached the last tree and jumped to the back porch the bullets stopped. There was no sigh of relief as they knew now, they were waiting for the next trap.

"I'm not a big believer in luck, but damn I'm glad it was on our side. Now what is our next move," Pon asked with a slight chuckle?

"There isn't really a plan, because no matter what we think of he will have an answer. Right now, our only responsibility is to be careful and find Anna," Rob stated as he caught his breath from the run. They crept into the house where there was no light to be found and the daylight was slowly slipping away. If darkness falls completely, they would be at the disposal of Gene and the Fool.

They began the search, looking in every door they found, but there was nothing; no Anna and no light switch. As they found dead ends and failures, they grew frustrated. They were stumbling around in darkness and wasting precious time. Though they were frustrated they were still pleasantly surprised that they hadn't ran into any traps or enemies. It was impossible, but the house felt completely empty. However, they could still feel the danger in the air even though nothing had come after them yet. Gene had just shot at them, he had to be planning something. It felt as if they were being watched and studied. Gene and the Fool were stalking and hunting them, yet they could do nothing to stop it. They found an old-fashioned lantern and candle just before the sun had fully set. They hurried to light it before it was too late, but what they didn't know was that danger would soon follow the glow. As soon as it was lit something launched itself from the shadows and knocked the lantern to the ground. The figure then drew two knives on them.

"I see Gene has sent his lap dog to face us and I must say you have earned your name Fool if you plan on taking us on without any backup," Pon said with a smirk knowing that the Fool would not stand a chance.

"No, Rob is the real fool, he always has been," the figure replied with an arrogant tone as if the situation was flipped.

"Jackson, is that your voice I hear? I can't believe it. I never would have imagined that you would be working with Gene again. You two never had the best relationship even coming to blows on several occasions if I recall. I must say though it all makes sense now. There are few men or women that have such control of a blade to remove eyelids without harming the eye itself," stated Rob with a touch of amazement in his voice. The men stared each other down waiting for one to make a move, but this tension distracted all three as the flame escaped the lantern. It begun to grow on the wooden floor of the old farmhouse. At first it was only a slight flicker, but the inattentiveness of the three men would cost the farmhouse. By the time they noticed it the smoke had already begun to rise and the fire was becoming larger than anything they could control with the simple tools available to them. Understanding that the urgency had just tripled Pon through himself at Jackson. Rob couldn't waste his time in a fight that Pon felt he could handle his own.

"Go find Anna! I'll take care of him and don't you dare argue with me there is no time just go," Pon ordered! Rob gave Pon a nod of thanks and ran off to find her, leaving his friend to take on the Fool.

"You think that you can beat me? You must be an idiot my friend. The last time we met I was ordered not to kill you yet and still won. This time I was given the go-ahead to make this your fiery grave," Jack smirked as he took up his stance. Pon readied himself as well, but smirked when he saw that Jack's right hand was wrapped and swollen.

"Did Gene leave you alone to play with that tiny blade of yours," taunted Pon as he glared at the injury? At first Jack was unsure why Pon seemed so confident, that was until he looked at his own hand again. He had forgotten about his bandages and realized that Pon now knew about a weakness. If he stood around too long Pon would capitalize so he decided to make the first move. Uncharacteristically he did not draw his blade right away, he instead tried to overpower Pon with his bare hands. Their fight was one based on speed as both moved with such speed that the normal eye could barely track them. Each man moved from one combo to the next with an effortless flow that look choreographed and planned. Neither was the expert that their respective partners were, but they could out dual nearly every other man. It quickly morphed into a stalemate between the men and with the stalemate dragging the fight on, the flames were allowed to grow. Unfortunately, they could not break to deal with the flames as each man would kill the other in a moment if they diverted their attention.

While the fight and fire intensified behind him Rob remained focused on the job in front of him. He had to find Anna, but every door he opened led to a dead end. Before he lost all hope, he came across an open door with a dim light shining through it. This light led him down a hallway which was connected to the basement. While he stood at the top step his heart began to race. He knew this was a trap in some form, but there was no other option. More than likely Anna was somewhere in that basement and this was going to be his one opportunity created by Pon's actions.

Before he began his descent, he felt his pocket and found the bullet that Gene had left the first time he made contact as the mysterious Eye. He didn't understand why it brought him comfort but it had. His heart slowed down and his breath returned to him. It was at this moment he knew he was ready. He took his first steps towards the end of a journey and the man that started him on his current path.

At the bottom of the steps Gene stood with his battle armor all polished and clean. His mask still covered his eyes and yet he could tell they were honed in on Rob. The two men locked eyes and the history between the two of them collided with their presents in a singular moment. Two men who had loved each other were now preparing to destroy one another.

"I know it is you Gene! You can take off that mask," Rob started, yet Gene stood doing nothing, "take off that damn mask and face me like a man! Don't I deserve at least that much from you?" Rob was physically torn by what he was being forced to do. This man had once taught him everything and both these men had put their lives in one another's hands, yet they now stood as enemies. One held an innocent hostage and the other a broken soul. After a long stare Gene finally removed the mask and threw it on the ground.

"Kid, you were always one of my best recruits and what you did all those years ago in North Dakota was important to me. It is because of that relationship I'll extend you one final kindness," Gene grabbed the metal staff that had been used in their prior fight and threw it to Rob, "The old monks who taught us the art of fighting with these passed this one onto me. They said it was a sacred weapon passed down through the generations, but I was never a true fan. It lacks that feeling a weapon gets when it is stained with blood. You see I've always believed that when you stain a blade it takes a piece of that person's soul. Today my blades will take at least one more soul and it will be the greatest one yet." Gene drew his double blades and prepared himself for battle. Rob had a fondness for staffs such as this and accustomed himself with the new tool.

He found that the weapon represented his own fighting style better than a blade or gun ever could. It had the ability to crush a skull with a well-placed blow, deflect the sharpest steel, and be used to merely guide momentum. It could kill a man, or gently nudge a puppy without harm. This staff in particular could be compressed into a small handle and extended to its full length on command. It was easy to carry and versatile. The handle was encrusted with gold and silver characters that spelled an old Japanese proverb "Keizoku wa chikara nari", to continue is power. Rob felt the weapon and spun it a few times to feel its weight. There was something perfect and eloquent about it. There was balance across it and it felt made for him. As he prepared to engage, he at last noticed the door behind Gene.

"Is that where you are keeping her Gene," yelled Rob in an attempt to intimidate the old veteran, despite knowing it would not work? Gene simply responded with a smirk knowing it would irate Rob. They engaged at last with Rob striking the first few blows. It was a master vs apprentice confrontation and they knew each other perfectly. Rob had modeled much of his fighting style after Gene, but had enough variation to still keep him guessing. They were renowned for being master strategist and had the ability to analyze opponents during battles. They used each attack as a data point to study technique. They would give-up minor blows early to gain the knowledge to counter larger ones later.

Their minds made them experts at counter maneuvers and knew how to use the opponent's own ability against them. They were a perfect match for one another. Each would wait for a move and then respond with precision only to be met by a counter by the other. They would rattle off several blows at a time, but were unable to land a single hit. Years of fighting side-by-side had eliminated all surprise and much like Pon and Jackson they fell into a deadly stalemate. Regardless of their inability to strike one another it was still pure poetry as they moved from technique to technique. They would alter their fighting styles in a fluid motion in an attempt to gain the upper hand, but the other would do the same in an instate. It had been a long time since the world had seen art such as this. Two masters of combat had not met since the end of the War and their battle would be legendary if there was anyone else to see it.

"For a man who hasn't battled in years your technique is still pristine kid," admired Gene as the men circled one another preparing the next move.

"For someone that is older than dirt you still move well," complimented Rob. The men may now be enemies, but their former bond was still strong. Gene transformed Rob from a weak naïve child and made him into the force of nature that was feared by all enemies that now stood in front of him. In return Rob gave Gene purpose again and saved his life. On top of the instance in North Dakota Rob was reason Gene gave-up his position as drill sergeant. There was something about this kid and Gene had to see what he would become.

These two respected each other and owed their lives to one another, but this only made the fight more intense. The blows became filled with passion as they knew one of them would likely die from this battle and they owed it to one another that they give their greatest in this death match. They both had the soul of a warrior and as such wanted to die as they lived, with passion flowing through their veins. After a moment of catching their breathes Gene raised his blades and Rob lunged in return. As the fight dragged on and the frustration mounted both started to become sloppy. Rob's week of constant fighting was wearing on him and Gene's age and the battle from Anna early in the morning were catching up to him. Their blows grew larger and they began to let emotion take control. The battle would not last much longer as Rob began to land small blows to Gene's core and at the same time Gene was able to make small slices along Rob's body. The beauty was gone from the fight and it was turning into an ugly slugfest. They were growing bloodier and bruised. It seemed like the fight would end in a double loss, but before they could land their final blows the fire collapsed the ceiling and separated them.

Though they were always aware of the danger the fight proposed, this new development worried Gene. A fire was something he could not predict or control, he retreated down a dark corridor to his left. Rob was ready to chase him down, when he remembered the first priority. He rushed into the room Gene had been guarding and to the woman who had always been there with him, even in his most dire of circumstances. It was there that he found her tied to the floor and unable to move more than an inch.

"Anna I may have a reputation, but I don't have time for this kind of excitement right now," he laughed as she began to both cry and laugh at his obscene comments.

"I see so this was your plan all along," she answered with tears in her eyes as he undid her binds. She hugged him with all the strength she had been using to fight and tried her best to hold back her tears. She wanted to be strong until they were officially out of this Hell.

"I need you to go help my friend Pon upstairs. He will need your help versus Jackson, then I'll need the two of you to get out of here before this place burns to the ground. He'll know the way out," Rob ordered as he pulled away, but before he did, he had to clear a single tear that had begun to roll down her cheek.

"What about you," she asked knowing what he was going to say, but trying to deny the truth?

"He is still down here Anna. If I let him escape now this will never end. He'll come back and then he'll come for more people I care about. I fear you and Iris would become victims of my failure. Now go, and don't worry about me. I'm not going to die down here," he assured her with a smile. It was the largest smile she had seen him flash in a long time. His mouth had stretched from ear to ear and his eyes had shut. After he stopped his smile, he hurried down the hall to chase Gene down.

"Goodbye Rob," she said softly unsure of whether she would ever see him again. After letting her fears of losing Rob pass. She moved towards the stairs and began to ascend from the dark Hell she had been stuck in.

At first Anna found no trace of the battling men. Instead all she saw was the fire and despair filling the farmhouse. She started to walk around the fire pit being cautious with every step when she suddenly heard cursing coming from the floor above her.

She arrived at the source of the noise and found a desperate situation. Pon, was pinned to the floor with his head hanging over an opening that led to pure fire. His metal arm had been detached and Jack was straddling him with a knife in his good hand.

"I told you that you were a fool. I have killed more men than you can imagine and that is what gave me the advantage today. Do you understand that I wanted you dead more than anything and I was willing to do anything to accomplish that goal? You didn't want to die nor did you want to kill and because of this indecision you and Rob will burn," taunted Jack as he raised his blade for the kill strike, but before the blade could penetrate him, Jack was on the receiving end of a kick to the temple that sent him flying off Pon.

"I must admit I was not expecting that," Jack said as he wiped his blood from his lip, "I guess I can finally kill you and pay you back for this bite." He rose and faced the young woman. Pon prepared himself to help, but she held her hand out to stop him.

"I'm a doctor and I'm ordering you to stand down big fellow. Trust me I can take care of this idiot," she said with a smile. Jack charged at her, but she dodged his strike and returned his arrogance with a kick to the gut. He bent over in shock and looked at the woman. He had forgotten that she had gone the distance with Gene earlier in the day. He tried to charge again, but was quickly put in his place by her again. One more kick to the head and he was unconscious. With the enemy down, she turned back to her new comrade who was in utter shock.

"I told you I was a doctor. It means I know how to fix people and make them hurt. Now I'm going to assume that you're Pon, so let's get out of here. Rob's orders and he said you'd know the way," Anna said gingerly helping him to his feet. Pon knew not to question what was going on and the pair began their exit.

Down in the catacombs of the old farmhouse Rob was growing closer to Gene. He started to hear the footsteps of the old man as he ran faster and faster. Then suddenly to Rob's surprise the footsteps stopped. Rob slowed down to prepare for a trap he figured Gene would be setting. It was then that a shot rang out echoing throughout the tunnel until it scraped Rob's leg.

"We both could have lived Kid! All you had to do was let me go! You had Anna, you won. But no, you wanted to come after me when we both know each other's moves. We could fight forever and never get past our stalemate Rob; you know this! So why won't you just give-up," Gene yelled? Rob stood in silence refusing to respond.

"On top of those facts, there is something more at play. This building is filled with explosives and is surrounded by a minefield!!! You know what that means don't you? As soon as the fire reaches my store room this whole property is going to be a pit of nothingness! You are skilled kid, but even you can't survive that," shouted Gene furious at his former student!

Gene slowly began to inch closer to Rob. As he came into sight Rob saw the damage that had been inflicted. The old man had blood dripping from his mouth and his arm was shaking uncontrollably making it impossible to fire another shot straight. The hits may have been small, but with Gene in his sixties those blows were more than enough. Willpower and stubbornness were all that kept him on his feet now. In that moment Rob looked at his own body which was not much better. The small incisions were growing from the strenuous activity and blood was oozing out of his body at a terrifying rate. On top of the new injuries the ones from the previous week had mounted. Neither man could last much longer.

"Why won't I give up," Rob mumbled as he moved closer to Gene, "I don't really know. When you left me that bullet and note, I considered its meaning greatly. I've wanted to end this pain so badly. I've thought about ending it for so long. Yet I couldn't do it, and I couldn't let you do it either. After putting a gun to your own head, a hundred times you'd think that at least once it would go off, even if it was just by chance. I couldn't do it though, why? It appears that something keeps pushing me forward.

At first, I didn't understand what that thing could be and it really didn't occur to me until I was forced into a nightmare state by Rick's toxin. It was then that I realized there are people that care for me and want me to survive. I kept running from that idea because I thought I was better off alone because everyone I touched always seemed to end up in pain or dead. That is one hell of a burden, but these people think their lives are better off with me in it and who am I to disagree with them. I don't live for myself; I live for the people who need me. I live for the same reason you do because the people that I care for and care for me still give me purpose. Once I figured that out, I made a choice much like the one you made all those years ago to live. More importantly I made the choice to stop you from hurting people anymore," Rob proclaimed as he prepared himself for one last strike. Gene grabbed his blade with his good arm and raised it as well. They each were now faced with a choice, one that every person faces in their lives, to act upon their destiny or let it pass them by. Gene made the first move and Rob followed.

Above ground, Anna and Pon had cleared the tree line and made it a safe distance away from the fire and minefield. They thought they were in the clear, when they turned to see Jackson moving after them. He nearly slipped at every turn due to the dizziness he felt from Anna's kicks. He continued to push forward unaware of the danger he was in. The fire had finally reached the storage room and in a flash the house, the field, and Jackson were gone. A crater now filled the space that once had been a home and hideout.

"ROOOBBB," cried Anna and Pon!!!! Their cry was met with pure silence. The birds no longer chirped and the crickets were terrified. They both began to weep knowing that their friend was gone. That was until a rustling started coming from a bush behind them.

"Glad to know you guys actually like me," a voice said. The pair turned to see Rob standing with an unconscious Gene draped across his shoulder. Rob was missing his left shoe and his pant legs were seared, but both of the men were alive.

"Gene was always a careful one only one way in, but he always had two ways out. Maybe I'm not supposed to be dead quite yet," Rob joked as his body gave out and collapsed into Anna's arms.

Chapter 23
Or...

Seven days have passed since Gene was finally brought to justice. The city had begun to move past the acts of violence it had just experienced, but something was different about the city now. It wasn't just the deaths that had changed the city, but also the response. Rumors had spread through the underworld of the city that Rob and a man with a metal arm were taking a stand with the newly formed police department. Light was shining on the darkness that had plagued the city and now small-time criminals were giving up their ways afraid of the consequences they may face. The city was breathing fresh air again. Hope Tower had been finished and inside of it sat the new maximum-security prison for one criminal, Gene. There were always at least ten guards surrounding him, guarding him, and trying to interrogate him. He said nothing to them. The only response they would get was spit.

As Gene sat in prison Anna and Pon had taken up jobs in Ascension rebuilding the science department and purging it of Rick's influence that was still being kept secret from the people. There was no need to reveal the truth to them not now that they were finally learning how to trust in the world again. The first project Anna and Pon took on was building a new arm for Pon and they made it far superior to what he had before. It was now lighter, faster, and filled with new toys that could help him fight the brave criminals that still remained. After Anna had helped Pon she took over a new science division created by the new Ascension C.E.O. which was solely responsible for medical advancements like prosthetics for people who lost limbs during the War. She wanted to give the world something it needed and new medical technology would move them one step closer to a better world.

As for the new C.E.O. of Ascension she was on her way to lunch with the man she had once agreed to marry. It would be the first time in years there was no agenda, no motive, nothing of greater importance in mind. This time they were there for each other. As she made her way, he sat at the table thinking about what he was going to say and what she might ask. There was so much that could happen and he was afraid that he didn't have all the answers she would need. He had charged at the most dangerous man in the city without hesitation, but was terrified of lunch. All he knew was that he couldn't freeze. When she finally arrived, he stood and froze. Her hair was draped across her shoulder and she wore a striped strapless dress. The new CEO who was elected by the remaining board and workers always carried herself with grace beyond his raggedness.

"Hey," was all she said as he fell back in his seat and she sat in hers.

"How are you today Iris," he asked her as he became lost in her navy eyes?

"Well I'm better now that I'm here with you. It has been a transition shifting from John to myself and covering up that little explosion," she explained as she began to look through her menu.

"I have no idea what explosion you are talking about. I haven't heard anything about one," he answered hiding behind his menu. After they had both ordered they got past the small talk and pleasantries.

"I've been curious Rob. Why didn't you kill or leave Gene behind," she asked him as she took a sip from the water that was delivered?

"I didn't want to be that man anymore Iris. I didn't want to be the soldier that just killed people because that was easier. I wanted to be the hero so many of the kids around town believe I am," he explained looking out the window towards the tower Gene was secured in.

"I think I like this new man you are trying to be better anyways. The one you've been the last few years was a complete ass," she laughed commenting on the man Rob had pretended to be in the past, "Now what brought you to this change of heart. I mean it isn't just the leaving Gene alive. You also just look happy again."

"It was you and Danny, Iris. I was forced into a nightmare reality where I was forced to go through Hell and face my demons. The biggest one was that I could end up just like John and the monster he could be, but then I was saved by the two of you. Just before I was cut down, I saw the two of you. She protected my body from the blade and you looked me in the eyes and protected my soul by reminding me I wasn't alone. It has been hard getting to that decision, but I think it was worth it," he said as he placed his hand down on the table where she reached out with her own to grab it.

"I miss her too Rob and I'm sorry about that outburst the other day of whether or not you loved her. I know that relationship was complicated," she said as she gripped his hand tighter.

"No, you were right I did care for her and still do. I'm not sure if she is dead or missing somewhere, but never mistake that you were never the second options. When I first met her, I connected with her, but regardless she was happy with someone else and that is all that matters to me. I don't know how I felt about her in truth, but it wasn't what you think. Then I met you through her and I found someone who was too good for me. Someone with a heart so pure I didn't even belong in the same room as you. I couldn't see that you loved me and you were becoming a part of me. You didn't complete me nor did I complete you. Instead you made me want to be better than I was," he said lifting her hand to kiss it.

"Does that mean the wedding is back on," she asked with a smile and a tear?

"Yes, just not yet. I have a few more loose ends to tie up. I just want to make sure you are getting the best Rob possible, but do not get discouraged that moment is closer than I ever thought possible. I love you Iris and soon I hope I can be the perfect trophy husband to a powerful CEO like you," he joked as tears formed in his own eyes.

"I hate waiting, but I think after all these years I can give you a little more time. Now there is something else I want to discuss, but not here so let's eat for now," she said as the food arrived. They continued to catch-up as they ate their dinner. As they finished Trisha came rushing in the door of the restaurant. Where she met the couple at the table.

"You're still coming to the ceremony, aren't you," she asked looking at Rob? With the criminal jailed and the city recovering a mass funeral was to be held for all the victims later that afternoon. John was to be the main subject of the funeral and Rob had agreed to do the eulogy for him and Carly. On top of that it was meant to be a dedication ceremony for the opening of Hope Tower.

"Of course, Trisha. Iris and I were on our way now," Rob answered with an innocent smile. They had a few moments to spare as the ceremony wasn't supposed to start until seven. Trisha took the lead as she said she had found a shortcut to the tower and wanted to ensure they got there on time. The trio had been walking for a few moments when Trisha's shoe came untied and she had to fall behind the other two. She insisted though that they just keep walking, so they did understanding her urgency.

Eventually they came across a small clearing that overlooked the tower. They stopped to admire it for a moment, for some reason they had found some peace in it. After all the struggles of the past week they had found moments of happiness. This peace did not last long as they both felt a sudden pinch to both of their spines. This pinch dropped them instantly to the ground, their hearts slowed dangerously low, but they remained conscious if only slightly.

Over in the tower Gene was becoming restless as he looked to the clock:

"We're getting close boys. I enjoyed this game even if it was a part, I hated playing, but it is almost over and I will be free," he laughed until a guard struck him. Back in the clearing the couple were still trying to figure out what had happened.

"What is going on," uttered Rob in a terrified voice as he lay on the ground? The only response was a hauntingly familiar laugh. It echoed and it was a sickening sound. The source walked closer to them and knelt over their frozen bodies. The figure then rolled Rob over and all he saw was the pasty white skin of a dead man. John lived and he stood over them taunting Rob. He was enjoying the struggle in Rob's eyes as he remained helpless on the ground. John could do anything with no consequence.

"Did you miss me Robbie," John begun, "I must say that you executed your part of the plan perfectly. I wasn't sure if you would put that bullet in your skull or not, but it was fun seeing you struggle from afar. And in the end, you didn't pull the trigger I'm so proud of you." John stood gazing at his masterpiece that rose above the rest of the city. Now that it was complete it utterly dominated the skyline. He then glanced down at his watch and his grin grew larger.

"Let the real fun begin," he remarked. Off in the distance the clock tower began to ring. Every gong forced John's smile to grow larger and larger. Suddenly, it hit the seventh gong and for the first time in years it rang. John threw both hands to the sky and Hope

Tower began to explode from within. The blast started on the prison level and forced the tower to collapse in on itself.

"Man, I love you Rob. You put my ignition device in the tower, you helped organize a gathering of mass proportions, and while also helped prove that Rick's internal explosives idea would work. I must give myself a round of applause for this one. A plan of this magnitude is hard to pull off," John began to laugh again and clap to himself. He sat down next to Rob as he continued to laugh.

"Now I know you are dying to know how I survived. More importantly you want to know how and why I did this," he said laughing and running his fingers through Iris's long blonde hair, "I think you already know the first one. Rick created a double for me and you failed to notice that he was right-handed while I am left-handed. Quite a misstep for someone of your caliber, but peace makes even the greatest blade dull. Now the how I organized all this was easy. I have been setting this up since I moved here and watching you the whole time, figuring out what your responses might be. Then I started pushing you in the proper directions when I needed to. First, I reintroduced myself to you at the top of that building and shot you. This accomplished two things: I tested out this paralysis serum you now have and made you talk about me to everyone. I knew that on rough nights you and Kendra used each other for support which meant Carly would be easy prey. Having someone hire that thug to beat on you in the bar was child's play I just needed the right people. Then in a beaten state I knew Anna would force you in my direction after you had just told her how powerful I was. Are you still following this Rob," he asked as he paused for a moment to observe the smoke rising from the tower in the distance and the screams from the innocent people who were there for the ceremony?

"The next step was using Pon. I knew who he was from the day I met him. I remember his pathetic pleading and as soon as he went full hero, I knew a meeting with you was imminent so I placed you in an area that took you to his favorite bar. He is smart, but predictable. From then on it was small things like leaving his office stocked and the conference room open. God, I played you two like a fiddle. Knowing all that I bet you are wandering why would I do this? The simple answer is I wanted you to see the truth, not about me like Gene was instructed to make you think. No, I wanted you to know the truth about yourself and the world around you. These people haven't changed they are one incident away from falling back into chaos and that will be the end of this world. I wanted you to see that, so when we reset it, we can build a better one. As you can tell I want you to be a part of that world so I wanted you to see that you are just like me or at least that you are capable of being me. I just have to remove the distractions," John gloated as his eyes turned cold and deadly.

"For the longest time I always thought you were a monster, but you were also my friend so I didn't let myself believe it. Now I know you truly are nothing, but a monster," grumbled Rob struggling to speak. John rose to his feet again and pulled a gun from his belt.

"We're both monsters Rob. I was hoping that you'd understand that. I guess Rick's toxin did fail. Oh, well I guess if you want something done right, you have to do it yourself. Now I have one bullet in this gun Rob. The whole time I've been standing here I've been trying to figure out who I want to shoot with it, then it came to me. There is one last button I can press that will make you snap, one more that will turn you into me. Her, if I shoot her, you'll follow me, and from your willing participation in our game you will realize that you want to be just like me. You want to see the world burn because all it does it hurt you," John said as he pulled the trigger. The shot went straight through Iris. John turned and walked away grabbing Trisha who was standing nearby and pulling her with.

"Nooooo," screamed Rob as he saw the life slowly draining from Iris!

"It is amazing to think what I have taken from you. First, I took Gene who sacrificed himself under the condition I spare Iris," John started causing Rob's face to turn, "Oh yes Rob he did all this because of the promise he made to you after this city fell the first time. He was not loyal to me, but deep down this was for you. Of course, I lied and took the love of your life. In a matter of 5 minutes you lost your mentor, your love, and me your closest friend on top of all the other bodies this journey has created. Now hunt me, search for me, let every moment of your existence be filled with feelings of hate you have for me now. I'll be waiting for you back where everything started," John said as he continued to walk away laughing, but just before he left, he threw something towards Rob and Iris

"I won't let you get away with this," Rob exclaimed, but it was too late John had already left him! Unsure of what to do he looked at what John had left behind. It was another bullet casing with the letter "D" engraved into it. Unable to process what it meant; he turned his attention to Iris who was slipping fast.

"Iris don't go! Just hold on someone will come for you," he pleaded as he started to gain some motion in his arm. He tried to raise it to her face one last time. This was his second experience with the serum and he now had some resistance to it, "Please Iris I just found my way back to you. You can't leave me now!" Iris looked over at Rob as tears ran down both their faces.

"I have always loved you Rob and I'm just glad in my final moments I got to be happy with you again," she said trying to raise her own hand to his. She managed to grab it and he held tight.

"I love you too Iris. I will not let him get away with this," Rob responded gripping tighter.

"I know you won't, but I don't want you to. I want you to be happy Rob and chasing him will not allow for that. Please don't let him consume you. Don't become the monster he wants," she begged as she took her last few breaths holding his hand tight and mouthing 'I love you' one last time. Her grip then lightened and she was gone. Rob cried and cried unable to do much more. He had never been so close to happiness and now it was gone, Iris was gone.

"I'll find him. I will make him hurt Iris, because he's right I have to. I love you and always will, but I can't just let him go, I thought the War and this ordeal with Gene would be the end of it. In reality for John this was just the beginning," Rob proclaimed as anger filled his eyes replacing the sadness that had been there. He laid on the ground with her lifeless body crying unable to do anything more.

A few days later funerals were being held for all the victims of the tower collapse, but they waited on Iris'. The people had waited and made sure that she was the last one, so that everyone in the city could attend. Everyone did except for her former fiancée who had gone missing shortly after he brought her body to Adam and his new police force. There was mass confusion surrounding the events of that day. No one knew who detonated the building or shot Iris except for Rob and a few of his closest friends. Then he had vanished and the city was left without another hero in their minds. Pon had dedicated his days to assisting Adam keep order after the buildings collapse and despite the ongoing tragedies it was clear that the city would survive thanks to the leadership of Anna, Adam, and Pon.

The funeral itself was simple and yet beautiful just like the woman it was for. Anna gave a eulogy that brought tears to the mournful crowd as they missed the woman who was taken so abruptly from them. As each mourner passed the coffin to pay their respects they cried as they recounted a memory of her or thanked her for all she had done as the main psychologist in the city. She had kept the city from falling apart even if she hadn't known it in life and it was tragic that they could never express their true gratitude. Up on a hill overlooking the funeral Rob stood behind an oak as he hid from the city. Gerald approached him one last time.

"Why don't you go say goodbye? The city wants to know that you are at least alright. They need to see their hero again before he goes off chasing the madman who did this," Gerald pleaded with Rob.

"Gerald I am not a hero. I've told you that before, I am merely a soldier who has done some heroic acts. If you want to see a hero look at the woman in that coffin. She was just a normal person with no fanfare or accolades and yet she made it her duty every day to make others' lives better. She didn't do anything extraordinary that others can't do, all she did was care about people and you are seeing the payoff. If you watch closely more than half of them are placing a rock with their initials next to her grave. Those are all her patients or people she has helped through hard times. They are giving her one because she gave them one with her initials 'I.K.' engraved. It was meant to symbolize that she would always be their rock, their foundation, that she would always be there for them during hard times. I know because I have one of my own. Now Gerald that is a hero. I want you to tell all your kids that. Tell them a hero is someone ordinary making the choice to care about and love others when they need it. If we have more people like that, we will need fewer of me to avenge the fallen ones," Rob stated as he looked to the sky again and felt the breeze pushing against him. He saw a single dove flying above him following the current and knew it was time.

"I'm sorry Gerald," Rob began as he wiped the tears from his eyes, "She says it is time to go, don't worry I will find him and I will end this!"